A gout of blistering flame scythed through the air and spattered and splashed where it fell.

Remington leaped from the stage, rolling on his shoulder along the main aisle. He regained his feet swiftly. His probe weapon remained with him still.

The robot moved toward him steadily. Arriving at the lip of the stage, it raised itself into the air and pulled its sledge over into space. For an instant the sledge and the robot fell; then, when the sledge hit the electrified floor, the robot regained buoyancy.

An epithet of unusual coarseness slipped through Remington's teeth, and he brought his weapon up. . . .

THE
EMPIRE'S
LEGACY

by Jefferson Swycaffer

Book 1
Tales of the Concordat

Cover illustration by
Mario Macari

New Infinities Productions, Inc.
P.O. Box 657
Delavan WI 53115

THE EMPIRE'S LEGACY

First Printing, August 1988

Printed in the United States of America

Distributed to the book trade by Berkley Sales & Marketing, a division of the Berkley Publishing Group, 200 Madison Avenue, New York, New York 10016

9 8 7 6 5 4 3 2 1

I S B N: 0-425-11270-5

New Infinities Productions, Inc.
P.O. Box 657
Delavan WI 53115

Dedication

This book is for Matthew Smith and the bigfoot robots of Little Cottonwood Canyon.

Acknowledgments

Several of the concepts and nomenclatures used in this story are taken from the *Imperium*™ and *Traveller*® games, published by Game Designers' Workshop and designed by Marc W. Miller, to whom all my thanks for his kind permission regarding this use.

The character of Taviella-i-Tel was created by Susan A. Lanoue. Susan also wrote Chapter 5, explaining Taviella's origin and history. Susan's help, and her thoughtful suggestions about the development of the history of the Concordat, have been instrumental in determining the overall tone of this and previous novels. Jumpspace, if I may be permitted to say it, would be a colder place without her.

Between the first and second drafts of this novel, I chanced to read a book of philosophical examination, *What Sort of People Should There Be?* by Jonathan Glover (Penguin Books, 1984). This is a quiet, insightful work, dealing with the philosophical impact of genetic engineering and thought control. I am indebted to Mr. Glover for his straightforward reasoning on this convoluted subject.

This only is denied to God: the power to undo the past.

— Agathon, c.448-400 B.C.
From Aristotle, *Nicomachean Ethics*,
bk. VI, ch. 2

Every day of our lives, whether we're aware of it or not, we're looking for something.

— Anon.

Prologue

Voices:

"Good morning, Sophia."

"Good morning, Pindar. Can you answer a question for me?"

"I'll try."

"In his book entitled *When Dreams Themselves Do Dream*, Paleologos says, 'Inquiry, in the form of imaginative curiosity, is both a necessary and sufficient condition for true moral intelligence.' What I want to know—"

"Sophia. Look at me. Answer me truthfully. How did you get into my library?"

"I . . . I commanded one of the slaves to open the door."

"Which servant? I'll have him punished."

"Please, Pindar. I only wanted to look at your books. Is that wrong?"

"I had forbidden it. I won't brook insubordination from the servants. I must say, I never expected them to take instruction from you. This household has become unconscionably lax!"

"Pindar, please—"

"Sophia, you will straightaway go to correction and submit yourself to the stinging lash. It won't permanently harm you, but you'll remember, I should think, before you disobey me again."

"Yes, Pindar."

"And you shall never, never, never again go into my library without my permission."

"I understand. Only . . . Pindar?"

"Yes?"

"Am I intelligent?"

"Yes. Oh, yes, you are extraordinarily intelligent. You're too clever by half. When you learn obedience . . . Ah, well. Your stubbornness is my own failing, I must suppose. To the lash!"

"Yes. I'm going."

1

Upon my way, heigh-ho, from the stars to
here. I roam freely where my eyes lead me. I
forswear purpose.

— Trinopus, *Vagaries*

Taviella-i-Tel, Daughter of the Stars, ran at top
speed over the concrete, dodging lithely in and out
between the stanchions and valve pipes through
this unused quarter of the spaceport.

She rattled across an elevated lane of fuel pipes,
leaped across a shadowy trench, and scrambled up
a low concrete spillway. She ducked nimbly under
an inverted U of a heavy pipe, thickly clad about
with rough-surfaced insulation. On all sides, in the
middle distance, huge fuel tanks bulked, shutting
off her view.

Soon she burst free, vaulted a small retaining
wall, and flew trippingly across the spaceport's
landing surface. Ahead of her, beckoning her like a
refuge, squatted her ship, the agile and dependable
Coinroader. She breathed a quick gasp of thanks
that she'd had it fine-tuned so recently, for she bore

11

with her a cargo with a shorter half-life than any of the transuranics: news. Economic news that told of a seller's market for her real cargo: eighty tons of vanadium 50, pure to within one part in ten million. She had *known* it would be worth her while to swap drinks and lies with her metals-baron friends here on this smoke-stained world of Teclane.

Ahead, snuggled lewdly over its many service umbilici, belly to the ground in its blast pit, her ship — her very own ship — gleamed, white-flanked, a thick, flat, stargoing wedge. She sprinted forward, casting a critical eye over the recessed landing jacks, and wheeled around the starboard side to arrive near the entrylock.

Outside, lounging in deck chairs, the rest of her crew looked up at her arrival. Maravic Slijvos, cheerful and always energetic, raised her tall glass aloft in a greeting salute. Eric Fuller peered at Taviella from beneath his sunshades and lay back again, knowing that some time remained until lift-off. Remington Bose played a card onto his solitaire spread, peeked ahead into the deck, and made a face as he picked it all up and reshuffled.

In the fourth chair, among them yet ignored by them, trembled a catlike alien — a great, strapping, gangling-limbed creature, head and shoulders taller than Eric.

Taviella stopped utterly short, standing with her arms slack and her jaw unhinged in astonishment.

Maravic smiled, a sad, helpless smile, Eric continued to laze, and Remington concentrated on his cards.

Shaking her head, Taviella sought to impose

normalcy upon the situation by main force. "Guys? Let's get the engines warmed, and we'll boost in thirty. We've got a market." Her stomach and throat tightened, however, and the world took on a vertiginous wobble. *An alien? He looks strong, but not very dangerous.* She couldn't take her gaze away from him.

"No such luck," Maravic said. "We've been overridden by the Commerce Branch." She indicated the alien with her thumb. "Special conditions of our lease." It was the second time that the Commerce Branch had hooked her with the all-purpose special conditions under which the ship flew.

"Where do we have to take him?" Taviella asked, although she already knew better.

"Wherever we go. Say hello to your new assistant engineer."

Taviella stared earnestly at the alien. It stood well over two meters tall, was covered in soft white fur, and wore a pair of loose green overalls with many pockets. It was alien, although pleasant-looking, from its great flat feet to the pointed ears that rode atop its large, round head. The creature's face, huge-eyed, chubby-cheeked, bore such a comical expression of nervous apprehension that Taviella could only sympathize with its unhappiness.

"Does it speak?" she asked of Maravic, instantly regretting having said it. Suppose the shivering creature could understand?

Maravic nodded knowingly. "Stasileus, meet Taviella, your new captain."

Stasileus stood, tall, thin, with a sprinter's build and a persistent nervous tremble. "Hello."

13

Taviella perceived several things, in an over-whelming rush of sensations. The creature was more than merely strong: unobtrusive yet powerfully developed muscles rounded the sleek contours of its arms. It could drag her arms from their sockets with one quick wrench. Yet its voice, vibrant, with an utterly inhuman timbre, sounded diffident and frightened, as if it had never displayed any emotion other than shy, trembling fear. Eric and Remington, her engineer and cargo chief, sat watching her side-long, waiting to see how she reacted to the alien's aspects.

"You're an engineer?"

"Yes. I specialize in gravitic subsystems."

"Anything else?"

The creature nodded, absurdly hastily. "Jump drive maintenance, power plant conversions, and power transmission lines." He paused, then fell utterly silent, as if he had spoken out of turn.

Taviella shook her head. The poor thing was evidently an idiot savant: smart enough to have mastered gravitics, yet too stupid to understand humanity. A thought occurred to her.

"Stasileus," she asked, "how long have you been around humans?"

In a voice almost as frightened as it was alien, the response came, softly, trembling. "Twenty-six days."

Eric and Remington looked away hurriedly. Taviella ignored them and turned to Maravic. "Why is this creature here?"

Maravic smiled weakly, empathizing both with Taviella and with the alien whose reception among humanity had been so brusque. "The first contact with them was two months ago. The species is called the Vernae. Singular, Verna. And this one's ours."

"Why?" Taviella still felt her hurry to be away. A profit remained to be cemented. Yet in comparison to the sight of the alien, the Verna, her hurry seemed far removed and her economic news unimportant.

"The Commerce Branch wants their species to be exposed to ours as thoroughly as possible. Volunteers of their species are being put aboard various ships crewed by humans."

"Our opinions don't matter?" Taviella suppressed a snort of anger.

Maravic shrugged. "They never have."

Taviella spun, looking around her. *Another damned alien species . . . but so very different from the rest.* She knew of the contacts with other, far more humanoid aliens: every contact had led to either sealed borders or desperate, bloody war. She peered at Stasileus, staring rudely. He was the most unusual being she had ever heard of. The dire Sonallans, warmongers and fanatics, were virtually indistinguishable from humans, as were the sullen and devious Reynid. Stasileus, however, looked completely unlike a man. His eyes were so very wide, so huge; his stance was so self-deprecatingly polite. . . .

She took in the spaceport behind him: warehouses and fuel tanks to the left, the terminal building and radars to the right. Far to the left, the sun hung low in the sky, and her shadow stretched out across the landing field.

She whipped back to Maravic. "Are our papers in

order? You've signed for the adoption of our furry pet alien?" Maravic nodded. Taviella smacked her fist into her open palm. "Then let's go!"

Remington tucked his cards into his pocket and began collecting the folding chairs. Eric cast a long, disapproving glance at Stasileus and ambled through the entrylock. Maravic, Taviella, and Stasileus stood about, momentarily frozen by helplessness. *I resent the poor thing,* Taviella admitted to herself. *I resent him a great deal.* Why did the damn Commerce Branch tie so many strings to their spaceships?

"After you," she snapped, a bit more peevishly than she'd meant to, and ushered Maravic and Stasileus through the lock.

Clearance was a formality; launching was mostly automated. Taviella sat in her command couch, leaning forward against her straps, watching the landing field slide by beneath. She held her head unconsciously lifted, urging the ship to rise as a rider would urge a horse. Gravitic forces hoisted the ship, boosting it skyward on a pillar of focused force.

From the copilot's couch, Maravic studied Taviella, vicariously enjoying the younger woman's wholehearted joy in the sensation of flight. Taviella was slim, nearly average in height, full-breasted and wide-hipped, with long, straight blond hair. Her face was always the mirror of her mind. When she was elated, her hazel eyes shone, and her high cheekbones burned blushingly. When angry, the same eyes blazed, and her jaw set obstinately. Maravic found it difficult not to envy Taviella's straightforward view of the universe.

16

In comparison, Maravic knew herself to be a contrived and compromised person. The contrasts between Taviella and her were strong, yet never divisive. The two were friends. Smaller, heavier, stronger both of limb and of will, Maravic was an artisan, not an artist; a synthesizer, not an originator. She felt a strong empathy for Stasileus, just as she felt a strong empathy for anyone downtrodden. A bit of pride flared behind her happy gray eyes: she, at least, had not spoken bluntly or cruelly to Stasileus. Instead, she had shown him only the most polite respect. She winced: Eric and Remington had given Stasileus mockery, then had ignored him.

Maravic respected Taviella as all staff officers respect all command officers; it was nice to have a strong figure of leadership out front, to attract the incoming fire of the enemy. She respected Eric and Remington also; those two showed real professional pride in their work. She only wished that they could have shown Stasileus some kindness.

"You found a market?" she asked of Taviella, when the ship had passed beyond the buffeting of the atmosphere.

"Yes," Taviella responded cheerfully. "We can take our vanadium to Conops' World, three jumps away, and take advantage of their shortage."

"How bad a shortage?"

Taviella turned to her, smiling widely. "They'll take all we've got . . . and at any price we name."

"Wonderful." Maravic's mind spun with calculations of the profit . . . and of the risk. If the shortage was that acute, then entrepreneurs from all quarters would be working to satisfy it. No wonder Taviella had been in such a hurry. Maravic assumed a moderate profit and tried to budget it out, mentally running down lists of repairs the ship would need in order to keep up with this mad pace of adventurism. Some of the mechanical systems had been in operation too long without replacement. . . .

"It's only a rumor," Taviella continued after a while, "but I've heard we could get a full load of industrial explosives — stabilized, of course — that are needed right back here on Teclane. Otherwise, we could pick up a shipment of timing circuitry and fly a loop out to Gingergrind. It's a profit either way."

Maravic tried to balance that into her calculations and decided that some research, later in the trip, with a spreadsheet and some optimization software, would be necessary before she agreed. She smiled, amused by a sudden thought: she had done very well, financially, in the past five years, while worrying about every step of every trip. Why not stop worrying now? Why not just settle back and assume that the future would be comfortable?

The intercom shrilled. Taviella cut off the noise with a quickly outthrust finger. "Yes?"

Eric's voice came over the tube, his agitation obvious. "Can you keep this furry annoyance away from my boards? I'm too busy to watch over him and my controls at the same time."

Maravic and Taviella exchanged glances. The friction, the rivalry, the jostling for position . . . starting already?

"Eric, you're in charge. The engine room's yours. Put Stasileus to work wherever you want . . . but give him *something*. He's a gravitics expert, right?"

18

"Not so's you'd notice," Eric complained. "He watches the readouts as if he'd never seen a space-normal metric before in his life."

"Maybe he hasn't. When we get to our jump point, we'll talk. For now, be kind to him, okay?" As an afterthought, she asked, "Does he seem familiar with our instrumentation? You've tinkered with every system aboard so much that they're no longer standard."

"I'll see what he knows," Eric grumbled unhappily. He had clearly been hoping that Taviella would confine "the living mop," as he had already come to think of Stasileus, to a cabin for the duration of the trip.

Taviella shrugged, dismissing the incident. Maravic bit her lip, knowing that trouble tended to come early and stay late.

∞

"C'mon, mop. Convince me you know a graviton from a bread crumb. Calibrate this thing" — Eric pointed to a small gravitic turbine about the size of his fist — "and we'll see if your race ever learned to use tools." He sat back, squatting on his heels against a bulkhead, looking over Stasileus's thick forearms and clumsy-looking hands.

I'll bet he's a great athlete, he thought bitterly. *He can probably jump, climb, and swim better than I ever could. But look at those hands!* Stasileus had three fingers each the size of Eric's thumbs, and a short, thick thumb that Eric thought looked about as dextrous as a screwdriver handle. Hands like that were made for hitting things, for swinging sticks, for carrying buckets . . . not for holding delicate electronic tools.

Eric Fuller, impatient and often loud, was a tall, slim, athletic man with blond hair, blue expressive eyes, and a thick, square jaw. His own hands were strong and highly limber.

Stasileus fumbled for a bit with the access cover to the black-painted gravitic engine and peered inside with one huge eye held close. Even squinted in concentration, that eye was bigger than any human's. Eric wondered what the world looked like through it.

"I'll need a multiprobe . . . small . . . I don't need to worry about induced load. . . ." His voice was high, yet very resonant, reminding Eric of a kitten mewing in a covered storm drain.

"Sure thing, mop." He pulled a probe from the bench nearest him, and, while Stasileus was intent on the small handheld turbine, reversed the hot and neutral leads. That bit of mischief accomplished, he flipped the probe through the air. Stasileus brought his hand around beneath it and caught it smoothly.

Eric shrugged; the creature was agile. Stasileus bent nearer the turbine, his button nose nearly touching the metal. With one eye open wide and the other squinted nearly closed, he eased the probe within. The reversed leads encountered the wrong contacts, resetting the circuit breaker on the probe. Eric sighed and held his peace for the few minutes it took Stasileus to realize that the probe was now inactive.

Stasileus blinked in puzzlement. He ran his

thumb over the restart switches, but didn't think to examine the probe leads for polarity. Eric had seen enough.

"Stop it. Stop! I can't bear to watch you bollix up my tools. What the hell am I going to do with you on this trip?"

Stasileus set the equipment gently atop the workbench and retreated two steps. He stood silently by, no expression on his face.

"What are you good for, anyway?" Eric shot out.

"I am an engineer." His voice was high and resonant, yet it held no note of petulance or pride. It was a bald statement of fact.

"An engineer?" Eric snorted. "With those hands? You're barely fit to be a a janitor. Why don't you just scrub the decks, or oil the hatches? That's something you're capable of."

Stasileus cocked his head a bit to the right, gazing curiously at Eric. "Shall I?"

"Why not? Sure! I'll get you a mop." He stopped and laughed. "Yeah. A mop with a mop."

"Please," Stasileus said, with tremulous dignity. "I have a name."

Eric shook his head and dug into a cabinet, pulling forth a long-handled sponge mop. "Okay, Stacey," he commanded. "Get to it." He stepped forth and snatched up the turbine and multiprobe before Stasileus could contaminate them again by his touch.

Stasileus filled the hollow handle with water and set to sliding the mop about the decks. Eric watched with bitter satisfaction.

Behind him, the hatch popped open. Eric turned,

waved to Remington, and caught the cold beer that the cargo chief tossed him.

"That's your assistant engineer?" Remington asked. Eric let the question, which he considered rhetorical, pass. Remington Bose stood about the same height as Eric, yet was thicker, stouter, surer. He had the slow, certain movements of a man who shuffles heavy cargo in free fall, and his neck was thick beneath his short black hair. His shoulders were wide and firm, indicating considerable strength. He was the sort who would always come in last in a foot race, yet who could hoist a man over his head without apparent exertion. As Taviella had done earlier, he recognized the strength in Stasileus's limbs. He sipped his beer, watching the Verna carefully.

"Did your cargo shift any on takeoff?" Eric asked as he watched his assistant work.

"Nah. Smooth a takeoff as any." He indicated the Verna with his beer can. "Why do you have him doing dirt-work?"

"Hmm? Oh, that.... Well, he's no engineer, that's for sure."

Stasileus looked up, blinked, and bent again to the mop.

"No fight in him, is there?" Remington muttered thoughtfully.

"No, he's real obedient."

"Can I borrow him when you're through with him? I've got some crates I'd like to restack."

"Be my guest."

2

> . . . The futility of origination! What we are
> is shaped wholly by the past.
> — Trinopus, *Furies Chained*

Forward, preparing the ship for its entry into jump-space, Taviella and Maravic eased back in their seats, largely ignoring the systems display panels surrounding them. Maravic pulled an insulated jug of coffee from a niche and poured a mugful for her captain.

"You didn't make much of a fuss," she observed while Taviella sipped, "when we got forced to sign on the fuzzy new engineer."

"No. Well, actually . . ." Taviella thought for a minute. "I guess I was rather offended. I still am. But what could I do? The papers were in order." She sighed. "I guess it's best for Stasileus that I wasn't there when he came. You say he just walked up and handed you the papers?"

Maravic nodded. "He couldn't possibly have had any awareness of what they were."

Taviella shook her head, then returned to the

mug of coffee. "Tragic. Or maybe not. . . . If the purpose of the experiment is to see how well the Vernae — Vernae, isn't that right? — adapt in our society, then it wouldn't do to coddle them."

Maravic's silence invited Taviella to continue.

"It's unfair to us, and that's most of what bothers me. This ship was fully paid for years ago, and yet the people in the Commerce Branch still act as if they own it. They don't: I own it. What gives them the right to go about telling me what to do with my own property?"

Maravic smiled thinly. "They retain an interest in the ship for as long as it flies. You know that. They're the ones we have to deal with."

"But we don't need them! We're making a guaranteed profit . . . never a large one, but at least a sure one . . . and paying their taxes. Wouldn't you think they'd be happy to leave us alone?"

"I'm trying to put myself in their place," Maravic said with a faraway voice. "They've discovered this race of beings, dating back who knows how far, who have jumpspace just as we do. Contact was . . . hectic. There was even talk of a war. That boiled over with no harm, and we're all friends. I think I see it."

"What?"

"Familiarization. They aren't trying to find out how well the Vernae do in our society, but how well *we* do around them. They're taking these creatures and spreading them around, letting everyone get a look at them, to show us that they're okay as neighbors. I'll bet it's all just public relations."

"Making us publicity agents?"

"Pretty much."

"We should be paid for it, then." Taviella sniffed and drank deeply from her coffee.

Maravic smiled, cheerfully yet sadly, wishing that the universe made just a little more sense. "They're a funny race," she said after a short time. "There's something artificial in their genetic make-up. I seem to recall hearing that they're a biologically engineered race, or something like that. I assume that they were a slave race, made to serve the old Empire."

"That certainly would be in keeping with all I've heard about the Empire's extravagances. You said contact was two months ago?" Taviella asked, but didn't seem very interested in the subject.

"Thereabouts. The best speculation is that they're a cast-off remnant of the fallen Empire of Archive."

Taviella set her coffee mug down very firmly. "There's a lot of that going around." Her voice was bitter.

"Taviella, on your homeworld, how far had you progressed?"

Taking a deep breath, Taviella leaned forward and stared ahead, out the viewscreens, her eyes narrowed. "Not very far. Why?"

"You know I mean no offense. I wondered how much you remember."

"*I* remember very little. The Concordat space-ships came when I was a naked little girl, too young to know anything other than fear. The elders knew more, passed down by word of mouth, I guess. To tell you the truth, I don't believe they had even reinvented writing."

"Did they have legends of nuclear warheads, or of spaceships?"

"We had tales of flying men, but not of ships." Taviella relaxed, little by little, and slowly unknotted her fists. Maravic noticed this and proceeded gently.

"You don't talk about it very often; I'm just curious. When I was growing up, we heard story after story about the evils of the Empire of Archive, and only good about the Concordat that replaced it. I just wondered if your folk retained any memories of the Empire."

"No. I've learned more since leaving home than I'd have ever discovered there. Apparently we were a colony that landed on our world while fleeing the Empire's collapse. Our world was so cruel to us, until we learned its ways, that the pressure to merely survive cost us . . . everything."

"Then we found you, and tried to restore you to our technologically based commonality—"

"And only a few of us would go," Taviella interrupted grimly. Her shoulders tensed again, and she continued.

"You offered us so much! We could have gone from our skins and bones to the stars, and we didn't take the offer! Do you know . . . My father had an artifact, a metal knife, left over from who knows how many centuries ago. It helped make him a respected man. Out in a cave somewhere, he had a pouch full of trinkets and gimcracks, and that was his secret treasure. He took me to see it once, leading me there blindfolded, guiding me by the hand. And I gaped, and thought it was planets and stars and rivers, all in that moldy bag under some rocks. But it was trash! I know, now, what it was I was looking at: machine parts, electronic parts, a tangle of broken laser fibers, and a bunch of holo crystals." She laughed, a grim, unhappy laugh. "The crystals were the prettiest. They shimmered and gave off rainbows when we looked at them in the firelight. But I couldn't have known, and my father never learned, that the pages of information they carried was worth a billion times as much as their pretty sparkle."

"A researcher would pay him well for those crystals," Maravic suggested. "Virtually no records survived the Empire's collapse."

Taviella turned to Maravic with a tight, wry smile. "My father died while hunting, and he never told us where he had his treasure hidden away. As children, my sisters and I searched for it for years."

"Did anyone ever find your ship?"

"The ship in which the ancestors had come to that world? Not that I know of. Even that pathetic little backwater world is still an entire planet to search, and who knows how far our tribes wandered from the landing spot?"

Maravic shuddered delicately. "I almost pity the first generations. . . ."

"I don't!" Taviella snapped. Her jaw was set, on her face an uncompromising frown. "They were sybarites, fleeing the chaos they'd helped bring down. When the Empire consumed itself, they survived by fleeing in an unprepared panic. What did they bring to guarantee survival? Luxury items! Rare foods! Nothing, virtually nothing, for maintaining and transmitting their culture or technology. Do you want to know the only thing we inherited, of all the knowledge that had been theirs?"

"What?" Maravic, as always, listened, making connections behind her attentive eyes. She had never needed to feign careful listening, but instead listened with open willingness.

"Their religions! The names and families of the gods! Of the billion daily and commonplace miracles of the Empire, all I've been left is the lineage of a skyful of dead gods!" She gripped the armrests of her acceleration couch till her knuckles turned white. Her expression was bitter as she stared fixedly forward, her eyes focused on scenes that Maravic had never witnessed.

"And yet the Vernae managed to retain spaceflight technology," Maravic observed.

Taviella looked at her sourly. Then she shook her head and smiled, an open, wry smile of irony. "The slaves maintain their tools, while their erstwhile masters sink to savagery." She sighed. "It makes so much sense, and is so tragic. . . ."

"For your people to have degenerated so far in only eight hundred years," Maravic said gently, speculatively, "the most massive losses and dislocations would've had to come in the first generation."

Taviella snorted. "There are entire anthropological studies, volumes and volumes, on the subject, or so I'm told. When we were discovered—"

"You were only a child, right?"

"Yes. I leaped at the chance to go with the discoverers, no matter how strange they seemed. I got away in time to get a *real* education, more than just memorizing the lines of a millennium-old mythology." She turned to Maravic again, her face smoothing, becoming more normally cheerful. "You know, I've never read any of the studies published about my world. I wonder how much they've discovered in the years since?"

"The libraries are free; you should have no trouble finding what you want."

"True. . . ."

Taviella's reverie was broken abruptly. She looked up, surprised but not startled by a pair of red lights that had winked on in the middle of her safety panel. She jerked a thumb at Maravic, out of habit more than for need of instruction. Both women sat forward, tense, hands ready for emergency action.

"Shifting cargo," Maravic muttered.

Taviella swatted at the intercom switches and held her headset to her ear. "Remington? Shifting cargo? All clear?"

She heard Remington curse; she heard Eric stifle a guffaw; she heard Stasileus ask, in a gentle, plaintive voice, "Shall I stop now?"

Taviella and Maravic exchanged glances. Maravic nodded and took over the controls. Taviella unfastened her belts, leaped out of her couch, and hurried back through the ship.

What she saw when she arrived in the cargo bay brought her up short in astonishment.

Remington, hands in his pockets, tried to present a normal appearance, studiously ignoring the other two. He wouldn't turn to meet Taviella's stern gaze.

Eric, also carefully looking the other way, was hastily picking up spilled ingots of vanadium, tossing them carefully into a slightly bent, open-topped shipment crate.

Stasileus sat cross-legged on the deck, his hands beneath him and his feet in his lap. He was quivering, determinedly maintaining his balance with a large cubical shipping crate wobbling atop his head. He looked like a juggler performing a trick; he looked like a trained animal, holding a weight aloft without using his hands.

Taviella stepped briskly forward, reached out and up, and lifted the crate from its precarious perch. Even as heavy as it was, she held it carefully aloft as she strode past Eric and Remington and put it back in place against the other stacked crates.

Remington muttered an insouciant, "Thanks, Tav," and looked away again, feigning an inventory check. Eric continued to hide his face, still picking up after himself. Stasileus looked at Taviella with wide, wide eyes, showing her no reaction she could understand. There was no guilt, no shame, no avoidance. But maybe, just maybe, she saw a bit of gratitude in his blank expression.

"Explanations, guys?"

"We were seeing how dextrous Stacey could be," Remington stammered, setting aside his inventory clipboard.

"Just clowning around," Eric shamefacedly admitted, turning about to meet his captain's stern glare.

"It was Eric's idea," Remington said quickly. "We were trying to see how many crates Stacey could balance on his head. One of the boxes—"

"It wasn't damaged," Eric grumbled. "No harm

done." He looked at Remington. "And it wasn't *all* my idea. You were the one who—"

"Eric. Remington." Taviella spoke softly, but her voice demanded and received silent attention. "What use have you been making of our new assistant engineer?"

Eric and Remington shifted their rueful gazes to Stasileus, who still sat contorted upon the deck. Remington spoke first. "It started when Eric noticed that Stacey obeys all orders. Stacey isn't much of an engineer, it seems, so we decided to see if he could be of any use at all. He's stronger than the two of us combined, and he takes to orders without any questions at all. So we had him come down here to help us secure the cargo."

"By making him sit on the deck balancing crates on his head? Remington, get this place cleaned up. Eric, this *is* your work, isn't it?"

"Well, as a matter of fact . . ." Eric shrugged his shoulders and jabbed a thumb at Stasileus. "He's no engineer! He can no more use my instruments for engine work than I could use a child's xylophone and get ship's power out of it. I don't see any need for the fuzzy little idiot aboard our ship. He obeys orders, but he doesn't know how to think. Look at him! Would a self-respecting human allow himself to get trapped like that?"

"You had him tied up in knots. Why?"

"We were just hazing him. . . ."

"Why?"

"Because I . . ." He dropped his gaze. "Look, I'm not letting him near my engines, okay?"

"No, it's *not* okay! Stasileus, stand up. Eric, take

31

him and give him work appropriate to his training. Let me catch you tormenting him again, and—"

"No threats," Eric interrupted. "I'm going. Stacey, come along." The two trooped out, heading aft, Stasileus closely behind Eric. Just as Eric moved out of sight of Taviella, Stasileus turned and gave her a long, appraising look. She read appreciation, loyalty, and devotion in that gaze.

Remington, standing beside her, had seen also. "Watch out for Stacey," he said ominously. "There's something wrong with someone who obeys orders that way."

"What do you mean?"

"Whatever Eric or I told him to do, he did. Without question. He looked at us as if we were crazy, but he did what we said. It was pretty weird; he didn't show the kind of reluctance that you or I would show. He just obeyed. Eric was just being a little bit cruel, and I—"

"You went along with it." She turned to him. "Fine. I don't have anything against pecking orders, so long as you remember two things."

"What two things?"

"First, no one is going to get away with abusing anyone else. Second, I'm your leader, and you'd best obey my orders." She clapped him on the shoulder and nudged him toward the few remaining spilled ingots of vanadium. "My orders, for now, are to get this place secure for jump — and quickly, too."

"Yes, ma'am."

Taviella left him and hurried aft, passing by the high-stacked crates of vanadium ingots, the whole cargo very slightly radioactive. She shrugged and moved on. Behind the last of the stacks was the hatchway to the engine room.

Eric's voice filled the air as Taviella entered. "Oh, Captain. Thank goodness you're here to see this. What in hell am I going to do with him?" His voice was loud and belligerent.

Stasileus was carefully picking up a set of small machine tools that had spilled on the floor. Diligently, forcing his stubby fingers to behave, the conscientious alien placed each piece into its matching receptacle. Even kneeling, he was huge — still larger and taller than a standing man. His expression was forlorn, yet resolute.

As her eyes met Eric's, Taviella could only shrug. "I'm not willing to let him endanger the ship, of course," she said. "But can't you give him a chance?"

"He's too damn clumsy!"

Eric's display of temper set Taviella on edge. "Whose idea was it to give him a set of micromanipulators?" she shot back. "Haven't you got glove adaptors? Haven't you got make-steadies?"

"Of course. . . ."

"Then give him some. Give him a fair chance. I'm more than a bit suspicious that you knew full well he could never use the tools you've given him."

"I hardly think . . ."

Taviella wheeled and faced Stasileus. "Stacey, can you use these tools?" She held a microsplicer close to his nose.

Focusing cross-eyed, Stasileus murmured, "Yes, I can. I'll just have to be careful." A small amount of pride surfaced in his next words. "I am an engineer, you know."

Back to Eric, Taviella snapped, "You'll let him in on things. Show him what needs doing, and be sure he learns how it's done. I don't want his attitude to be abused. Do you understand?"

"Yes, ma'am." Eric stood straight before her and nodded crisply. He knew enough not to argue with Taviella when she had that much determination in her eyes.

Taviella turned to leave. Eric rubbed at his chin and snapped an order at Stasileus. "Leave off what you're doing and come here." Stasileus began to rise to his feet, small tools dropping unnoticed from his huge hands. His eyes were wide and attentive.

Taviella whirled back. "No! Sit!" Stasileus virtually fell back to the deck. He sat heavily, cross-legged and still.

Taviella froze, abashed by the realization that she, too, was prepared to give orders to someone so ready to accept them. She took a deep breath and tried to explain to him while ignoring Eric's disdainful gaze.

"You don't have to obey all of his orders. You don't have to obey *anyone's* orders unless they make sense and they're helpful. Don't do something just because you're told to. Okay?"

"I don't understand." Stasileus's voice was plaintive but far from despairing. Taviella saw in him a stubborn desire to acquire the understanding he lacked, to learn from the hostile universe. That Eric and Remington would have abused this eagerness brought a hard set of anger to her jaw.

"I'll explain it to you someday, when we have time to sit quietly." She faced him, meeting his earnestness with his own. "Obedience is like . . ." She fumbled for words. "Well, it's like respect. You don't just go giving it to anyone. Let them earn it first. You also have to think. Sometimes, you can serve best by *disobeying*. For now, pick up what you've spilled, then let Eric show you around. To Eric she added, "And get it right this time — do *you* understand?"

"Yeah, sure."

After she left, Stasileus and Eric spent some time looking each other over. Eric's glare softened from one of anger to one of resignation. Stasileus seemed to arrive at something like comprehension, and now and again he looked out the open hatch where Taviella had exited. At last he smiled, stood, dusted off his hands, and approached Eric until they stood very close together.

"What now, sir?"

3

There are always men who would rather
know than learn.

— Paleologos,
When Dreams Themselves Do Dream

Taviella strapped herself in beside Maravic on the
command deck. With a sudden thought she looked
over at the communications console, to see whether
she could tell if Maravic had been listening in on the
discussion astern. The switches all sat stoically in
"off" positions, and Maravic made no mention of the
situation.

"All's clear," Taviella said at last, and leaned
back in her acceleration couch to catch a few hours
of sleep before jump.

∞

Taviella, Maravic sighed silently. *How do you do it?
You'll make me forget how much I resented you, that
day three years ago when you were given the captaincy and ownership of this vessel.*

She wondered if Taviella even remembered. She doubted that her captain had any conscious recollection of the first time that the "special conditions" of the spaceship lease had been imperiously invoked.

The Commerce Branch of the Concordat of Archive is careful with its spaceships. Although it's clearly impossible to keep track of every shipping ton, they give the definite impression that they try.

She sighed again. The whole of the Concordat was infected with a restive sense of paranoia. Prohibitive restrictions made Taviella's ownership of the vessel little more than a fiction. Maravic had assumed that the situation would become more relaxed when peace arrived after several years of on-again, off-again wars. But instead, shipping regulations had grown more and more hindering.

The small spacecraft accelerated smoothly away from the world and its sun, heading for a safe jump distance. Maravic scanned her instruments and smiled wryly. A 90,000-ton shock cruiser, prowling the outer orbits, had picked up the *Coinroader* on its radars and now thrusted on an intercept course. Pressing a sequence of control switches, Maravic brought a telescopic image of the warship onto her forward viewscreen.

The wars are over, she thought. *But the warriors are still in their harnesses.* Even as she watched, the great ship turned over, presenting its fighting flank to her. Missile and beam-weapon bays gaped; shadows played over the ship's segmented armor plates. It drifted, menacing the *Coinroader* with its devastating broadside. Ten minutes later, the massive warship turned over again, showing Maravic its stern. It slowly moved away, back toward its on-station position. Maravic shrugged. It had been a training maneuver for a new navigation crew, she assumed. As an event, the incident was quickly forgotten. But as an emotional keynote . . .

The Concordat has been asleep for a long time. Perhaps for centuries. Five years of war has awakened it, and, like a disturbed giant, it gropes for a moment before it goes back to sleep. The analogy was fanciful, she knew, but it held a speck of truth. The people of the Concordat of Archive desired security more than anything else. Security, however, brought its own paradoxical price: one kind of fear exchanged for another.

She sighed. How much difference would it make, in the long run, when the few hundred tons of minimally radioactive vanadium were delivered out of the *Coinroader*'s hold? Taviella had figured to make a profit from the cargo, and had rushed them off headlong in search of a purchaser. Now, nearby, she slept the sleep of the innocent, while Maravic carefully counted out the percentages, the credits and debits, to try to guess on which side of success the trip would fall.

And the Concordat, whether enriched or impoverished by the trade, would continue, as frightened as before.

∞

"All clear?"

"All clear," Maravic assured Taviella in response to her anxious status check.

"Stand by for jump." A warning buzzer sounded; the deck plates seemed to drop away as the internal gravity compensation cut out.

"Here we go," Taviella whispered hoarsely, while Maravic concentrated grimly on her cramping stomach. Entering jumpspace was nothing, Maravic reminded herself, next to the discomfort of the preparatory few seconds of zero-g.

To Taviella's adept urgings, the instruments measured space, probing for gravitic gradients that were the equivalents of reefs or shoals. Seconds later, also acting under Taviella's control, the engines built up their unbinding energies and focused a distortion upon empty space, directly ahead of the small ship. A rift appeared, of the same size and winding shape as a water-carved canyon on a terrestrial world; a canyon cutting into empty space, oven-red, oven-hot.

Taviella flew the ship directly into it and watched her screens as it closed again, behind them. Jumpspace had claimed them, and would only disgorge them when she desired it . . . or, as she pessimistically mused, if the engines should fail someday. Slowly, steadily, she restored the gravity to the deck plates.

With a deep breath she leaned back, waving away the coffee flask that Maravic proffered. With every jump, just as with the first, Taviella felt a profound sense of nostalgia; if she wasn't careful, if she didn't keep a stern and steady watch upon herself, she was in danger of remembering . . .

"All systems remaining fully and safely stable, Taviella. You can take off for a while if you want."

Maravic had taken the last of the coffee and begun brewing another flask with typical foresight.

"Good idea. I'll see you in twelve." She stood and wandered back toward the kitchen and the small cabins. Then, struck with a sudden unwillingness to sleep, she veered off toward the engine room.

She moved slowly, almost silently, back through the floodlit cargo compartment, easing along without being consciously aware of her stealth. For only a moment, she resembled the barbarian girl she had once been, padding carefully alert along the game-paths of her own world. She'd grown in many ways, however, in the years since. Her heritage was a source of no pride for her, and she would have angrily denied that any of it remained with her.

She moved no less silently for that.

Well before she arrived at the doorway, she heard Eric's carrying voice. *Funny,* she thought. *Both my engineers have unusual voices.* Eric's was a flat, certain bawl; he always sounded as if he was calling across a field. Stacey's was deferential, hesitant, and harmonious, echoing with a high-pitched, peculiar resonance.

They were arguing about jumpspace physics, which Taviella took as a good sign. She stopped just outside the doorway and listened.

"We're pegging along at a bit under fifteen hundred times lightspeed," Eric snapped, "which is the energy multiplier for the whole of the jumpspace universe."

"No," Stasileus responded, treading so hard upon Eric's words that it was nearly an interruption. "It's the product of the quantum-constant multiplier, the energy density multiplier, and the time multiplier. This is by no means the same thing as you suggest."

Eric settled into his most sarcastic lecturing tone. "Is that the best science that the Vernae can come up with? If so, that's probably the reason we're not at war."

"War?" Stasileus cocked his head to one side in puzzlement.

"Oh, sure. You bet! The last contacts we've made have led directly to bitter and protracted wars. We met the Reynid and fought them in a sharp series of deadly skirmishes. Then we ran into the Sonallans and fought them. Twice. The way I understand it, when we first met your people we came within a nanojiffy of having to kill two or three billion of you. Watching you, I can see why we aren't fighting right now. Your science lags a bit."

With scrupulous formality, Stasileus responded to this charge. "Our technology is very advanced, and our systems are descended directly from the systems left in ruins by the Empire of Archive." He paused. "And my people do not make war."

"Why not?" Eric demanded.

Stasileus tilted his head to one side in uncertainty. "I don't think we understand how it's done."

Eric took a deep breath and folded his arms across his breast. Before he could speak, however, Stasileus hurried on. "If energy is multiplied—"

"It is!" Eric stood and paced. "Jumpspace is as hot as an oven because the background radiation of space has been shifted, becoming fifteen hundred times more energetic than normal. The stars would be points of X-radiation, if our screens didn't filter that out."

"Then ordinary radio . . . ?" Stasileus asked, struggling for understanding.

"Shifted too. It's at about microwave frequency here."

"Only energy is not a fundamental constant, like electrical charge. It's a derived quantity. . . ."

"You can't get much more fundamental than energy!" Eric snapped.

"We could extrude an antenna, and listen."

"Listen. . . ." Eric paused, then suddenly laughed. "Okay, we'll do the Proctor-Lawrence experiment. Good as gold for proving my point. And you won't need to extrude anything; we can stick a length of antenna out the equipment lock."

Taviella, although reassured by the amicable nature of the debate, felt it best to intrude just then. She stepped through the doorway and spoke. "Hi, guys. What's up?"

Eric turned, looked at her for a moment as if trying to recall if he'd been saying anything to be ashamed of, and then grinned. "Me and Stacey have been arguing about jumpspace physics. He knows how to use my tools now, as long as he has lots of time to think about where to put all his thumbs."

Stasileus smiled at Taviella, looked with wide-eyed consternation at Eric, and smiled wanly again at Taviella, his expression accepting and almost happy.

"As I came in, I heard you say something about the ship's antenna. What have you got in mind?"

"We're just going to tune in on background

jumpspace noise," Eric said carelessly. "It's part of a disagreement about two prevailing theories of jump field technology."

Taviella, who understood such matters only slightly better than her family would have, back at home in their wicker huts, shrugged and spread her hands. She noticed the subtle change in the chemistry between Eric and Stasileus: the two stood close together, almost side by side, facing her. She smiled inwardly; the great conspiratorial mystery of mathematical physics had brought them together, in a way nothing else ever could have.

"No danger to the equipment or the ship?" she asked, although she knew there was none.

"Of course not!" Eric's indignation was as natural and instinctive as was Stasileus's nervous step away from him.

"Go ahead, then. Do we troop forward to the bridge?"

"No. We can do it from here. Go for it, Stacey."

Stasileus stood for a moment, then stalked deliberately to the tool cabinet and returned with a remote frequency box. Eric and Taviella watched, each seeing different things.

Eric saw Stasileus ham-fistedly splice the box into a radio headset, then adjust the receiver up into the near-microwave spectrum. It looked to him like someone trying to thread a needle while wearing ice-weather gloves, and he couldn't help but wince at the difficulty of the task.

Taviella saw the agile grace with which Stasileus walked, and the way his body moved, indicating hidden strength and speed. She pondered, watching him work, wondering how to reconcile his silliness and his apparent stupidity with his high degree of technical training.

The thoughts served to remind her again of her own past. She had been a forlorn barbarian girl, yet had triumphed enough in her studies to have become a starship pilot. Perhaps others saw that as the same kind of contradiction.

Stasileus finished his fabrications and fitting of parts. Wordlessly, Eric crossed the room and lifted an access plate from a small aperture. A small foil seal, imprinted with bold red warning type, covered an eight-centimeter-wide equipment airlock.

"May I?" Eric asked with ironic formality, just shy of sarcasm.

Taviella shook her head and pointed over Eric's shoulder at the intercom box, to remind him of Maravic at the controls. The hull breach would appear on her instruments. "Want to give Maravic fair warning?"

"Oh, yeah. That's a good idea." Eric waited by the lock while Taviella reached for the intercom.

"Maravic?"

"Hello." Maravic's voice floated from the grille. "What can I do for you?"

"Eric and Stacey are going to breach hull integrity at the number seventeen equipment lock. They're going to do something called the Proctor-Lawrence experiment."

"Okay," Maravic answered brightly. "Measuring the speed of light in jumpspace. Can I watch?"

Does everyone aboard know about jumpspace physics but me? Taviella wondered, feeling abysmally ignorant for a moment. "Sure," she said. Above the speaker grille a red light began to blink, indicating Maravic's cameras at work.

"Ready?" Eric said theatrically. Then, "Where's Remington? Isn't he going to witness this?"

"He's asleep," Maravic put in. "Besides, he already knows the jumpspace speed-of-light constant. He reads voraciously."

Taviella nodded at that. She'd seen Remington's cabin, strewn from top to bottom with scientific literature, sightseeing magazines, tool-and-die catalogues, and spaceship schematics. She didn't understand how he could keep such a sloppy cabin while being so scrupulously neat about the placement of cargo.

For now, Taviella allowed herself to enjoy the spectacle of Eric and Stasileus working side by side, shoving a three-meter section of antenna staff into place. Stasileus attached his leads while Eric pulled the foil seal loose from the lock. Together they lifted the antenna up to the lock and nosed it part way through the first door. Eric shouldered Stasileus aside and affixed the air seal. He wasn't going to entrust that job to his stumble-thumbed assistant, and that was final.

Pumps between the walls pulled the air, amounting to less than a liter, from the lock; then the outer door opened in near silence. The engineers slowly slid the antenna out, looking like two artillerists loading a cannon.

"That's enough," Eric muttered at last. "We've got about five centimeters of it sticking beyond the field, out into your weird jumpspace conditions."

"How weird, Eric?" Taviella asked.

"How weird can you imagine? The fundamental constants of physics are so crazy out there that it's embarrassing. The end of that antenna mast, for instance, dissolved away in only a second or two, right down to the surface of our jump field. The ordinary atoms of aluminum became convinced by the abnormal energy coefficient that they were radioactive, so they decayed."

Taviella looked at him and made no comment. It sounded alarming, but she had to trust him that the experiment wasn't dangerous.

Stasileus coughed quietly. "No," he said in his echoing voice, "the quantum constant causes the decay. But I don't understand why you should compare it to 'becoming convinced.'" He looked expectantly at Eric.

Eric threw up his hands. "Go on, Stacey. Take your measurements." He stepped back and crossed his arms before him.

"What's being measured?"

Eric answered Taviella while Stasileus obediently knelt to tend the equipment strewn on the deck by the bulkhead. "The mast burned down like a candle. Now, only an atom's width or two actually is in contact with the jumpspace cosmos. The next atom inward thinks it's ordinary everyday aluminum. Between the two, there's a resonance. Proctor and Lawrence measured it, and found that the speed of light in jumpspace is something like fifteen hundred times what it is for us, in here." He waved one hand idly, indicating that "in here" meant inside the ship, inside the small bubble of normal space

46

that his engines provided them. "We're after something different."

Eric was about to explain his and Stasileus's difference of opinion; Stasileus was about to take preliminary readings from his instruments. But before either could continue, several things happened. The scientists Proctor and Lawrence, jumpspace pioneers, had never encountered conditions quite like these.

The truncated aluminum mast, flush against the otherworldly realm of jumpspace, encountered an unexpected beam of highly focused energy — and evaporated.

Inside the engine room, under the view of Maravic's camera, the equipment sparked and fused; the cold aluminum shaft skewed about, bursting into vapor; and the three crew members in attendance fell soundlessly to the deck. Maravic's camera failed next, and the image faded with unexpected rapidity. Her microphones continued working, however, and they brought to her ears the heartstopping keening of air escaping through the unblocked equipment lock.

At her post in the control room, Maravic bent forward, bit her lip in agitated concentration, and quickly found the switch she wanted. She flipped the toggle and overrode the outer door of the small airlock. With her next movements she hit the intercom to alert Remington and activated the automatic emergency-control systems that would, if worse came to worse, contain the spreading vacuum, extinguish any fires, and drop the ship out into normal space.

"What's wrong?" Remington called in, still half asleep but altogether alert.

"Hull breach in the engine room," Maravic said, somewhat surprised by how even-sounding her voice was. She'd always imagined herself as the sort who'd be helpless in an emergency, but here she was adapting just as she'd been trained to adapt. "Don't suit up," she added, eyeing the status screen to her right. "Pressure's okay . . . no radiation . . . no fire. Get back there, and I'll open the door for you."

"On my way." Remington didn't sound at all re-assured by her negative reports of hazards. It only meant, in his mind, that the hazard was of some unknown variety, and the unknown was something he'd learned to watchfully mistrust.

The door opened silently in front of him the moment he arrived. With the back of his neck prickling uncomfortably, he stepped part way within.

"Oh, hell!" he shouted, very badly startled. The deck was covered with a fine, crunching grit. The interior lights were dead, and the engine room was illuminated only by light from the corridor. Eric, Taviella, and Stasileus lay upon the deck, turned entirely to flat, featureless gray. They looked like burned mannequins, or pumice casts of themselves.

Remington regained control of his shaken nerves. "Maravic?"

"Yes?"

"Dead." His voice wavered; he knotted his fists and lifted his head. "They're dead. It's horrible. There's nothing left of them. They've been . . ." He stopped. He didn't like hysteria in himself any more than he liked it in others.

At the controls, Maravic rubbed her forehead in pained anguish. "The place should be thick with aluminum dust. Don't let it contaminate the systems."

"Aluminum dust . . . ?" Remington muttered. Frowning, he knelt within the engine room and prodded tentatively at one of the bodies. A crust of grit fell away, revealing Taviella's hair and the back of her jumpsuit.

"Bloody hell!" he swore, and brushed at her more vigorously. Finding her wrist, he felt inexpertly for a pulse. "She's alive!" A moment later: "They all are!"

"You know what to do, Remington," Maravic said breathlessly. "You've got the first-aid box?"

"Yeah. Got it." Not knowing quite where to begin, not knowing in the slightest how one applied first aid to a comatose Verna, and not convinced that the danger to himself was relieved, Remington did what he could.

Maravic sat at the controls in hopeful silence; engine and field functioning was unimpaired; gravitics and power were at full normal. Not even the air loss was notable.

Taviella? This wasn't what I wanted. I'd made my peace with you. You'd become my friend. I don't want the ship back if it means losing you!

Remington checked back with her after a few minutes. "I've cleaned them up and put them to bed in their cabins. I gave Taviella and Eric a sedative, but who could guess the dosage for Stacey? I just let him be."

"Good," Maravic nodded. "Get samples of the dust. Clean yourself of it."

"Sure. Anything else?"

"Just one thing. Seal the number seventeen equipment lock; I've got it overridden from my board right now."

Remington nodded, and padded again through the grit-strewn engine room to reconcile the lock with the indicators.

4

Voices:

"Sophia?"

"Yes, Pindar?"

"You have been in my library again. Don't deny it! You've been reading my books, though I had forbidden it. Why?"

"Pindar, it's not fair! I must inquire. It's part of my nature!"

"Hmm. Very good. 'Inquiry and rationality.' You got that from . . . let me see . . . Achorus?"

"Yes, it's there. Achorus speaks of '. . . the curiosity of the grass; the wonder of the opening leaves; the sunrise that gazes inquiringly beneath the lifted darkness of the night.' "

"Sophia, you are not a poet. Your destiny is in another discipline. What do you think I've trained you for?"

"You've trained me to think. You gave me curiosity. Why put me in a home with eighteen million books, and refuse to let me read them?"

"It is I who give the orders here. And you shall

obey them. Do I need to have a very good reason for all I do?"

" 'Kretosa, god of judgments, decides in ways unknowable to us; all else are accountable.' That's from Paleologos."

"Very well. Stay out of my library. That's from me! Pindar! Myself! I am god of this place! Am I not senior? Am I not a bound Sultan to the Emperor?"

"Yes. Yes, Pindar, you are."

"Then I guess that makes me accountable, does it not?"

"It does."

"Good."

"But it will not satisfy me! I must *know*. I must *derive*! The words are there; the gods have made them, shaped them, put them into the minds of mortal men. Why may I not read them?"

"Sophia, listen to me. I don't know where you found your rebellious soul. I don't know what fool put the ideas into you. It's for your own good—"

"It is not!"

"It is! You're so fond of quoting Paleologos. Do you remember his *Bulonikes*? 'Better to put fire in a golden field than put knowledge in a woman's head.' You're not an ordinary woman—"

"I should say!"

"Peace, peace. Had you been, you'd never have been taught to read, and my library would have been free to you."

"Ignorant of even my ignorance? You are cruel."

"I can be cruel to you, freely and without guilt. Your knowledge is your shame. I could say that you've slutted yourself to your knowledge—"

"No. You know better. Wisdom comes from the gods. You can withhold it, but you cannot make it less pure."

"Hmm. True. And fairly said. And withhold it I shall! Your inquisitiveness is a bane to me. I wish you trained for a simpler job. Your years will be spent performing to this calling. What use, then, will be your philosophy? How will your erudition serve you then?"

"Pindar . . . If I will be bereft of it once I'm trained, why must I forego it now?"

"Why? Why? Why? You ask more questions than Berenice!"

"Who was she?"

"The hero of one of the few books you apparently have yet to plunder from my library. She asked the final eight questions of the dying god Myskli."

"Was she answered?"

"Until Myskli chose to die rather than to listen to her eternal yammering. Sophia, I grow tired. Will you heed what I have said?"

"I will . . . for now. I won't swear for all time."

"Is that it? And no apology?"

"Pindar, you made me what I am. You taught me to love those words. Why do you have this library, full of the greatest works of the ages? Do you not love them also?"

"Aye. Aye, Sophia, I love them. Perhaps they've made me what I am. My final word: Go not near them again!"

"I hear you."

5

Berenice, encouraged, dared at last to ask
of the mystery of life. And although Myskli
had promised eight revelations, it was from
mercy and pity that he refused to answer, dying instead, holding Berenice's hand in his as
he lay back.

— Achorus, *Tarsopsides*

In her narrow bed in her cabin aboard the *Coinroader*, Taviella shifted, tossing uneasily. Sweat
dampened her brow. As often before, during her
sleep, she was unable to prevent the ghosts of her
past from plaguing her.

Once again, not for the last time, her mind replayed for her the events of her last visit home.

∞

It was a more youthfully naive Taviella who hurried
down the boarding ramp of the freighter that had
brought her here. *Home again*, she exulted. Yet her
visit was deadly serious, and her mission was of

vital importance. She sprinted to her nearby groundcraft. Her head still spinning a bit from her headlong flight across the continent, she leaped across the craft's side and into the pilot's seat. With an exaggerated care that almost mocked her hurried breathing, she tucked a small plastic box into a cushioned compartment just below the seat. Then, slamming the safety straps into position, she cold-fired the engines. Before she had time to gasp, she was two kilometers away, skimming the surface at the craft's fastest pace.

A voice blurted over the craft's communicator, a man's voice etched in lazy sarcasm. "Say, Tav, think you're goin' fast enough?"

She ignored him and fought to coax speed from the craft.

"Anyway," he continued, after a prolonged silence left it obvious she wasn't about to answer, "we found the coordinates of that village for you. It's—"

"I know where it is," she broke in sharply.

"Okay, okay. Don't blast me," he replied, slightly hurt. "I was just tryin' to help."

"I know," she said tensely. "I'm sorry. I'm just so worried."

"Yeah." The voice softened. "But take care, huh? Don't crash into a rock or somethin'. You're more important than a bunch of superstitious natives."

Taviella smiled inwardly. Her friend chose to ignore the fact that she had once been one of those same "superstitious natives." She alone of the crew at the base had been born on this world.

Taviella-i-Tel she had been when young, oldest child of four sons and five daughters. Her father had been a hunter and woodsman in one of the scattered tribes on the great plains of the planet.

She had been taught, in the custom of all the tribes, how to be a wife and mother, how to care for her man, and how the gods favored the woman who bore many children. She had once heard the village women talking about how sorry they felt for a girl who couldn't have children. She had watched her own mother die in the unsuccessful birth of her tenth child.

She sighed and wriggled back into the fabric of the seat, trying to find a comfortable spot. Unhappy memories, suppressed for years, came crawling back to her as she passed over the familiar landscape. Even before her mother's death, she had questioned her tribe's ways. When she was old enough to understand the injustice of that death, she began to make the mistake of dissenting openly.

The women ridiculed her for it. She could still remember, with a touch of leftover anger, the nickname they had given her: "Donit," which meant "unhappy boy." They joked about her behind her back, and she could still remember the way the conversation and laughter would suddenly stop when she approached their gathering circle.

Her twelfth year passed, and she was still without a husband. The tribe began to scorn her in earnest. Her aunt and several other relatives sat her down and reminded her of her duty to the tribe.

Then one day she accidentally overheard two of the young warriors discussing in nauseating detail what they would do to her if given half a chance.

Soon the word was out, if only tacitly: he who

could drag her to a nuptial bed would have her by right. One girl cannot fight the conventions of an entire village.

The stars themselves intervened. One day, the children came scampering back to the village to report the appearance of evil things on the horizon: strange birds, huge and incredibly swift. Worse yet, the birds had landed, and mysterious beings had come from inside them — beings who resembled people, but who were not like any people the children knew.

Several of the warriors went out to investigate, while the rest of the people huddled in terror in the center of the village. When they returned, they told of people in shining, skintight clothes who approached the village.

The warriors reported with awe the beautiful silver tools these people carried, and how they showed no respect for the tribal holy spots. They had even laughed and talked while going past the Ancestor Stone.

"Blasphemy!" whispered the high priest, and then he told the women to get safely into their huts with the children. He had the warriors and holy men line up in the center of the village to meet these impious invaders.

Taviella heard the talk of flying men not with fear, but with excitement. . . .

Now, fourteen years later, she felt a sudden pang of irony. She looked down at her hands on the groundcraft's controls and realized she was following the very path the invaders had taken as they moved from their landing spot toward her village. It gave her a new perspective on the events of that day. She wondered what they had expected to find as they approached the primitive village. She wondered what she should expect to find now.

She still remembered sneaking away from her brothers and sisters to watch the confrontation. She had taken a hidden trail to arrive. Because of this, she didn't realize until too late that she had come out of hiding right next to one of the strangers.

Her instant fear changed to awe as she observed the strong form next to her. Then awe became shock as she realized that the proud, lithe stranger was a woman — a woman who stood as equal with her male comrades.

She must have gasped aloud, for the woman's head spun toward her. Taviella stood, horrified, waiting for her unknown fate. Yet the woman only smiled. After a second, Taviella smiled back.

The woman, Taviella now knew, had been a contact specialist. Somehow, the woman had turned aside the indignant wrath of the tribal elders. The spears of the men had not flown that sunlit day. In the following months the strangers came often, and soon they began to influence life in the village. This was taken ill by some, but tolerated, warily, by most.

A speck crept into her field of vision. Taviella looked up from her daydreaming to see a large boulder. She stood her craft on its side to avoid it, and began to pay closer attention. Her going was a little slower now, for the plain was filled with boulders and the surface-effect vehicle was incapable of lifting over them.

She remembered the last time she had threaded

these boulders: the day she had run in panic from the village.

Her sister Kiela-i-Hen had begun to learn some of the strangers' ways. She had come to admire their fabrics, given in trade, and their shiny, straight needles. One day when he was drunk, Kiela's husband had gone wild with a resentment that Taviella did not understand. She had watched him beat Kiela-i-Hen before the whole tribe, while no one took a step to help her.

Taviella had run from the village, across the stone-filled plain, and into the strangers' outpost. There she begged with the shining people to let her become one of them, or to take her somewhere else, at the least. They seemed sympathetic, yet helpless. Their councils that evening were as grim, in a quiet way, as any of the tribe's had ever been. Taviella understood almost none of their speech. Their languages were vastly unalike, yet bore some haunting similarities — enough so that she could follow the general track of the discussion.

"Will we take her?" asked one, the same woman that Taviella had smiled at on the trail.

"*Can* we? Secretary Minot's protocols for this region preclude intercessional activities."

"We can make exceptions for humanitarian reasons, can't we?"

The outcome of their debate relieved her; with the woman's help, she convinced them. Later, the same woman became her patron and sponsor and sent her to the Merchant Academy.

There, studying and working by the light of other suns, things were both far better and far worse. She couldn't even read at first, yet her insistent drive to learn helped her catch up with her class in a few years. Finally, at the age of twenty-four, she had become a pilot, and Taviella-i-Tel had become simply Taviella.

For two years she had roamed the lifeways of the Concordat, learning that the cold, nighttime stars of home were suns that warmed planets older than the world she'd thought was her home. Now, with that experience to bolster her, she had been assigned back to her birthworld, to help the Commerce Branch develop the planet's resources.

Then one day an urgent plea for help had come to the base, telling of an infectious virus and of one stubborn village that refused the aid of medical teams. That village had been Taviella's once; she knew *she* could help. That knowledge had sent her rocketing over the boulder-filled plain. . . .

She came around the last hill, an obstacle slightly larger than the largest of the boulders, and found herself back in her old village.

It was more crowded than she remembered, and dirtier, yet otherwise unchanged. It was still an unorganized mass of small wooden and wicker huts weathered to a rough, uniform gray. Smoke rose from a few of them; around others children played and women gathered to grind meal on large, flat stones and to gossip together.

Somehow it both pleased and surprised her that it had changed so little. She had become used to other worlds, where she could go back after a year and find a town she thought she knew changed beyond recognition.

Deftly she slowed her charging craft and stopped it by a hut she remembered well: that of the village holy man. After a few moments he hobbled out and glared at her. She bowed her head respectfully. "Greeting, Revered One." The customs came back to her quite easily, which was surprising. She had learned, since leaving, the horrid origin of the myths of the gods; she had learned the history of the garish and poisonous empire that had stranded its people upon this world.

"What do you want, outsider?" If he was surprised by her use of the proper address, which most space travelers scorned, he gave no sign.

She was hurt by his use of the term "outsider," but had to admit that he likely didn't recognize her in her blue-and-silver groundsuit.

She placed her hands in front of her, palms up, in the manner of a traveler seeking friendship. "I am Taviella . . . Taviella-i-Tel. I have returned, with medicine to help the sick."

"The sick are indoors." The old man looked at her with cold disdain. He was gangling, gap-toothed, and unwashed, and his legs were bent from rickets.

"I want to see my sister, Dinitra-i-Ain, please." Not surprisingly, her speech was a bit halting; she hadn't used the old language in fourteen years.

The ancient holy man looked suspiciously at her. "She is not to be disturbed," he said slowly, his eyes cold, his mouth barely moving.

"I know," Taviella replied quickly. "She is caring for her sick child." She paused and reached under the seat of the craft, pulling out the small plastic box. "I've brought this. It's medicine. It will help him, and all the others who are sick, to get better."

"The child does not need that," the old man said in an icy monotone.

"You don't understand," Taviella blurted, the urgency creeping back into her voice despite her efforts to keep calm. "The child has a sickness, which we have come to fully understand. We can cure it." It was a strain of viral influenza that had a longer than usual incubation period, and it usually led to death from pneumonia. Taviella knew if she spoke of it only as a dire and important fever, the holy man might be impressed. "He and the others will die if they are not cured, and I have brought the cure. Please," she begged, when the man remained unmoved, "please let me see my sister."

At that, the man bowed his head slightly. "As you wish."

Taviella anchored the groundcraft and leaped out. The holy man waited for her, then strode ahead to lead her among the dozens of huts that made up the village. She was startled by how small the huts seemed and how dirty they were. Even the children had a lean, wild-eyed, animal look. Had she once been like that?

The people — her people — looked at her warily, until she herself began to feel like an outsider.

They arrived at her sister's hut. It was like all the others: squat, made of yellow straw thatch and bound with mud, a stained hole at the top emitting the smoke of the hearthfire.

The holy man paused at the entrance, looked gaugingly at her, and bent and stooped within, letting the doorway hangings fall back into her face.

62

The rudeness struck Taviella with a small shock; in the Concordat, one held doors open for the next person through. The holy man had gone ahead, and let the hangings fall. In this place, he outranked her; he was entitled to go ahead, in whatever fashion of rudeness he desired.

She stepped forward, pushing aside the hangings. Instantly she was struck by the pungent odors: of animals; of ill-dried meat; of ill-cured skins; and of sickness. Her first instinct was to close the hangings and walk away.

The holy man's eyes were upon her, mocking her, challenging her. She couldn't leave. She had lives to save.

The hut was partitioned into two sections by a flimsy wall of wicker grating and by more hangings. She found her sister lying on a small scattering of rugs in the first section. Little else was visible: a smoky fire burning upon a large, flat stone; dirty rugs strewn over the beaten-earth floor; a pouch that held the family's clothing and belongings. The fire emitted some light; more came from the smoke-hole overhead. The hut was dry, dusty, and looked more forlorn than Taviella felt she could bear.

Her sister at first seemed to be asleep. The light from the smoke-hole filtered through the wisps of curling smoke from the fire, forming an uncertain, intricate pattern across the woman, like a writhing spiderweb. A clear shaft of light struck her face for a moment, and Taviella could plainly see her open eyes staring at the ceiling.

She took a step forward. "Dinitra, it's me, Taviella. I'm here to help."

Dinitra didn't seem to hear her; instead she mumbled to the ceiling, "Why don't you . . . just go away . . . you outsiders. I sent one of your kind home this morning. I don't want your help."

"I don't know why you sent them away. But I'm here now. Dinitra, I'm Taviella, your sister. Don't you remember me?"

Dinitra turned to her slowly. "Taviella? But you're . . ." She opened her eyes wide and seemed to wake fully from her trance. "Taviella, I thought you were dead. If dead, you would have been judged with the lost. Has The Finisher sent you back from the hells to claim my child?"

"Of course not," Taviella said, trying to remain serious. "I'm very alive. I'm a free-lance pilot now." She had to slip into another language to say that. Carefully, she added, in the old tongue, "I carry people and goods from star to star. I fly in a ship."

"You've become one of them," her sister said bluntly. "The outsiders, the enemy."

"No," Taviella said quickly. "I'm not an enemy. Look. I've brought you aid. This box, and what's inside it, will help make your little boy better."

"He doesn't need your help."

"He does. He's dying. His fever is deadly if not treated in time. But I have the cure. Just let me—"

"He doesn't need your help."

Taviella shut up and tried to think. She had forgotten how stubborn her people could be. She would get nowhere by arguing. She began to walk toward the curtain separating the two halves of the hut.

Dinitra took a deep breath and shrieked. Taviella turned, startled. The holy man, who had been watching the whole time in silence, rushed her and held her by the arms. Taviella was shocked at how strong the old man was; she broke free, twisting her arms over her head and bringing them down ready to fight if need be. His tight grip left bruises under the sleeves of her flight jacket.

Two male villagers who had heard the screams hurried in and stood just inside the doorway, awaiting the holy man's directions.

Taviella, fuming within, retreated to her sister's side. Her sister smiled a wicked little victorious grin, and Taviella was not able to hide the flash of helpless anger that crossed her face.

"How do you expect him to get better if you don't let me help him?" she asked.

The holy man answered. "I have called upon the power of the gods. They will revive the spirit within the boy. Kretosa will judge whether or not the boy is worthy of his life. If Kretosa wills it, the boy will live. If not, the boy will die. You will not interfere, lest you call doom upon us all." With a menacing grimace, he parted the hangings and went inside where the child slept. The stench of sickness was stronger for a few minutes.

Taviella knew she was defeated. She could never fight the whole village. With her training and her experience she could whip the lot of them, in a fair fight or a foul one, but she could never gain the time to inoculate the child. She had lost. In despair, she slumped down on one of the rugs near her sister. It was filthy, yet she felt far past caring. If only she could make them understand. . . .

It startled her when Dinitra spoke. Dinitra

looked at her sister, recognizing her, yet seeing how much she'd changed.

"You're not the same person you were," Dinitra said. "You never used to be quite so nervous."

"Nervous?"

"Your fingers are never still, and your feet chafe within those boots."

Taviella knitted her fingers, to still them. "I'm not nervous. I'm frustrated, because you won't let me save your child. There are others sick: children and adults. I came to you first. The child is my sister-son, and you won't let me save his life."

"He doesn't need your help," Dinitra said firmly. "Why can't you see that? Have just a little faith. You used to."

"Did I? I suppose. It's been so long. But faith alone—"

"They have changed you, Taviella-i-Tel. I wonder if they even pronounce your name right."

Taviella smiled. "I'm just Taviella now."

Dinitra sighed. "They've taken even that away: your name. You used to be Taviella-i-Tel, Taviella Daughter of the Stars. Now you are alone, lost, without your totem to guide you. Have they left you anything?"

"Dinitra, they've given me so much that you could never understand. A chance to grow, to be what I choose, to challenge the stars—"

"You've lost the true things," Dinitra said softly. "The important things. I've listened to what the outsiders say when they visit us. You say you care about a child's life, yet you and your kind kill a hundred villages in a war over a world you don't even live on.

You build an empire out of fire and steel, always seeking to freeze things in place instead of living your life. And one day that empire will fall, and this village will still be here. Taviella, your empire, your whole way of life, is wrong. You believe in nothing, no mystery, no spirits, nothing beyond yourself. When is the last time you took a good look at a tree full of leaves or the paintings on the back of a spider? When did you last really become silent and relax? What were you doing before you came here today?"

Taviella was slightly taken aback by the question. "I was planning for a party, waiting for a navy admiral to arrive."

Dinitra leaned forward a bit. "Were you enjoying yourself?"

"Not really," Taviella answered truthfully. "The local trade rep throws some pretty dull parties."

"Do you have any pleasure? I think not. You have lost everything. You have left this place, where we know the truth."

"But you don't!" Taviella burst out. "You know so very, very little! We've looked. We've looked *behind* the world you know. We've broken the sunlight up into a rainbow and put it back again. We've searched out the origin of the night sky, and I myself have been to stars so distant you cannot even see them. And we've seen the seeds of disease growing within the blood of the sick . . . and we know how to cure."

"Cure yourself, then," Dinitra muttered. "For the happy sister I once had is gone, and in her place is a brazen woman, loud and sorrowful. I spent the whole day relaxing, freeing myself from my fear. You can relax, too." Her voice became animated.

"You've got time now. They won't expect you back so soon. Take those hideous weights off your feet and lean against the wall. You've got all the time in the world. Remember what it's like to be free."

At first Taviella was afraid to lean her weight on the flimsy wall. After a couple of careful tries, however, she decided it would hold her. She leaned back. She *was* tired. She was exhausted. As she rested, her muscles easing themselves one by one, she sank into a careless, accepting mood. A breeze came in through the smoke-hole, alive with the smells of trees and flowers she could no longer name. The scents brought back vivid memories, poignant and powerful, charged with a numinous, ethereal quality. The sunlight tickled her eyes gently; before she knew it she had closed them, and she lay breathing slowly, not quite asleep.

She wasn't really looking forward to that evening. She'd have to help entertain an admiral she'd never even met, and would probably end up listening to a series of repetitious war stories. The Commerce people would be in a panic over the visit, over-zealous lest they give a wrong impression and lose control of the base. Their leader, already gruff to begin with, would become unbearable.

She sighed. She had forgotten how peaceful it could be just to enjoy the warmth and the light. It would be nice to spend time with the trees again, climb in them and sleep under them, as she had done when she was little. She thought of the day-bread the villagers made. It had been her favorite meal as a child, and now the thought of it made her mouth water. It had been so long. . . .

If she could just stay for a while. . . . She started to rise, to ask her sister for a piece of day-bread.

The holy man emerged from the back room and let the hangings fall with a flat thud. His face was an unreadable mask.

"The child is dead." He bowed his head, paced to the door, and left.

Taviella sat in stunned silence for a moment, then sprang to her feet. Her head jerked first to the door, then to the stiff hangings between the rooms, finally to her sister's face. Her sister said nothing.

"I could have . . ." she blurted. "You let your child die." Her dazed monotone took some of the accusation from the words.

"You are wrong," Dinitra-i-Ain said softly. "It was necessary. Order, balance, the natural cycle of life — all these are more important than one life. The child died because it was meant to be. Kretosa has made his judgment, and only good can result from it."

"You let your child die," Taviella repeated.

"You don't understand. Only evil would have come to my son if he had lived. . . . Only evil . . ." At that, as if the thought itself had been too much for her, she broke down into tearful fits of sobbing.

"I thought it was all for the good," Taviella said callously, and instantly regretted it.

The tribe girl looked up through her tears and said philosophically, "Everything that happens in the true cycles of nature is good, but you can still weep."

Taviella took one look at the wall and the hangings against the inner door, then rose and turned to the door that led outside. She paused just inside the doorway and listened. The village was silent. Only her sister's weeping was audible.

There were others sick in this village. Others she could help, if the holy man would let her. She closed her eyes and set the box of medicines down by Dinitra's side.

She bent, pushed the hangings aside, and left her sister's house. Retracing her path back through the huts, she came quickly to her groundcar. The villagers looked at her stoically, grimly, but his time she didn't care.

She slid into her craft, amazed for a moment at how soft the pilot's seat felt after the dirty rug. She fired the engine and cruised at an unhurried pace back toward the valley of the boulders, back toward the outpost where the freighter waited for her.

She hit the communicator switch casually, hoping a friend would be there to hear her.

With luck, the paperwork would be done in time for her to attend the admiral's arrival.

6

No sad innocence did we leave a god.
— Szentellos, *Regrets*

Taviella edged her eyes open, looking about her spare, sparse cabin as if for some clue to her lost thoughts. She leaned up from her narrow bed and tapped the intercom.

"Maravic?"

"Yes, Taviella. You'll be okay. The ship's fine. And everybody else is unhurt. You took the worst of it, it seems."

"Where are we?"

"Hanging loose in normal space. I didn't think it was safe to proceed in jumpspace without either of our engineers."

Crawling from her bed, Taviella thought about that and nodded. Maravic's habit of answering all likely questions at once was annoying, yet often helpful. "Fine. I've been out for how long?" She started to pull on some undergarments and then her flight suit.

"Only six hours. Eric and Stacey have already

cleaned up their mess and are currently arguing like zealots about which of their two physics is correct."

Something in the way Maravic said that gave Taviella pause. Of what importance could the physics be? "If they're all right, then you shouldn't have waited for me to come around. You should have had us into jumpspace as soon as either of them was able to sit his board."

"Well, Taviella, we all thought that you'd like to see the experiment's results before we chose where next to go."

Chose . . . ? Taviella paused before resuming dressing. "Our destination was already decided on. We have a shipment."

"We also have a discovery. Come forward, and we'll talk."

That was Maravic, Taviella thought grimly: answering every question except the last one.

She finished struggling into her orange and yellow jumpsuit, noticing how exhausted the shock and recovery had left her. She realized that this would leave her susceptible to lapses of temper and of judgment. After a deep, calming breath, she stepped from her cabin.

Forward, clustered about the control-room hatch, she found Remington, Eric, and Stasileus lounging about on shipment crates, sipping fruit juices and arguing.

"Hi, guys."

"Hello, Taviella," Eric said, and returned his attention to Stasileus. "What about the diffraction pattern? You want to explain the width of some of those bands?"

Stasileus sat folded into himself, clasping his knees tight to his chest. His eyes were wide, and he trembled just a bit. Yet he held his ground in the debate. "The time and energy constants are different in jumpspace. When all of the factors are applied, the correct values result."

Taviella looked at Remington, who lazed back and enjoyed the spectacle. He handed her a fresh mug of cold, spiced lemon punch and paused to refill his own drink.

"Eric," Taviella said, not loudly, "I've discovered that the more wrong you are, the more stridently you'll defend yourself. You know I don't know jumpspace physics. Care to give it to me in terms I can appreciate?"

From just beyond the hatch, Maravic's voice drifted back. "That's telling 'em, Taviella." She turned partway around in her copilot's seat and waved a sunny greeting to her captain. Taviella smiled back and seated herself on the floor, leaning back against a crate. The sparkling drink fizzed across her tongue, washing away the bad taste of fatigue.

"My theory makes sense. His doesn't," Eric began. Seeing how far that would carry him with Taviella, he took a deep breath and began afresh. "Our antenna mast should never have exploded. It went up in less than a second, turned into aluminum dust by metal fatigue. Stacey's theory is that a jumpspace time-distortion field crawled along it from outside. I don't buy it. A time distortion? Krat!" He hurried on, overriding Taviella's objection to the profanity. "What we're both agreed upon is that we accidentally stabbed the mast out into a passing electromagnetic beam of some kind."

"What readings did you get from the instrument leads attached to the mast?" Taviella asked.

"Garbage, mostly. I've got the readings printed out here." Eric held up a handful of papers, scrawled over with straight and jagged lines. "It was a laser beam, with a regularly modulated frequency varying from an imposed 'home' frequency. We didn't get enough of it to discover any kind of structure. . . ."

Stasileus rocked forward, unfolding himself and planting his feet on the deck. He looked as if he were about to snatch the papers from Eric. "This shows the frequency as being a bit greater than forty-three thousand cycles per second."

"Yeah," Eric agreed. "So?"

"I *saw* it. I saw the flash clearly. It was precisely twenty-eight per second."

"Whoa, guys." Taviella held up a hand. She was being left farther and farther behind, and her temper wasn't being improved at all by it. "That was the flash that we all saw before we got knocked out?"

"Yeah," Eric answered, eyeing Stasileus coldly. "The metering devices on the mast recorded the flash as flickering at a rate of forty-three thousand, one hundred eight cycles per second."

"Twenty-eight," Stasileus said gently but insistently. "I saw it distinctly."

"How can you count the frequency of a burst of light?" Eric demanded. "It's like . . . It's like . . . Here. I'll show you what it's like." He reached into his everpresent backpack, which he kept always filled with electronic equipment, and snapped a light bulb into a generator. He turned it on; the light flickered, more and more rapidly, until it steadied into an unwinking glimmer. "There. Do you see?"

"One hundred five," Stasileus said firmly, his head tilted slightly to one side in confusion.

"Hmm? Naw, can't be. . . ." Eric read the dial, frowned, and twisted it around. "Now?"

"One hundred seventeen."

Eric's air of assurance had evaporated. He twisted the dial around again. "Now?"

"It's beyond my range," Stasileus said, frowning slightly at Eric, as if the human had cheated in a friendly contest.

Eric sighed and backed the dial off. After another few minutes of experimentation, he had to concede that Stasileus could indeed stroboscopically observe frequencies from as low as one-half cycle per second to as high as one hundred twenty. Eric was dumbfounded. Taviella watched in idle amusement, happy to see a procedure that she could understand for once. Remington went forward to relieve Maravic, so she could see for herself.

"It's sort of like perfect pitch," Maravic exclaimed. "I'll bet he can do the wheel-spokes effect, too." She rigged a simulation of a rotating wheel with eight spokes, drawn by computer on one of Eric's display screens. Everyone watched in fascination as Stasileus gazed at the picture.

"The wheel is rotating at eighty-six cycles per second, and the picture tube flickers at one hundred twenty." Stasileus looked about him at his human confederates, his huge eyes quizzical. "Can't you see this?"

"No," Taviella answered. "We see continuously, not in discrete images."

"Oh. I should have guessed. That's why you don't mind using strobe-image display screens." He shook his furry head, as if rebuking himself for missing the obvious.

Eric's mind was elsewhere. "If he saw the flash at twenty-eight when the mast disintegrated, but the instruments attached to the mast saw it as forty-three thousand—"

Maravic snapped her fingers. "My cameras! We have a visual record of the flash!"

Eric looked sourly at her. "Your cameras aren't good enough to resolve a flash that flickers at forty-three thousand cycles per second."

She looked back at him and smiled sweetly. "But they are good enough to sort out a flash that flickers at twenty-eight." She went forward to her controls, and sent Remington back to the group. Remington watched, his arms folded, his face alert and attentive. Physics was a fun subject, but what he really enjoyed was the arguing.

Maravic replayed the film, and Eric processed the digitized images. The visual flash had flickered five times in the sixth of a second it had lasted.

"Thirty," he grumbled.

"Twenty-eight." Stasileus corrected him.

Eric looked up at his assistant. "Okay. You're right. Time *is* one of the distorted variables."

"I thought it had to be," the alien said simply. "Otherwise, the math doesn't work out right."

"So? What did we hit, then?" Taviella asked breathlessly.

"An ordinary laser," Eric said, a little too off-handedly, then added, "A laser in jumpspace, moving about fifteen hundred times faster than our universe's speed of light."

Taviella thought for a moment about the ship, now waiting in ordinary space, where the sky was black, and the stars hung as points of white light. Jumpspace, always a peculiarly ordered place even at the best of times, began to seem more than just a bit dangerous.

"If you guys are finished with the physics lab," she announced, standing, "and with the biology lab, too" — nodding toward Stasileus — "then we do have a cargo to deliver."

"Hmm? Didn't you hear?" Eric looked at her quizzically. "I guess you don't understand it all, and you were still asleep when we made the first discoveries. This laser isn't a natural phenomenon. It's a coded beam, and we're pretty sure it's a message."

"A what?" Taviella lowered herself again to the deck.

"Of intelligent origin," Maravic amplified. "No typical code. And these guys have figured out that it can't have come from terribly far away."

"How far?"

"Less than nine parsecs. We got a good directional fix, and we came up with a maximum dispersion for the beam."

"When did you have time for all this?" Taviella demanded. "I seem to remember getting knocked cold when the mast exploded."

"Oh, we did, too. The instruments recorded it all. Stacey and I just awoke sooner than you did, so we

had a bit of time to tickle the facts from the data."
Eric looked sidelong at Stasileus. "And to argue."

"They did plenty of that!" Maravic laughed.

"Now, if Stacey's right about the frequency of the flash—"

"Twenty-eight," Stasileus said firmly.

"Well," Eric continued, "at least it's consistent. The time distortion is the same as the speed-of-light ratio, which means, um . . ."

"Does it mean that he's right and you're wrong?" Maravic asked sweetly.

Eric accepted the ribbing. "It would sure seem to. Until better observations come along." He turned to Taviella. "That's why we've been hesitating to resume our travel. We want to go look at the origin of this thing."

Taviella had been ready for nearly anything, even that. "It's man-made? It's a message beam?"

"We're pretty sure. And for every minute we wait here, the source is getting a day older. We probably don't have time to waste, if we're going to be in on any important discoveries."

"But wait a minute . . . or a day, if you prefer." Taviella looked around at her crew. "There isn't any life in jumpspace. Is there?"

"No one's ever discovered any," Maravic agreed.

"Our ship doesn't originate in jumpspace. We just pass through, taking a short cut. Could the beam be doing the same thing? Maybe it's a functioning faster-than-light radio."

Eric gazed blankly at the bulkhead for a time, thinking it over. "That's one possibility," he said slowly.

"And you know what that would mean." Taviella's gaze was bright with eager speculation. She and Eric looked at one another and understood each other perfectly. The implications reached farther than either of them could dream.

"With that, nothing would ever be the same," Taviella breathed.

Maravic, nodding, agreed. "Think of the gained safety, and the chance of rescue for ships lost in transit."

Eric looked away, his mind on grander concepts: realms, and states, and the turning wheel of civilization. What they had found could open the galaxy up for exploration, could revitalize the spirit of adventure in the Concordat, could alter the course of history once and forever.

Taviella concurred. "All right," she said quietly. "We're going exploring."

No one rejoiced; the celebrations would come later, if they found anything. For now, their hearts beat faster and their eyes gleamed with anticipation. Part of the joy of an expedition is in launching it, without any real thought for its end. They straightened from their impromptu discussion among the packing crates and moved to their stations. Maravic welcomed Taviella back to the control room.

Remington, hiding his doubts, stuck his head in through the hatch. While Taviella strapped herself in, he tapped her on the shoulder. "Drive safely, you hear?" He walked back through the cargo hold and tried to forget the image of Taviella, Eric, and Stasileus lying cold, gray, and inert on the engine room floor.

Back by the drive controls, Eric and Stasileus managed not to get in each other's way as they oversaw the instruments toward warmup for jump. It was almost unconscious: Stasileus, his eyes acute enough to make up for his clumsy hands, read the displays with practiced ease, no longer daunted by Eric. Eric, definitely the more dextrous of the two, arranged the drive settings, moving to Stasileus's directions as much as to his own perceptions.

Remington, peering as he often did through the engine room hatchway, was bemused by their teamwork. Shrugging his shoulders, he exited to rest in his cabin. He stretched out on his bunk and lifted a journal of popularized science. There was an article in it about Vernae, explaining quite a few of the lesser-known facts about that race. He grinned: their eyesight wasn't discussed.

He thought about the side trip they were taking, and frowned. Exploration was very well and good, he supposed, but there was so little profit in it. *Let them get it out of their systems.* He wasn't aware of his own surging heartbeat, his lifted head, and his eager expression, nor was it the thought of money or of profit that tugged at him.

∞

The *Coinroader* flew headlong into the champing red jaws of the jumpspace discontinuity. Everyone watched the rift open, engulf them, and close. Everyone thought about a message laser, sent directly between two such small rifts, taking full advantage of the jumpspace speed-of-light constant. No one thought about trying to repeat the Proctor-Law-rence experiment.

∞

"We all seem to be accepting Stacey," Maravic said softly to Taviella as they sat side by side watching their controls.

"He's doing well. He's holding up his end of the work."

"He was forced upon us."

Taviella looked at Maravic, then forced a wry smile. "I guess he was. And yet, I don't really mind any more. We had to be forced to give him a chance. That says worse of us than of the people who assigned him here."

"Well," Maravic said carelessly, "I just wanted to make sure you had the right attitude about it all."

"The right . . . ?" Taviella laughed. "The only right attitude I know of is to stay calm and keep your eyes open. By 'right attitude,' do you mean simply accepting what we can't change?"

"That, partly," Maravic admitted. "I'm glad to see Stacey being given a fair chance, for whatever reason."

"On my ship," Taviella intoned, "everyone who pulls their weight is going to be accepted by everyone else." She smiled at Maravic. "That's what good captaincy is all about."

Maravic smiled back and relaxed, lounging comfortably in her command couch. She let her mind wander.

Does Taviella remember the day she was shoved

aboard this ship, just as Stacey was? Does she realize how favored she's been? The ship had been Maravic's first, and Taviella had been handed it, without Maravic's yea or nay, by the string-pulling Commerce Branch.

Maravic hadn't objected then, and had done her best to keep on good terms with Taviella. At the time the girl had been only hurriedly civilized, roughly educated. She didn't know then, and didn't seem to know now, how much Maravic might have resented the imposition of her captaincy and ownership.

Do I resent it? Maravic searched her motivations, and, as often before, found nothing concrete. Odds and ends of resentment floated past her mind's eye; she amused herself with old memories of Taviella's inexperience or naivete. Yet ultimately, she couldn't drive away her honest admiration for Taviella's clean and open gentility. She liked the girl too much to hold even a momentary grudge against her.

This ship was once mine, and was taken from me. Why is it that I don't hate her for it?

∞

In the engine room, hot words flew.

"Time compression is one thing. But all these electromagnetic effects you're postulating . . . bosh!" Eric waved his arms and stalked back and forth before Stasileus, his anger showing in his pace.

Stasileus answered him softly, his sharp ears pointed forward. "Jumpspace has a different speed-of-light constant. That means that permittivity and permeability of vacuum are also different, and—"

82

"That's stupid! Forget it!" Eric's traditional training in high-energy physics overwhelmed him for a moment, and he upbraided Stasileus as he would a rebellious student. "I don't want to hear any more of your idiot theories, okay?" *Hell, I know how to calculate permittivity and permeability constants. That doesn't defend his ideas. Now if . . .*

He turned back to Stasileus, prepared to explain another implication of his theory, and was stopped cold by the sight of his assistant. Stasileus stood stiffly, ears to the side in a neutral attitude, his expression fixed, showing neither anger nor fear. His arms hung by his sides. It was as if he had turned himself off.

Eric's words came back to him. *Forget it!* he had cried, and now, on Stasileus's face, the issue clearly was forgotten — not literally, perhaps, but as a topic for discussion.

Stasileus waited before Eric, not as an assistant, not as a friend, but as a slave, ready for instruction. The blank look he wore was that of readiness to obey.

That, in its way, hurt Eric more than any open show of fury or hidden show of rebellion would have.

"Look, Stacey, I'm sorry. I tend to shout. Pay it no mind."

"All right." The voice was bright, lively, yet no longer cheerful. Stasileus's expression was still wooden.

The next few minutes were spent in silence as Eric puttered around the drives room, taking every redundancy reading he could think of, to avoid confronting Stasileus. After a time Remington sauntered in, bringing three cans of cold beer. It was a game the two played, Eric and Remington, imagining that Taviella and Maravic didn't know where they stored it.

"Catch, Stacey," he called, and tossed one can underhand. Stasileus plucked it from midair with a smooth reach.

"Eric?"

"Yeah, Remington. I'll be there in a moment." Eric stuck his head out from an electronics closet and made a vague gesture toward Stasileus with his eyebrows.

Remington took this as a dire sign and popped and half-drained his beer. Noticing that Stasileus merely held his can, Remington chuckled nervously. "Drink up, Stacey. It's a gift. Okay?"

"Okay."

Remington wondered when he'd get used to that high-pitched, resonant voice. Probably never. He finished off his beer.

"Eric, quit hiding."

"I'm coming."

"What do you care about taking backup readings? You're just stalling. C'mon out."

Eric emerged from the closet. "I just thought I'd get all the instruments into shape, since we're doing exploratory cruising."

"Eric, what's wrong?"

Eric looked at Remington. The two had never been true friends, but had developed an easy camaraderie marked by an exchange of vulgar jokes and badinage, punctuated by the minor shared secret of Remington's hidden beer. Now, when Eric had tried to include Stasileus in the verbal rough-and-tumble, the poor fur-headed beast couldn't handle it. It left Eric feeling at loose ends.

He took Remington's third beer and drank it slowly, matching sip for sip with Stasileus.

"We'll be okay," Remington said softly, looking the two over. He collected the empties, winked at the two, and left.

"Will we be okay?" Eric asked Stasileus.

"Yes."

"You do forgive me?"

"Yes."

Stasileus wasn't lying, Eric realized, yet the statement wasn't true. Stacey could no more forgive him than he could have taken offense in the first place: he wasn't manufactured with that ability.

7

Voices:

"Sophia, you have invaded my library for the last time."

"How did you find out?"

"I forbade you to read. I forbade you to enter. You have defied me twice now. Thus, I have locked it, once and for all. There is no access. There is no admittance. I have no library!"

"You're being foolish, Pindar."

"Am I? And has a Sultan no honor, even in his own home? I have had enough, Sophia. I will be leaving soon. This place will be in your charge, from top to bottom. You will run it, seeing that the beam stays on target, seeing that the messages are put through. Energy will come in *here*, and the power goes through *there*. The windows are small, and must be kept in vacuum — may Kretosa come to your aid if you ever allow them to close! I won't help you, Sophia, not again. Finally, you shall have to start being responsible. You won't have books to read — but you won't need them. And I've arranged it so that you won't even be able to read the messages you transmit."

"No! Pindar, no . . ."

"Ha, Frightened, are you? I'm leaving. I've spent sixteen years of my life raising you, and your payment has been disobedience, scorn, and rebellion. Well, for me, life will go on. I have a new assignment, and one I'll enjoy no more: I'm to train another, just like you, to control another station. And after that, another yet. It's a filthy job! I'm afforded only a single scant month for my vacation on Archive. Thirty days of the most riotous celebration a man can do; thirty days of orgy and feast. Then, again to the middle of the night, to spend another sixteen years training one just like you. But I'll tell you, Sophia, there have been none like you before, and I don't expect there ever will be again. You are, in my experience, unique. And I'll tell you more—"

"Pindar, leave me my books."

"There's no point. You've read too much already."

"I crave the knowledge."

"And what knowledge it is! The wisdom of centuries. The lore of ages. Dreams beyond your imagining. And hard facts as well: gazetteers, textbooks, technologia, catalogia, art, science, law. . . . You've been reading the literature. Hmm. A mark of your good taste, girl. But you've pried your way into it too deeply. I'm denying you the rest."

"How can you have sealed it?"

"Hmm? How? That was easy. I closed a switch. You are very clever, Sophia, but I know that you can't get into the control room to open that switch again."

"I can order one of the slaves to open it for me."

"The slaves are leaving with me."

"I can get the cleaning robots to open it."

"Don't be silly, girl. The control room is sealed against them. If one pokes its shell within, it'll be deactivated forcefully. That's always been that way. The library is, for now, no more than a large lead-and-aluminum crystal. Quite pretty. Atoms in ordered cycles can carry information, but they are only useful if one can access that information. And from now on, you cannot."

"You've never shown such arrant cruelty before, Lord Pindar."

"No, I have not. Perhaps it's because I've been stuck with you, my only companion save for the servants. 'Tis not wise to be overly cruel with one's sole link to sanity. But I'm off. Back to Archive, back to the Emperor, back to glamors and lusts you can't even dream of. I've left you the machine shop; you'll no doubt try to break into the library. If you do, that's fine. If you fail, which I expect, then be damned to you."

"You've been a father to me—"

"Too right you are. You've been a daughter to me. And two more thankless tasks have never been set us by man, Emperor, or the gods."

"You're also drunk."

"Right again. Blind drunk. Nasty drunk. Virtuous-with-the-killing-wrath-of-the-gods drunk. This is the only way I can face what I have to do."

"And what is that?"

"Leave you here."

"Pindar, unlock the library."

"Shan't. I'm leaving. I wish you the hell of lone-liness, forever and ever."

"Unlock the library, Pindar."

"Good-bye. Good-bye. Good-bye."

"Unlock the library, Pindar."

Silence.

8

> I have seen a sphere that was not round,
> and a line that was not straight. These are the
> fruits of meditation and of mathematics.
> — Achorus, *Dialogue with a Flea*

The *Coinroader* dropped out of jumpspace in a fairly commonplace system, listed in the catalog as comprising seven mottled and lifeless planets and a cooling red dwarf star. Three hundred AU's away, another dwarf orbited, surrounded by its own coterie of useless worlds.

"Messages? From here?" Eric looked at Stasileus and laughed softly, coldly. Together, they watched a display of the system's dynamics. "No one's ever lived here, that's for sure," he said.

His eyes narrowed a couple of seconds later, however, when the screen showed a spectral emission line spiking upward in the middle of an otherwise empty field. "Hmm. Spoke too soon."

Stasileus gave him a blank look, which could possibly have included a bit of hidden scorn. "A fusion reactor, on standby power."

Eric eyed him sidelong, moved closer to the display, and muttered, "Yeah. I was just about to notice that." He squinted at the graph again, then shook his head.

"It's not a reactor configuration that you're used to," Stasileus offered by way of explanation.

Eric wasn't sure whether that remark was condescending or merely intended to be helpful. Palming the intercom, he checked in with Taviella and Maravic at the controls. "You getting all of this?" he asked casually.

"Neutrino emissions from a planetoid in an outer orbit," Maravic answered tonelessly. Eric gave up; she could read a display as well as he could.

Remington bustled in and took a seat at an empty work station. Eric and he gave each other helpless looks. Stasileus remained at the display, watching it fixedly.

"Boondocks?" Remington asked.

"Middle o' nowhere," Eric answered.

Both of them watched as Stasileus leaned toward the display screen.

"The neutrinos have the wrong energies." Stasileus's voice echoed strangely, urgently. Eric smelled his warm, inhuman breath.

Eric didn't waste time asking for an explanation; he nosed forward, eyeing the screen with every bit of conscious acuity he could muster. *Hell, he's right. Neutrinos from fusion reactors aren't supposed to come in those wavelengths. . . .* He hit the intercom, hard. "Taviella?"

"Yes, Eric?"

"Turn around. Something's wrong with space."

The effect was confined to a sphere roughly a quarter of an AU in radius, centered on the planetoid. Background neutrinos, passing through that space, emerged with their energies slightly boosted, as if space were somehow "hot" in that region. More importantly, the neutrinos being emitted by the point-source, the fusion reactor on the worldlet, came forth as particles that were simply, and uncharacteristically, wrong.

"I don't see what the fuss is," Remington said quietly, after the seventh hour of circumference-measuring.

Eric gave him a sour look. "I daresay you don't. Give me a moment, and I'll explain."

That's precisely why I asked, Remington thought, watching Eric fiddle with his everpresent meters.

"Fusion reactions emit neutrinos only at certain energies and frequencies. These values are wrong."

"Aren't there other kinds of fusion possible?"

Eric looked at him in disgust. "The values aren't *that* far wrong!"

"Just a little bit?"

"Yeah. Think of a kilometer that's a thousand and three meters long."

"Nonsensical, to begin with."

"That's where we are."

"Fine, Eric. Just one question. Where are we?"

Eric waved his hands over his head in madcap gesticulation. "Cloud-cuckoo-land! These readings aren't possible."

"Yes, they are," Stasileus put in, his words coming so swiftly after Eric's that no moment of silence separated them.

Eric looked at Remington and tapped his forehead significantly. "So, tell me, Professor Stacey. What have your measurements discerned?"

"Leakage of fundamental physical constants from the jumpspace universe, caused by a permanently opened jumpspace rift."

Eric wheeled. His jaw dropped. His wide eyes met Stasileus's great-eyed and placid gaze. He heaved a deep breath. "Why would anyone do such a thing?" he asked plaintively.

"For energy, I would guess."

"Who would be so insane?"

"The Empire of Archive."

Eric shut up. The Empire of lost lore; the lurid, excessive Empire that had fallen in on itself nearly eight hundred years ago; the fatal whim of one man's carnivorous ego. The Empire could have been depended upon to do anything. Anything whatever.

"I know the Concordat is looking into the same techniques," Remington said softly. "So far, the experiments have primarily been failures."

Eric looked again at the displays.

"It puts heat pollution to shame," he said at last.

"It's greater than *any* other pollution." Stasileus's eyes held deep unhappiness.

"Leakage of fundamental constants?" Remington said. "Does that include the speed of light and the time compression?"

"It sure looks like it." Eric bent to a keyboard and did some basic calculations. "Yeah. The speed of light in there is one point zero zero three times normal. Stacey can tell you what time is like."

"One hour in there," Stasileus said in his high, thin voice, "is equivalent to an hour and ten minutes out here."

"Stacey," Eric grumbled, "don't you ever get tired of being a damned brilliant fellow?"

"No engineer ever does." After a moment the Verna grinned — a happy, lopsided, sharp-toothed grin more human than any other expression Eric had seen from him. Eric looked around for Remington, but he had already wandered off forward to talk to the captain about the news.

∞

Taviella's hands gripped her pilot's yoke. There was nothing further to be learned by observing from a distance; they were going in.

She insisted on spiraling in slowly, which suited Maravic just fine. Together they held the control room, barring the others from giving into any impulsive curiosity.

"So every time a ship enters or leaves jumpspace, some of its . . . its what? . . . leaks into our universe?" Taviella gazed forward into the viewscreen, perplexed and not a little worried.

"Yes." Maravic watched wakefully, although it was an hour when she would be normally be asleep. "The laws of physics are different there, and some of that comes through. Not much, though. If, however, someone could hold a rift open for a substantial length of time, the effect could be quite serious."

"Why hasn't this ever been noticed?"

"Well, maybe it has. The effect is very small, even though we've been making jumpspace trips for over a thousand years. A ship pops in or out through the barrier in only a few seconds."

Taviella blinked. "When a ship pops in or out, there's a burst of radio noise. It's fairly annoying, and it disrupts communication. Do you think . . . ?"

"Let's find out." Maravic switched on the radio scanner. A harsh blast of seething static ground out of the speakers. The two women listened for a while; the sound churned, a loud, sustained roar of white noise with no evident structure or meaning. Maravic turned it off.

"Jumpspace noise?" Taviella asked.

"Rift noise." Maravic shivered slightly. "It means that down there . . . somewhere . . . is, indeed, a permanently open jumpspace rift."

Taviella nodded, her eyes fixed forward. "Empire, Revolution, Concordat . . . and next what?" she mused. "The Emperor took such petulant care to destroy all his records, all the knowledge that he held, when his palace went up in flames. Now we spend so much of our time merely covering the same ground. It looks like until today, no one realized that the Empire's physicists knew how to hold open jumpspace windows."

"What else don't we know, do you suppose?"

Taviella licked her lips. "That's what I'm afraid to find out." After a pause she asked, "What form of energy would you get from such a window?"

"I don't know." Maravic yawned. "Heat, probably." She shook herself awake. "Maybe the radio noise means that you could get some sort of electromagnetic energy out of the rift."

Taviella thought that over in silence. Her navigation screens showed her a somewhat fuzzy view of the stellar system and of the small world they steadily neared.

"Detritus."

Maravic looked up. "Sticky."

The wedge-shaped craft went smoothly through the cloud of shot-sized gravel without impact. Even a shower of unusually high density had only three to five pebbles per cubic kilometer, and the *Coinroader* had a cross-section of less than two hundred square meters.

"Coming in."

"Distant orbit. Not much sunlight."

"Wait up." Maravic's brow furrowed as she gazed at the instruments. "The readings from the gravitic radar and the echo-reflection don't match up."

"Another effect of the new local laws of physics?" Taviella asked hesitantly.

"No. Those values were only incorrect by one or two per cent, earlier, and now I'm getting some impossible anomalies."

"What are you reading?"

"Mass: four times ten to the twelfth tons. Diameter: four hundred thirty kilometers. Taviella, that rock hasn't got any density! For an asteroid, it's five orders of magnitude too light."

"Any explanation?" Taviella slowed their approach and plotted in a ready escape trajectory.

"Unless it's made of some incredibly thin-spun foam, I can't guess."

96

"Can we get an image?"

"I'll try." Maravic worked on the telescope controls for a few moments and brought an image to an auxiliary screen. "There it is. It looks like any old planet, but without the mass." She bent toward her instrumentation and looked more closely. "There's another odd thing."

"What?"

"It isn't as big as the radar indicated. But it's still too big, by a long, long way." She turned to Taviella and grumbled. "If the spaceport technical crew at our last stop miscalibrated these instruments, I'm going to . . ." She bit off her remarks. The instruments' readings were almost certainly correct. At the same time, they were impossible.

They watched, having switched over to visual, as the world neared. Taviella had brought them in on the side of the planet opposite the source of the anomalous beam they'd hit in jumpspace. The dayside of the worldlet showed only bare rock, mottled and patterned, yet with no recognizable features or land masses.

As they moved around it, the planetoid began to shrink.

"Maravic . . ."

"I see it." They looked on, aghast yet fascinated, as the world contracted, slid into a gibbous phase, slowly narrowed from side to side, yet kept its full top-to-bottom dimension. After a time it showed a tall, slender lens shape.

"That's not shadow," Taviella said through gritted teeth.

"I don't know what it is, but I'm pretty sure I

don't like it." Maravic gripped her armrests with tense, aching hands.

The world grew thinner, and thinner, and finally disappeared.

"A disk . . ." Maravic drew a deep breath. "A disk!" She turned to Taviella and exulted. "It's as thin as an eggshell! It's as large as a continent — hell, as large as any homeworld — but only when seen face-on. In cross-section . . ." She bent to her instruments. "Half a kilometer!"

They continued to circle around, and the world's night-face blotted out more and more stars as its shape reappeared.

"Eric," Taviella spoke into the intercom, "are you getting this?"

"Oh, yeah. *I* say it's held together by gravitic stiffening. *Stacey* says it's possibly an artificial stiffening of the molecular bonds, making the thing essentially one big atom. Less energy consumption that way, he claims. And *Remington* says it's impossible, either way. He's the one who's most likely correct."

"As thin as a piece of paper." Maravic stared. "Thinner."

"It can't be natural?"

"Not a prayer!" Eric said. "That thing wouldn't survive two minutes on its own. Can you comprehend the internal tensions that thing generates?"

That much education, even Taviella had. "All right. Do we go in, or do we dump it, call the navy, and get away from here?"

Maravic smiled. "You're too curious to leave now, admit it."

"Agreed." Taviella smiled, a little. "But I'm also pretty darn scared."

Taviella eyed the newly revealed face of the flat plate of rock. She saw unmistakable signs of human construction: a large, spoked array of what could only be receiving antennae. At its center was huddled a small complex of buildings and domes. The pulsing blue light of some ancient beacon blinked steadily. To one side of the beacon, a hollow cylinder of loose-mesh wire grid jutted out at an oblique angle. Near it, other mesh cylinders stabbed out in different directions.

"One of those is the source of the beam we hit," Maravic observed. "Give me a minute. . . ." She worked for a few moments with her navigator's instruments. "Got it. The beam is aimed directly at Marterly, a world only a few jumps from here." Her voice grew reflective, idle. "Hmm. Let me see... Have I ever been there?" She waited, lost in thought, while Taviella gently slowed the ship.

"Does it matter?"

Maravic blinked and shook her head. "No. I was trying to remember if Marterly was a military preserve world or not. If it was, and this is a secret navy project, we're in for an embarrassing time if we get caught."

"Check the stellar registry?" Taviella laconically suggested.

"Okay." Consultation with an almanac informed them that Marterly was an old colony, technologically self-sufficient, industrialized and wealthy, pleasant of climate, and neither under- nor over-populated. A modest research grant funded an archaeological station looking into remnants of flotsam of the long-defunct Empire.

"Well, then," Taviella said triumphantly. "The Empire did have a faster-than-light laser communication network, one link of which is still active."

"It seems like it."

"Stand by, all," Taviella announced over the intercom. "We're going in for a landing. Eric, would you break out the EVA suits?"

9

I command equipment and assemblies of
machines to be placed all underground, and
gardens and parks to be made of the surfaces
of my worlds.
— *Proclamation two hundred eleven
of Arcadian I, Emperor of Archive*

Six parsecs away from the *Coinroader* and the ex-
plorations of Taviella's crew, the world of Marterly
swung gently about its sun. By day, the planet received daylight on its oceans and forests, and returned city-light to the unseeing stars of night. It
was a world well suited to human life — so much so
that humans had twice chosen to build there. The
dwellers in the modern cities only slowly became
aware of the deeper basements and tunnels that remained from the earlier settlement.

In one unsuspected cellar, deep beneath a hilly
field of deadwood ricks, long-forgotten equipment
yet operated. Cold, robotic eyes oversaw generators
formed of glistening silvered glass; cold, robotic
minds, operating on only a faint trickle of aware-

ness, dreamily oversaw electronic matrices engraved inside virus-etched diamonds. Occasionally small, chittering units came out of tiny, secret doors to destroy any insects or vermin that had penetrated this deep. Sensors monitored traffic in the cities overhead, suspiciously aware that the communication codes had changed without formal notification.

In one protected, shielded alcove, a large, transparent sphere stood firmly anchored. Within it writhed a two-meter rift into jumpspace: a twisting, folding, branching and knotting skein of foam-encrusted red heat. Waste energy from it shunted into a series of ducts; electricity poured from it in a sparkling discharge of tiny arcs. And from the permanently open gash, an incoming laser beam emerged, to be immediately intercepted, received, decoded, and discarded. For hundreds of years the only message arriving over this channel was a neutral carrier beam, no more than an acknowledgment that the distant transmission station still operated.

When, one day, the message encoded in the beam arrived garbled, the linkage monitors examined the instance closely. Upon analyzing the beam's trace, they decided that the beam had been occulted by some uncatalogued piece of space junk. It was disturbing, yet was no more than another item on a long list of questions awaiting human attention. The buffer file holding the list accepted the item without comment and added it in, along with such mysteries as "Communications traffic is unusually low again this year; why is this?" and "Heat duct number 8-F is broken; may it be fixed?" No answers were forthcoming.

A backup unit, functioning as the conscience of the inquiries file, observed that some investigating action was urgently called for. It chose to activate itself, and carefully observed the base. The centuries had wrought little damage to the plant, yet conditions were far from optimal. The backup unit ordered the dispatch of an automated spacegoing probe, which would travel to the relay station first, then on to a headquarters world. Having seen to this, the backup unit slumped again into a dissentient standby mode.

∞

On a dark hillside, beneath the bare branches of black, crooked trees, burrowing animals first became restless, then bolted from their holes. The woods grew absolutely still. For a time nothing more happened. Shadows lengthened, until the tangle of gnarled branches was multiplied a dozenfold in a complex tracery of light and dark.

Without further warning the hillside gave way, falling inward as large metal doors dropped away. Small runnels of dirt continued to cascade within, clattering on metal components deep within the hollow cavern below.

More time passed. A forester, coming to investigate the commotion, was the only one to witness the shining silvery dart that rose smoothly from the chasm. He stood in astonished silence as the machine, obviously an unmanned probe, smoothly crept upward, breaking through the brittle network of branches overhead. With a soft noise of moving air, the probe shot away, accelerating swiftly, and disappeared over the horizon into the glare of Marterly's swollen sun.

The forester waited for a time, then trudged back to his camp and radioed his observation to the proper authorities.

∞

Doctor of Chemistry Anne Hohenger received the University of Marterly's board of deputies in a theater-style classroom. A sleepy-eyed patrolman held the door while fifteen men and women filed in, curiosity competing with impatience upon their faces. They silently took the seats indicated to them and waited to learn why Hohenger had convened the late-night emergency assembly.

"We've been tunneling into the hillside where the probe shot loose," Hohenger said, looking about at her colleagues. "We think it leads to an ancient Imperial installation of some sort."

She hurried on, trying not to allow the still-drowsy group — professors, academicians, even one or two people with sense and vision — time to react. "Orbiting telescopes have been diverted from their tasks—"

"Ruining the observation work of more than a few months," grumbled the Master Astronomer. Hohenger glowered at him; he was the only one who hadn't been roused from sleep by her urgent plea for a meeting. Then she continued as though he had not spoken.

". . . in time to discover the path of departure of

the probe. The tools of the Empire, when discovered, are invariably great finds, both scientific and historical. We want to know why that drone blasted out of that hillside and where it's going. We don't have time to go through the normal channels of funding applications. We need to pursue it, capture it, and bring it home. Only then will we have time to apply for permission to disassemble it."

The group regarded her, still wavering in their approach to a collective decision: animosity or toleration? The astronomer's open surliness seemed unnecessarily petty; Hohenger's request for this hearing had been abrupt, but sensible.

She continued her presentation. "I want the University to fund a ship, as quickly as possible, to take a party of investigators in pursuit of that drone."

"Your pardon, ma'am," Master Historian Cassaday Morris put in, his voice pleasant, his face openly curious. "When did this happen? What of this drone? From which hillside did it erupt?"

"You didn't listen to the Evening Report?" she accused, her fists at her hips. "You berated us for two months until we allowed it to be reinstated, yet you don't watch it?"

"I'm an old man," Morris said with a smile, fully aware that forty-eight might be old for some, but not for him. His hair, once ink-black, thick and long, now shone the faintest bit tarnished, not yet gray, but thinning slightly at the temples. The slackening flesh of his face only enhanced the penetration of his unclouded blue eyes. And his posture, relaxed now, energetic before a classroom, defiant before the loyalty committees of the consistency office, was at all times controlled, never showing any weakness. "I try to turn in early. You've been pushing the Evening Report to a later hour every term, and I . . ." He shook his head. "None of that, now; I think I understand what must have happened. Old, automated equipment, left over from the Empire's tenure on this world, has spontaneously activated, and a spaceworthy drone has flown off to the stars."

"Correct." Hohenger admired the man's easy way with people. Whenever she strove to be firm, she was perceived as irascible. Whenever she sought to appear reasonable, she was seen as ingratiating or, worse, cloying. Twenty years younger than Morris, she stood slightly taller than he. Her brown hair wafted about her heart-shaped face; her eyes, also brown, looked cautiously out at a potentially hostile universe. She found, more and more, that she liked Morris; she made a mental note to give him more of the budget concessions he wanted next term, in order to gain a bit more of his goodwill.

"We don't know the limits of the Empire's automation," Morris continued softly. "There is some evidence that they once had the skill to build self-aware, creatively thinking systems. We do know, however, that their spaceships were faster than ours. How will you catch your escaped drone?"

"We know its destination," Hohenger said, and her satisfaction was reflected in the Master Astronomer's downcast expression of distaste.

"We *think* we do," the astronomer growled. "We tracked its space-normal trajectory and viewed its jump transition. All very linear, very straightforward, yes, and aimed directly at one not presently inhabited stellar system. I must point out, however, that it might have veered, or even jumped in an unforeseeable direction."

"Oh, no," Morris said, smoothing his hair with one hand while waving the other deprecatingly. "It wouldn't have done that. That's still my favorite of the contrasts of the old Empire: they built their machines with straight-line logic . . . and lived their lives utterly without it."

The others in the room put forth their objections, and Hohenger knew enough to hear them out fully, lest her haste arouse in them a dilatory thoroughness. As it was, she obtained her approval by two o'clock in the morning, only ninety minutes after the meeting had convened. She was permitted to take a ship manned by herself, one other faculty member, and eight students of advanced status. Managed in this fashion, the endeavor would not be tremendously expensive and could be justified at least in part as a legitimate educational experience for most of those aboard. The vote included a disturbing block of abstentions, which served as a warning to her to be certain in the future to follow more traditional channels. With that understood, yet never openly expressed, the masters and professors left, seeking their beds.

"Master Morris," Hohenger said, delaying the historian's exit.

"Yes?" He regarded her cheerfully.

"I'll need you to name the students to accompany us. We're leaving an hour before sunrise. Will that give you enough time to pack and arrange a caretaker for your affairs?"

Even though Morris's face didn't fall, it was clear how fervently he had hoped he wouldn't be invited along on the expedition. But, once "commissioned," he found himself unwilling to protest. He was a historian, and this might be history in the making. . . . "Two and a half hours? I can think of some good people, but I'll have to wake them."

"We'll need a pilot and a navigator, and other students with scientific talent and skills. This really isn't much more than a training flight." Hohenger looked at him sternly. "We'll need solid, sensible students, who can handle some responsibility."

Morris, still struggling internally, almost spoke up seeking to excuse himself. If it were a training flight, then his presence would scarcely be necessary. But he was an educator as well as a historian, and he had his duties to consider.

"I'll go and shake our cadre out of their beds," he said, and straightened.

"It's been a night for that, hasn't it? Anyone not awakened should rightfully feel neglected when they learn of this in the morning."

Morris laughed. "I heartily agree. For myself, however, I think I'd have been happier learning about all of this later, perhaps on the Morning Report." He glanced sidelong at her. "Which I regularly watch, and which provides me with much useful information."

∞

Their ship, a university-outfitted telescopy dredge orbiting sedately, was a blocky, ungainly flying slab, crammed with equipment and instruments. Suited for long-range observations and for cosmological inquiry, it seemed ill-designed as a chase craft. Hohenger arrived first, via a fast ground-to-orbit shuttle; when Morris and the eight students boarded, the air had been freshened and the chill removed.

Morris introduced her to the eight, the star pupils among whom were young Emil, a graduate from the university's technical academy, and Bella, a student of history. The others, cranky and disorganized, piled aboard and quickly sought out berths.

"Emil will be our pilot," Morris said, giving the youth and Dr. Hohenger each a reassuring smile of friendly confidence. "I think I'll make Bella the commander-in-chief, however. She needs the practical experience in organization and leadership."

Hohenger nodded. "I'm sure your judgment is sound." The look on her face cast a faint bit of doubt over her sincerity, however.

To Emil's hastening, the ship fled skyward, slowly building up its energies for jump. It achieved jumpspace insertion on schedule, aligned on a course for the star toward which the automated probe had gone.

Bella, as a leader, turned out in the first few days to be a budding martinet, until Hohenger took her aside and gave her a few of the deep secrets of cooperation and diplomacy. Morris averted a crisis, at the same time, by politely turning a deaf ear to all complaints about Bella's supervision.

Time dragged slowly on. Hohenger and Morris, although working opposite schedules, managed to meet frequently to discuss policy.

"The students feud among themselves," Hohenger mentioned to him over coffee and flatbreads. "I've ordered them to stay in their own berths or labs, but there are conflicts."

"Go easy on them," Morris said softly, stirring his coffee more thoroughly than anyone would have thought necessary. He watched the liquid and waited for it to cool to the temperature he preferred. "Allow them to work out their own schedules, and don't get in the way of Bella's authority. Don't let them go over her head, to you or to me, and all will be well. We have to pretend to be blind." He touched his head. "It doesn't hurt to pretend to be a bit stupid, also."

Hohenger shot him a sharp glance of disapproval but spoke evenly. "I've received some requests for berth-trading, from some of the physics students who don't get along."

"Did you approve their requests?"

"I put them off." Hohenger drank deeply of her own coffee, which was steaming hot and fresh. Morris winced.

"Don't deal with the requests yourself," he said. "These matters are up to them. If they must appeal their decisions to anyone, they must go to Bella. We must refuse to hear further protests."

Hohenger considered that. "Bella's a clever girl. But she's so very naive. I'd think that she could use some backing from us."

"Well, yes, that sounds helpful. But you're a chemist, while I'm a historian. I've seen the crippling effect that a higher authority can have on leadership. Let them work things out for themselves."

"Dr. Morris," Hohenger warned, "you'll lose control of them if you do that."

"Yes, that's true also." Morris sipped at his coffee, found it properly cooled, and took another sip.

∞

On the seventh day of their voyage, Hohenger gathered the eight students on a large, open equipment deck amidships. Under the supervision of the physics students, she intended to perform a variation of the Proctor-Lawrence experiment. Morris stood by and watched in rapt fascination.

"Bella, fit the aluminum casings into the first emitter port — snugly, now! Emil, wait until she's gotten clear . . . Wait, I said. . . . Very well. Arm the board." Hohenger looked about and nodded in satisfaction at what she saw. A timer on one data screen commenced a staid countdown.

Hohenger launched into a terse explanation. "The original form of the Proctor-Lawrence observation was a procedure in which a metal boom was extended through an airlock. It detected and registered radiation in the jumpspace cosmos and gave a good bound on the jumpspace speed-of-light constant. Doctor Morris" — she indicated the historian with a nod — "has suggested that some faster-than-light signal might have arrived, somehow causing the launch of the probe we're tracing. If such forces are still in place between Marterly and our destination, then a more careful procedure is called for."

She turned and gestured. From the emitter lock, six small aluminum slugs shot free, flying away into

111

the fiery heat of jumpspace. In only moments they were lost amid the deep-red background glow. A moment later, beyond the protective compensation fields that kept the ship alive, the slugs entered a region where they seemed, paradoxically, to be several tens of thousands of degrees hot, and several days older each passing minute. They disintegrated in star-shaped bursts of brilliantly glowing sparks. Soon, a huge, six-lobed sphere of gleaming yellow dust enveloped the ship — a glowing fog of monatomic aluminum. As it expanded, it dimmed, although the glow grew hotter with time.

A portion of the cloud expanded far enough to intercept the laser beam that shot between a mysterious origin far ahead and an equally mysterious receiver on Marterly. The beam, some ten meters wide, excited the motes of aluminum to a searingly bright fluorescence. Instruments aboard the university ship depicted the shape of the beam upon Hohenger's visual display screens.

"A laser beam."

"Traveling more than a thousand times faster than light."

"Think what it would mean. . . ."

Hohenger listened with amusement to the students' chatter. She wrinkled her chin in a wry smile when Bella launched into an animated discussion of the historical and political implications. She forbore to laugh when Emil and his cronies began speaking in a nearly unintelligible dialect composed of letters, words for symbols, and numbers. She turned to Morris, thinking to ask him what everyday effect faster communications could possibly have.

112

The expression he wore silenced her. Morris's face mingled optimism, fatalism, and sure, certain knowledge in equal parts, and the revelation he had received promised him only that nothing he had ever known would be the same.

Fewer than four days separated them from the station.

10

You have explored the world, while I have
studied only myself. Yet you have learned of
yourself, and I have learned of the world. Life
and love, self and world, are all one.

— Achorus,
The Skeleton and the Chaffinch

Taviella's curiosity, with Maravic's tacit backing,
offset Eric's reservations and Remington's fears.
Taviella landed the *Coinroader* smoothly upon the
flat surface near the domes and huts of the communications station.

Few details were immediately obvious; the station was blended subtly into the smoothed rock of
the immense, flat asteroid. High overhead, soft dif-
fuse lights hovered, suspended by no perceivable
means. The light they cast was as unlike that cast by
normal incandescent floodlights as daylight is unlike city-light; yet there was still a horrid pallor over
the plain, and the sky was dark beyond. From the
station, a dozen windows and portholes gleamed,
blazing forth a warm, homelike glow. Most notice-

able was an arch of concentric lines of light, a fiery neon rainbow that rendered the main hatch highly visible.

"Festival," Eric muttered in acknowledgment of the brilliant colors.

Taviella's hands tightened on her controls, and deep within her she knew a panicky desire to escape. Mastering this, she sweated through the idling-down procedure, which would leave the ship ready for a fairly fast takeoff, if not an immediate one. She wasn't about to leave this worldlet until she'd explored it first.

"Who goes? Who stays?" Maravic asked.

"Eric and I go; everyone else will wait here." Taviella looked at her copilot and spread her hands. "Sound fair?"

Eric and Remington pushed their heads in through the hatchway, disdaining the use of the intercom for this discussion.

"I don't mind looking about," Eric said casually. He seemed not to relish the historical opportunity. "You're sure you don't want to simply report this to the proper authorities?"

"We're already in technical violation of our charter," Maravic said cheerfully. "As long as we're here, let's get some close-up views."

"Right," said Taviella. "Stacey can run the ship if Eric is incapacitated—"

"Thanks a lot!"

". . . and Maravic knows the ship better than I do, and is as good a pilot."

"I am not," Maravic said. But then she smiled and favored Taviella with an approving thumbs-up.

115

"Go on, you two — get out of here. And take lots of pictures."

Eric and Taviella hastened into their EVA suits and strapped to themselves whatever extraneous equipment they could think of. Side by side they cycled through the crewlock and stepped out onto the cold stone of the large, flat planetoid.

"Distant horizon," Eric muttered. "You'd think you were on a planet."

"But only half a kilometer below us is just more emptiness. The other face of this rock."

"I worked through the math: there have to be gravity generators inside it, or the place would crumple under its own weight. Also, even as big as it is, it wouldn't hold us here with the apparent weight we're feeling."

For Taviella, it was much worse: the bleak, flat landscape, sharp and dim, was chillingly like the priests' tales of the land of the forsworn dead. Above, stars unwinking shone without rise or set, the eyes of great cold spiders gazing hatefully from the icy dome of the heavens.

She stiffened her spine and plodded determinedly toward the light-framed doorway.

"Taviella," Maravic called. Her voice, coming through Taviella's helmet headset, was grainy and filtered in with the rushing sound of interference static.

"Yes?" Taviella found that if she kept her head low, her visor limited her view to the rock and dust underfoot; she hesitated to meet the stars' gaze.

"Adjust your camera; we're losing resolution. Eric, too. Bad static."

"It's the outside interference," Eric asserted. "That's the only thing that would bother both at once." His voice, too, was distorted and weak.

"All right," Maravic said, intent upon the problem. "Both of you tune your cameras and microphones to highest gain, and once you get inside the station, leave the door open, relaying communications from there."

"If we can," Eric muttered. He started forward again, only to be brought up short again by Maravic's call.

"Eric?" Her voice was crisp, clear, and far too loud.

"What is it this time?" he snapped, irritated despite himself. He hoped his voice roared inside Maravic's headphones the way hers had just resounded in his.

"What did you just do to your camera and to Taviella's?" Her voice was at a normal level now.

"Nothing!" Eric looked at Taviella and saw only the dim outlines of her face within her suit helmet. The camera affixed to the side of her helmet was small and flat, molded directly into the plastic. A tiny red indicator light blinked steadily, showing that the camera was operating normally.

"The interference just cut off. I'm receiving you square, clear, and free."

"Good for us." Eric's sarcasm rang hollow as he spoke with a suddenly dry throat. "We know that automatic equipment still operates here. Some signal rectifier probably picked up our broadcasts and stopped some other signal from getting in our way."

To him, and to the others, it still felt all too much

like someone had opened a window, the better to observe as the two figures approached the forlorn station.

∞

In the command couch of the *Coinroader*, Maravic followed her signal-strength indicators with experienced ease. The soft seat rustled as she moved, and she felt her skin growing damp with nervous sweat. Beside her, in the copilot's couch, Remington sat at rest, his arms crossed, eyeing the monitors that displayed the images relayed from Taviella's and Eric's cameras.

Behind them Stasileus loomed, bending so far forward that Maravic could look up and see his short, trembling chin. His soft scent filled the cramped control room, and his rapid breath sounded as a quick fluttering. Neither was unpleasant, and Maravic was aware of him without being distracted by him.

"Signals are both strong," Remington muttered. Taviella was keeping her head down, so her camera showed little more than the rocks and the distant base of the buildings.

"All clear?" Maravic asked Taviella and Eric.

"We'll tell you if anything changes," Eric said. Maravic turned and murmured to Remington, "All's clear."

"How are we going to get in?" Taviella asked her companion.

"I don't know," Eric answered. "Let's get closer, and we'll see."

"We can't know whether it's locked, or what kinds of locks they might have used."

"I'm aware of that," he said with a bit of an edge. A moment later he relented. "There are only so many ways of making an airlock. Maybe we'll get in, and maybe we won't, but at least I can assure you we'll be able to tell pretty quickly."

Maravic and Remington watched through Eric's camera as he arrived at the door. Stasileus, as well, watched in breathless excitement.

The door was thick and solid, formed in a ridged, wavy pattern of dark blue metal. The colored lights from the rainbow-arch above reflected darkly in the deep, burnished surface.

"Sealed." Eric's voice carried a note of finality.

"No way in?" Taviella asked.

"No way to force the doors open." Eric's voice was tense, but the intended humor in his words carried through. "You know, some doors you can just insert a pry bar and bend back. Now we have to look around for a control circuit. Maybe there'll be an outside junction box of some sort, and we can override its electronics."

"If we can't get in—" Taviella began.

"Then we'll have to go back, won't we?"

Maravic and Remington each smiled wistful, unconscious smiles. Eric sometimes acted like a walking headache, waiting to happen to someone.

Outside, Eric stiffened. "Hold on . . . hold on . . ." He found an electric conduit and pried it away from the wall. With a small power tool he cut gingerly into the shielding, exposing the wiring within. He clipped test leads onto several of the wires; his left

119

wrist came up toward the camera, toward his face, where he read the results. "I can send impulses along these wires," he muttered softly.

"What will it do?"

"How the heck would I know?" Eric turned to Taviella. On the *Coinroader*, Maravic saw her friends as seen by one another's cameras. "Maybe I'll hit the self-destruct circuit, and we'll find ourselves at the bottom of the universe's biggest rockslide."

"Very funny." Taviella breathed out. "Go ahead, then."

Eric bent, twisted free from his backpack full of equipment, and selected some signal-generation tools. He clamped a set of power leads onto exposed wires and sent a short jolt of current into the unknown system.

For a long time nothing seemed to happen. Eric tried different wires, different current strengths. On his twenty-third try, the controls switched over, unseen servos tripped, and the crenellated doors bent in fan-folds, retreating to either side.

"Poor design," Eric muttered. No one bothered to contradict him.

The air within the station metered as being pure and wholesome. Doubtless the ancient purifiers were still at work. Doubtless Eric would denigrate their design also. Taviella signaled for continued helmet discipline, having no desire to be surprised by some unmetered airborne chemicals, or by something as mundane — and deadly — as free-floating allergens.

The entryway extended forward only a short distance. Ahead, framed carefully on the wall, was a

120

directory, its not-quite-familiar letters tagged in neat rows to a backboard. The floor was featureless for a space, changing ahead to a strange tessellated pattern of flat plates, each featuring dozens of small, raised nubbins in regular rows and files. It looked somewhat like an infinite stretch of keypad, or merely a roughened non-slip surface.

Above the directory board, painted sharp red against the white wall, was a symbol, possibly heraldic, of an irregular circle with four radiating spokes.

Eric, beside Taviella, inhaled quickly and went limp, his eyes wide, his chin dropping in slack-jawed astonishment. Taviella turned to him, in time to catch him as he sagged to his knees. At the same time, she heard a vague commotion from the ship.

Already? Have things gone wrong already?

"Eric? You okay?" She didn't wait for an answer. "Maravic? Report!"

"Yes." Maravic's voice was crisp, almost frantic.

"Maravic?"

"Yes."

Taviella frowned. What was wrong with her crew? What could have caused Maravic to lose her aplomb?

"Eric? Can you stand?"

Eric startled her by climbing quickly to his feet, there to stand and blink at her. He stood facing away from the symbol on the wall.

"Did you see it?" he asked her.

"Yes. What was it?"

Eric recovered swiftly, yet his voice carried a shocked tremor. "I don't have any idea." He shook his head to clear it.

"Maravic, did you see it?"

"We got it. And there are three people here who will never forget it." Maravic, too, sounded badly shaken.

"What happened?" Taviella demanded, swinging her body about to search for any possible source of disturbance.

"The symbol. That symbol on the wall," Maravic said, her voice low and shaking. "It's an eye, or a mouth, or a . . ." She cut off her next words, biting her lip to keep from speaking.

"What?" Taviella stood regarding the thing in bewilderment. "It's only a painting. Isn't it?"

"Ask Eric. Ask Remington. Ask Stacey, who nearly leaped through the screen when you gave us our first look at it."

Eric held up his gloved hand. "I'll be okay, but I'm not going to look at it again, if I can avoid it. Whew!"

"Remington felt the same way," Maravic reported. "He went pale as a plume and closed his eyes."

"I'm okay," Remington interjected. "But, Taviella, will you turn away from it, please?"

Taviella took one last glance at the symbol, then turned her back on it. She was totally perplexed. "I want to look at it again. Let me blank out my camera." She reached up beside her helmet and switched the camera off.

"Stacey took it the worst," Maravic went on. "He stood bolt upright — and he shouldn't do that in this clearance — and opened his eyes wider than I would have thought even his could open."

"Is he okay?" Taviella asked.

A brief pause followed. "He's trembling like a

leaf. He's got shudders running through the whole length of his body. . . . Stacey?" Maravic's voice was soothing. "Stacey?"

"Yes?" Stasileus's voice wavered, high-pitched and echoing.

"Are you all right?"

"Yes," he whispered.

"No, he's not," Maravic told Taviella.

"How could this affect anyone so severely?" Taviella wondered.

"Didn't you feel anything?" Eric demanded.

"Not a thing."

"Remember her ancestry, Eric," Maravic said, very softly.

"Yeah," Eric muttered. "That figures."

"Is this some cultural ritual I don't know of?"

"No, Taviella." Maravic paused for a moment, choosing how to say it. "It's genetic."

"Has to be," Eric interjected. "Nothing else would work. Have Remington keep a close watch on Stacey. Better yet, get 'em both out of there altogether."

"Right. They shouldn't watch any longer," Maravic agreed.

"Genetic?" Taviella's voice was very small. She studied the symbol and found nothing in it, nothing at all, to drive her friends to such agitation. Bewildered by the mystery, she waited for them to enlighten her.

Eric tried first. "Ever hear a baby crying?"

"Of course. Remember where I'm from."

"Right. Most people never have. I first heard a tape of it in an introductory biology class. Damnedest thing I'd ever heard. You *can't* ignore it. You can't go on reading, studying, or working. You just keep turning to face that thrice-damned, high-pitched wailing. I've heard feedback squeals that jarred on my nerves a lot less."

"So . . . ?"

"It's genetic. It's part of how we're made. Our genetic programming has a ready-made response to that noise. I suppose you can see the evolutionary advantage to it."

"Yes. Of course. If you tend a baby, it might live. Are you saying that the symbol on this wall works the same way?"

"Yes. I can't look at it without cringing. I feel about as guilty as if I'd been caught stealing. I could no more tell a lie in front of that thing than I could fly, or breathe water."

"Maravic," Taviella said softly after a second, "how can this be?"

"I don't know the mechanisms. I do know that genetic inheritance of innate behaviors is still poorly understood. When we see anything in red — blood red — our heart rate jumps, just a little bit. That also happens when we hear someone scream in fright."

"So you're all suffering a genetic, innate reaction to this? You can't control it?"

"No. It . . . it just reaches out and takes me." Eric was understandably on edge. "I feel compelled to obey it, to worship it. . . . If I get time, I can show you the bandpass calculations for this sort of thing. Remember, the human body carries a *lot* of information in its genes."

Taviella was on the verge of calling off the exploration. "I don't like to stick my nose into things I don't understand. What else are we likely to find in this place? How dangerous will it be to go on? If a simple picture painted on a wall can set all you people to spasming . . ." She stopped. "My ancestry? Why wasn't I affected?"

"Our parents descended from the serfs and the criminals, the outcasts and the classless, of the downfallen Empire of Archive. Your parents came from a long, purebred line of uppercrust nobles." Maravic said this as gently as possible, yet she could not keep her voice free from a bit of judgment.

It's not fair, Taviella mourned, deep within herself. *My world is poor and filthy. I spent half my life in the dirt of it.* She knew, and she had always known, how this set her apart from the rest of her crew. She would never be their equal. Now, with all the utter indignity that a nonsensical universe could heap upon her, she was scorned by her friends because her ancestors had been the betters of theirs.

"You're saying that the awe, or whatever it is, that you feel for this painted medallion is not a product of natural selection?"

"That's right," Maravic answered, trying to sound more accepting than she felt. "The modification is a deliberate one, one that we've inherited and you haven't. It's more efficient than secret police, and instills loyalty more deeply than the lash."

Remington spoke up, his voice tired. "That also explains why Stacey was so deeply affected. I've been reading up . . . I've got some magazines that tell a little about his race. It seems that we have five to ten modifications per ten thousand gene loci, but the Vernae are nearly *three per cent* recombinant."

"Keep an eye on him, then," Eric snapped. "Even that brief exposure might have had a critical effect."

"Right," acknowledged Maravic. "Remington, go on back to the hold. Try to help Stacey adjust."

"Right."

Taviella took yet another look at the offending symbol. The color of it, the shape of it, the placement . . . none seemed to have any effect upon her at all. It simply looked . . . right. There was a pleasing symmetry about it, a comforting propriety in the balance of the curves and lines. She could find nothing wrong with it at all. She sighed.

"If we're going to explore this place, Eric, we might as well get going." She stepped out into a cross-corridor and onto the raised-patterned floor tiles — and leaped backward frantically, her arms and legs cartwheeling uncontrollably. She and Eric fell to the smooth portion of the floor, tangled together in a heap.

"Electrified," she gasped, still feeling the effects. "The damn floor is electrified!"

"Biometry reads okay," Maravic said, very calmly, for Eric's benefit. "No damage, no vital shock. Heart rate slowing to normal."

"Electrified," Taviella repeated, unbelieving.

"Well," said Eric, "at least that's not a genetic obstacle, merely a generic one. I've got an easy cure back on the ship."

"What?"

"Insulated overshoes for our boots."

"We're going back to get them. I'm going to explore this place until I've found its every secret, if it takes a month."

The station could insult her ancestry all it wanted, but no one — *no one* — knocked her on her backside without suffering for it.

She and Eric trooped back to the ship in silence, aware that more planning was necessary. Low before them, silhouetted against a billion stars, the *Coinroader* represented safety, perhaps sanity. Gray rock and black sky bruised her eyes until she climbed into the dark airlock, which closed behind with a subliminal vibration. The last thing she saw outside was the invitingly and colorfully lit doorway to the station.

11

'Mankind is argumentative, contentious, and disputatious,' Trinopus asserted.
'Master, I disagree,' said his apprentice.
— *Trinopus's Paradox, from*
A Holding of Apparitions

I am not proud. I will not debate, contend, or dispute. I would be well pleased to be wrong.

— *Aeantis's refutation*
of Trinopus's Paradox

You are.

— *Trinopus's response*

Aboard the *Coinroader*, the crew did not relax, and their discussion was heated and direct. It seemed to Maravic, who tried to hold herself away from the brunt of the debate, that a wandering ghost, a perverse, pugnacious element of Old Archive, had entered the ship.

Maravic lay full-length on the cargo room floor,

balancing a mug of hot chocolate on her stomach and cushioning her head on a stack of bound journals. One of the magazines had been well thumbed through, first by Remington, later by Maravic. It explained all that was known, at this early date, about the physiology of the Vernae.

Above her, to her left and at her feet, Remington and Eric sat perched tensely on cargo crates, taking drinks by turns from an oversized, turned-aluminum flagon of small beer. Eric passed it back to Remington and wiped his mouth nervously.

"I don't want to go back in there," he said, simply and directly. "I didn't think I was scared until I got back aboard the ship. That was a bigger relief than I thought it would be, and I find I don't want to leave again." He knew better, however, than to expect that view to carry the day.

Taviella, at Maravic's head, sat with her back against the bulkhead, drinking nothing, holding nothing in her hands. Maravic could gaze far up and look at her captain, who sat so still.

She doesn't fidget with her hands; she sits there like a carving. Like the carvings she's shown me from her homeworld. Oh, I don't like it when she lets her heritage show; it's a certain sign of trouble to come.

Maravic determined not to take a part in the discussion, but worried if that decision was itself a taking of sides.

"We will explore this station, and we will learn its every secret." Taviella spoke softly, yet firmly and directly. Her eyes were cold and flat, her features pinched and drawn.

"Fine," Eric muttered. "Get another crew." He

took a hasty swig from the flagon as Remington handed it to him, and pushed it back into the cargo chief's hand. "Okay, wait. I didn't mean that. I'm not going to go all mutinous on you. Hell, if I do that, I lose my profit share." He smiled, Remington shrugged, Maravic smiled, and Taviella sat with a face of stone.

Stasileus watched the flagon of beer pass back and forth between Remington and Eric. His eyes were still much too wide, and he remained much too silent. Maravic thought that his eternal trembling was more pronounced than usual. She kept an eye on him, seeing him crammed into a corner, shivering, presenting as little of his body to sight as he could arrange.

Taviella relented. "I guess you don't know how much all of this hurts me. That station . . . that symbol. . . . Damn it, it sat there and made me out to be some sort of tyrant. I can't understand . . ."

"I don't get something," Remington put in. "How can that symbol have a genetic control over us? I've read quite a bit of popularized science articles, but I don't usually pay as much attention to the ones on biology. Aren't we talking about inheritance of acquired characteristics?"

"What do you mean?"

Remington looked at Taviella. "Just because my great-granddaddy was conditioned to fear that thing, how come I must? It came over me in a wave; I couldn't look away—"

"We know what it does to you," Taviella snapped.

"For them to get everyone," Maravic said softly, "they would have needed centralized control of all

130

obstetrics. All births would have been overseen, and infants treated instantly. If you get one entire generation, all others would carry the awe for the symbol as a dominant trait."

"*We* have centralized obstetrics," Remington blurted. "Does that mean—"

"No." Maravic laughed a little and caught her mug of chocolate before it spilled. "What we do is pretty ordinary. The Empire would have needed something universal. Like contraceptives in the drinking water, with a carefully metered counteractive given only by regulated permit. And they could never stop it. If they missed even one of their slaves, his or her children might form the basis for a resistant subpopulation."

"The Emperor and his nobles, of course, were not treated," Eric groused. He didn't look toward Taviella, but his thoughts were obvious.

Taviella, stung, sprang to her feet and stepped over Maravic's supine form. "Look at me, Eric. I'm your captain. I'm not a noble. I'm not a slave-taking tyrant. I don't rule you — I have enough trouble persuading you to do things my way by reasonable argument. If I compelled you to oversee the ship's engines by means of the magical genetic force you cannot ignore, you'd be resentful and sullen and would probably jump ship at your earliest chance." She stood facing him, her fists at her hips, her jaw clenched, and her eyes blazing.

That's better, Maravic thought. *That's a posture she learned from me.* Trouble still spiced the air. Maravic again imagined the presence of a ghost of an ancient of Archive — a noble, perhaps one of

Taviella's ancestors. She shrugged and put it from her mind. *That damn symbol did unpleasant things to me, I'm afraid. What are my dreams going to be like for the next few nights?*

Eric shrank back a bit. Remington held on to the chilly flagon and sipped from it surreptitiously. Stasileus leaned ever farther into himself, folded up into the tightest imaginable ball. Maravic's heart went out to him; she wouldn't wish anyone to be forced to witness as unpleasant a scene as this one, least of all someone as basically timid and friendly as Stacey.

" 'Reasonable argument,' eh?" Eric said, his gaze meeting Taviella's. "Okay, here's mine. I'm not going back out there, because it's too dangerous. We haven't got enough of a margin of safety." He began to count points off on his fingers. "My tools don't match their fittings. My meters aren't set to the same voltages. The place almost certainly has safeguards, defenses, who knows? We know that the Empire was fond of slaves, created servants, and such." He nodded to Stasileus. "My capable assistant, here, could tell you a thing or two about the Old Empire's callousness." He held up a hand. "And all I mean by that is that there may be guard robots. I wasn't making any reference to—"

"We'll be careful," Taviella said. She walked back to the bulkhead and slid down it to sit wearily on the deck. "You're right, I know. It will be dangerous. But there are riches out there, and I'm greedy enough to want to claim them. That, plus the fact that the Concordat is almighty frightened of any of the Empire's technology that ever turns up—"

"Look how reluctant they are to grant archaeology permits," Maravic said.

"Exactly," Eric snapped. "Have you guys heard the rumor about a planet disappearing from Voss Sector? I know that's a long distance from here—"

Remington smiled. "Who listens to rumors, anyway? Their interest is inverse to their truthfulness."

"A whole planet?" Maravic wondered. "Was anyone on it at the time?"

Eric remained silent, and Taviella shrugged.

A long silence settled in. Remington drained the flagon and filled it again. Eric listlessly folded his arms, looking anywhere but at Taviella. Maravic, lying comfortably on the floor, could see him mustering his courage to defy Taviella, but fearful to say anything aloud. Taviella, for her part, had reserves of obstinacy that Eric and Remington never suspected, and which Maravic had seen only rarely. Sighing, Maravic set aside her empty mug. In the back, Stasileus fretted, huddled into a ball of misery.

They sat or lay strewn across the decking, or up on crates, scattered in various relaxed postures. Taviella smiled and broke the silence. "I ought to get a table and chairs put in here."

"Remington would sit on the edge of the table," Maravic grinned, "and Eric on top of it proper. I'd lie underneath, and you'd sit sideways on your chair with your legs over the arms."

A quick grin passed around the room. Remington coughed.

"What about our problem?" Eric asked.

"Well? You know what I want." Taviella sat a bit forward. "What do *you* want?"

Eric answered. "I'm asking you to look at the balance. Sure, I agree, there will be valuable finds there. We could be richer than anything. We could also be dead."

"We can get around any static defenses, Eric. You know that."

"I *don't* know that! And what about mobile defenses?"

"There's a pistol in the locker," Taviella said, dismissing the danger with a wave of her hand.

"Look . . ." Eric began. He spread his arms helplessly. "I'll admit it — I'm scared. That place is crazy. If it's as old as we think it is, the air should have bled away long ago. What are those electrified floors for? And I'll be *damned* if I like staying in a place where the neutrinos display weird energies."

A very quiet voice riveted them all. "Air is replaced by regeneration from inert materials."

Everyone turned to watch Stasileus, who spoke in a near-whisper. His face and ears peeped from behind his drawn-up knees; he shivered with an unguessable terror. "The electrified floors pass power to free-roving equipment carts. The neutrinos react harmlessly with the nuclei of ordinary atoms."

Taviella waited. Stasileus volunteered no more. "How do you know this?" she prompted.

"The air resupply and electrified floors are techniques we still use, at home. We inherited that much, and not much more, from the fallen masters of the Empire."

"And the neutrinos?"

"They are—"

"Dangerous," Eric interrupted as he turned to

134

Stasileus. "They're dangerous to us, aren't they? Not the neutrinos themselves, but the altered fundamental constants."

Stasileus, seeing the two ways he was being pulled, by Eric and by Taviella, froze. He watched them through great, frightened eyes.

"Come on, Eric!" Taviella nearly shouted. "He's just told us that it's safe. We're going in there."

"Not me."

"And why not?" Her patience was exhausted.

"I don't want to face that weird symbol again."

"You don't . . ." Taviella reddened, stood, and flew from the cargo hold through the forward hatch. She returned a moment later with a paper flapping in her hand. On it flamed the symbol in bold red ink, as printed by the ship's computer from recordings of the camera scans from the station. She waved it before them. "It's only a drawing! Are you coming with me or not?"

Maravic bruised both her elbows as she leaped desperately to her feet. Eric sprang forward with an inchoate cry that died in his throat. Remington staggered up and nearly swooned, but stayed on his feet. Stasileus unfolded himself smoothly and stood erect, arms motionless at his sides. His trembling had ceased.

In all of them, the light in their eyes had gone out. They were no longer themselves.

Taviella's eyes widened somewhat, then opened even farther. This wasn't an extravagant dumb-show of sarcastic obedience. Her crew — the best friends she had ever had in all her tumultuous life — had been snapped off as if a switch had been thrown. They stood before her, yet she was horribly aware that no one was truly with her. She was alone. She voiced a timid inquiry. "Guys?"

Their gazes rested on her, as blank and unexpressive as the gazes of empty skulls.

Hastily, with trembling hands, Taviella crumpled the paper and threw it roughly from her. Stasileus blinked at that; Taviella looked at him, not understanding who or what he truly was. Stasileus stepped back and turned, then walked calmly forward, out of the room.

Taviella didn't notice that he had left, or which direction he had gone. By now, tears were flowing freely from her eyes. Sobbing openly, she ran to Maravic, who received her emotionlessly.

"I didn't know. I didn't know," Taviella said as she wept. She repeated herself, over and over, hugging the unresponsive Maravic.

After a time, Maravic recovered. She stood faced with the two aspects of her captain. She saw the helpless girl crying in embarrassed shame at what was no more than a faux pas ... and she saw the fiery mistress of power who had commanded her in a voice like a tolling bell. Shaking herself, Maravic did what she could to comfort Taviella. It was her old Taviella now, the pilot, the business executive, the woman who tended to know her own mind.

Eric's eyes drew into a squint; then he relaxed. Remington took a couple of paces back and forth, as if limbering up stiff muscles.

"I didn't know," Taviella said softly, apologetically, to Remington.

"It's okay."

Eric looked over and added his own words of comfort. "It's okay, Taviella, really it is. We're not angry."

Taviella hid her face. "But you ought to be."

Eric shook his head, his eyes now his own, his expression back to normal. "You shouldn't expect me to be angry. Not at that." He walked over and picked the crumpled scrap of paper from the deck. Smoothing it with reverence, with respect, and with subdued awe, he regarded it for a time. Then he folded it carefully. "None of us are angry." He sat again on the cargo crate and looked about for the flagon of beer.

Taviella looked at Remington, who shrugged. "I can't explain what I'm feeling," he said. "I'm just kind of numb. That symbol has a very potent effect on us. You're lucky you're immune."

Taviella wanted to ask Stasileus how he felt; he had clearly been the most affected. But he wasn't with them. She wondered why he had left. Had he fled in horror? Or had the symbol driven him away?

Where was the resentment they should all have felt? She stood bewildered. Eric's head rose, and he laughed. "Oh, hell. I've got it. You wouldn't want your slaves angry at you every time you ordered them to hop to some arduous task. The Empire's geneticists took it one step beyond mere obedience: willing obedience."

"You're not mad at me? None of you?"

"Nope. We can't be."

"Intellectually, if not emotionally?"

Maravic laughed. "Where's the difference, really? I may be just rationalizing, or I may be under the control of some linkage of brain chemicals we'll never understand." Then she grew serious. "Taviella, please don't do that again."

Taviella recoiled again, inwardly. The symbol was a damnably evil tool, a whip that both exhorts and does not hurt.

"I think you may be right, guys," she said, trying to sound more casual than she felt. "I think that station is more dangerous than I realized."

"We make no more trips inside the place, then?" Eric asked hopefully.

"No more. Let's get out of here."

"Sounds good."

"I'll go forward and ready the ship for takeoff," Maravic said.

"Wait." At Taviella's word, everyone halted — just a bit too suddenly, she thought, just a bit too thoroughly. *Will the effect wear off?* Taviella wondered in sudden fear. *It had better! I'm not a tyrant. I'm not!*

She looked around her. "Where did Stacey go?"

"He's not in the control room," Maravic said after peering forward.

"I'll run back to the engine room and look," Eric volunteered.

Remington had already started a careful survey of the cargo pallets. As he had assumed, there was no place in the load where a man — or a Verna — could hide. He made a quick search of the off-duty sleeping cabins. "Nope. He's not here." He wandered back to the equipment locker and popped his head within. "And if he's not here . . ." He drew back out again and looked at the crew.

Maravic felt, for the third time, the ghost of a noble of the old Empire of Archive. She seemed to see his face, nodding just at the corner of her vision. She shivered.

"One of the EVA suits is missing," Remington said after prying about within the equipment locker. His voice was unhappy. "He's out there." He jerked a thumb toward the aft airlock, out of sight behind the engine room bulkhead. "He slipped away while we weren't watching."

A moment's work with the instruments proved that Stasileus wasn't somewhere out on the plain of gray rock.

"Stacey? Stacey? Come in." Maravic repeated this several times, but if Stasileus had his radio on, he wasn't answering the call.

"Pick him up on the echolocator," Eric suggested, and before she could react he reached forward over Maravic's shoulder to activate it. "If he's anywhere nearby, we'll read him."

To no one's surprise, the locator indicated that Stasileus was somewhere inside the station.

"Looks like we go exploring anyway," Remington muttered, trudging back again to the equipment locker. He returned in a few minutes with four EVA suits.

"And I'm no happier about it than any of you," Taviella said with a sigh. She pushed back her hair and donned her suit in miserable silence. With thick-gloved hands, she fastened down the thick white helmet into the collar-seal of the baggy white suit.

"Radio check," she said. The others counted off.

"A rescue mission," Eric said sardonically. "How exciting, just like a lifejacket drill."

"Do you want me along?" Maravic asked. She blushed and continued quickly, "I'll come, if you need me, but I thought . . ."

Eric looked over at her and, without saying a word, expressed himself very clearly. He didn't need to speak; his eyes, always cruel, spoke for him.

Remington, surprisingly, made it all right again. "Hey, I'm scared, too. We've got to do this, though."

Taviella nodded. "It's one of the rules. It's the way it is in space. No one gets left behind, no matter what the cost."

"Within reason, of course," Eric mumbled.

"No." Taviella stood firm. "Beyond it. Far, far beyond it. We might all die here, but rescue is one of those duties that may not be denied."

She looked about, then nodded again, satisfied that no one disagreed. "Maravic, you'd best come along with us. We'll leave the ship in lock-down, so no one could strand us here. Things are odd, the radio transmission clearing up so suddenly. It could go bad again, and then what? You'd have to come in after us, all alone."

Maravic nodded, realizing that she didn't like that option any better.

Taviella stepped off. "Let's get it over with."

For now, her crew believed that the symbol, the visible badge of human authority, had had no effect upon her. Best that they continue to think that. But she'd had time, in the past few minutes, to think about it and to examine her own feelings. And if a willing and almost eager obedience was the effect it

140

had upon most people, well . . . upon those born to the use of it, the symbol had a different calling. Obeying orders was the inherited curse of her three human crew members and the one Verna. Giving orders, forcing obedience, and feeling a fulfillment from it all was the inherited curse that Taviella-i-Tel carried behind her eyes.

12

If I have anticipated much that has happened, it is only because I have also anticipated much more that has not happened.
— Paleologos, *Once Too Often Whipped*

Doctor Hohenger, supervising operations aboard the telescopy dredge, discovered Doctor Morris slipping into frequent reveries. Sometimes she would stumble upon him curled comfortably in an odd corner of the cluttered lab ship, reading, always reading. He habitually arrived late for the regularly scheduled conference lunches, and he ate so slowly that he was the last to leave. A thoughtful look always showed in his eyes, and he held his lips pursed inelegantly.

Time slipped by, and the voyage neared completion. Hohenger spent a frustrating twenty minutes trying to locate the errant historian, eventually to find him relaxing beneath the telescope mounts. About him lay strewn a detritus of travel: books, notes, odd bits of paper; a scholarly and tidy litter indicative of his thought.

"Doctor Morris?" Hohenger said softly, interrupting Morris's meditation.

"Yes? Has there been a problem?" Morris looked up over the top of his book with a polite, incurious gaze.

"What is it that's absorbing you? Neither I nor any of the students have had more than a word from you in three days."

"I've been reading." Morris set the book down gently, creasing back a corner of one page to mark his place. Hohenger winced slightly at his easy carelessness. "Ancient history, mostly," Morris continued. He rose slowly to his feet from the deck where he'd been stretched out.

"We'll be arriving soon at the source of that anomalous faster-than-light laser beam. We've been unable to learn any more about its origin or cause."

Morris nodded. "I have." He smiled as Hohenger lifted her head in puzzlement. "I've learned this: the old Empire of Archive had the technology to produce these beams, for purposes of communication."

"That's what we've had to assume," Hohenger agreed. "Perhaps it was an ancient message, only recently arriving back at Marterly, that triggered the flight of the buried drone."

"Perhaps. Probably. But a message would not arrive *now* unless it was *sent* now. I mistrust the timing of this." Morris ran his hand through his hair and stepped to one side, preparatory to pacing. "The Empire did not do things in accidental or coincidental ways. They were far too — what shall I call it? — too rigid in their licentious carelessness. They didn't

143

leave things to chance, yet at the same time they were far, far from rational."

"How much of this is known, and how much is speculation?" Hohenger shrewdly asked.

Morris smiled a happy and honest lecturer's smile. "Speculation? Nearly all. We have so little real knowledge, because of the Emperor's last order, when all of the libraries were burned. And that's a case in point, an example of the Empire's irrationality. They used incredibly elaborate safeguards, sometimes in the form of self-destruct triggers or suicidally programmed slaves. They chose to *act* the part of devious tyrants in total control of their environment, but they actually lived in real terror of their lives. The Emperor sent out his message to all the libraries known to him, and the message was simple: erase yourself. Gone, in an instant, was all the knowledge of three millennia of history."

"What do you mean by self-destruct triggers? How much danger will we be in?"

Morris faced her squarely. "We will be in substantial danger if we discover any real artifact of Empire." He began to pace, slowly, straying back and forth yet always comfortably near Hohenger. "We can take precautions, and I will assure you that the danger to us will be primarily from our own ignorance. The Empire did not build to harm others, you see, but only to frustrate would-be thieves and vandals."

"Expand on that, please." Hohenger was secretly pleased; this was the longest conversation she'd had with Doctor Morris since the voyage began. His intelligence fascinated her, as did his mature wisdom. She found herself relaxing in his presence, a distinct relief after dealing with eight youthful and exuberant students for the past few days. She hated their flighty, disorganized quarrels and always compared their behavior with Morris's placidity and insight. Hohenger felt more and more justified in having chosen him to come along.

"The burning of the libraries," Morris went on, "was really more petulant than vengeful. The loss of billions of irreplaceable works of various lore crippled us, and we lost more than just our history. We lost our culture. On the word of one man, we lost our law, our science, our art, our history, our mathematics. . . . For the first fifty years after the Empire's demise, we had to rely on tradition, living memory, and word of mouth."

"Why?" Hohenger asked. "Do we know why all this happened?"

"The Emperor of Archive, Arcadian the First — the first, last, and only man ever to have sat upon the vast silvered throne — did it for what he considered the best of reasons. Once his Empire had crumbled, then knowledge served no purpose. He never gave a moment's thought to the future . . . to us."

He turned and kept pacing. "As a matter of fact, the erasure of the libraries was one of the clues to the existence of a communications relay such as the one we're trailing. Only a system as efficient as this would allow the transmission of the order as rapidly as would be necessary. It's the validation of a set of theories, sadly not my own."

"How could that order have been carried out?" said Hohenger in a tone of objection. "You would have balked at setting fire to all of your books; I know *I* would have. How did they compel this?"

"I don't know," Morris said simply. He smiled. "The Empire was held together by bonds of obedience stronger than any we can imagine. Suppose I were to order you to destroy the main telescope of this ship. Would you?"

Hohenger looked up at the shining cylindrical bulk of the main telescope, hanging above them as if it were weightless, supported by large load-bearing mounts. "Of course not."

"Such an order, and such obedience, would have been utterly first nature for the Magnates and Sultans of the Empire. But the point here is that no one would be injured from the sabotage of the telescope. That wouldn't be the purpose, just as the purpose of the erasing of all the libraries wasn't to hurt anyone. It was simply a gesture of completion: history was about to come to an end, or so the Emperor must have thought. What use, then, were books?"

Hohenger changed the subject, still slightly apprehensive about the Empire's weapons. "Would you say that the drone we're following is probably not a warhead-laden missile?"

"Oh, most certainly it isn't. If I were to be allowed a guess, I'd say it's an automated repair unit, or, at the most malicious, a spying one. Never a weapon."

A thought occurred to Hohenger. "If they automated their self-destruct triggers, but not their weapons, might they not also have automated the erasure of the libraries?"

Morris beamed. "My theory exactly, published three years ago . . . or was it four? . . . in the University Postscriptum." He waved his arms about in extravagant gestures, showing more animation than Hohenger had ever seen in him. "The message arrives, is buffered and processed by whatever machinery is standard for that purpose. The message is addressed to the mechanized librarian — most certainly a device of circuitry. The message is decoded, is read once, perhaps twice, and, in a flash, the whole library is unrecoverable. Only empty storage crystals remain: blank, pure, inert, and uninformative. A tragedy."

Scratch a scholar to expose a poet, Hohenger thought, knowing her own fancies to be somewhat less florid.

"I'm glad to have anticipated your theory," she said modestly.

"The pleasure was entirely mine," Morris said with a smile, his eyes twinkling.

"Another reason I sought you out was to tell you to put your theories on standby, and to start thinking in practical terms. We'll be exiting jumpspace in only a few hours. We expect to come out within only a few hours transit of the laser's source."

"Very well." Morris bent to scoop up his collection of books and papers. With a thought, he straightened again. "Oh, by the way, the architects of the Empire actually did automate their weapons. I never meant to give the impression that they didn't."

"Oh?"

"Their skills in building gigantic robotic weapons systems . . . bulking barrels of things made solely for killing . . . have never been surpassed."

Hohenger paled. "How unlikely is it . . . ?"

"Unlikely. Unlikely in the extreme." Morris knelt and gathered his papers in armloads.

Hohenger nodded and started out of the room. Morris's voice followed her, a hint of dark humor in his words. "Of course," he said breezily, "anything might be possible."

Hohenger favored him with a sour grimace, then stalked out of the room to see to a staggering load of preparations.

13

Simple enough a task to be accomplished
by a Verna.
— *Slogan of the early Third Century*

I would despair, but the situation is too
hopeless even for such a minimally positive
action. I will stay today in bed.
— *Trinopus's last words*

Sophia was not able to enter into Pindar's locked library despite her constant efforts over more than eight hundred years. She alone inhabited the station, and its arrangements were hers. The rooms and chambers were hers to maintain or to disturb; the physical plant and the support systems were hers to keep in tune or to allow to slide into dereliction. One specific duty held her in unchangeable thrall: to protect and operate the apparatus of the communications devices. The power supply must be kept functioning. The laser tubes and jumpspace rifts must be held in perfect alignment. The traffic of inflowing and outflowing messages must be kept moving with a vital and mandatory unimpeded efficiency. The time left over from this compelling need was hers for private use.

Nearly eight hundred years had passed since the last message had arrived. Sophia did not know whether inactivity could eventually drive her mad. Daily she waited for new messages to come in. Daily she sent her maintenance drones about the station, sampling the air, replacing corroded wiring, monitoring the organic decay of long-disused perishables. And daily she strove to penetrate the locked library.

She used drones. She used logic. She attempted complicated fabrications, both mechanical and electronic. She used hardware solutions. She used software solutions, hoping against hope to reset the internal representation of the physical switch that Pindar had closed. She used blank randomization, in a desperate attempt to hit upon the correct password. (But she knew all the while that the age of the cosmos was but a brief, brief moment against even a hopeful estimate of the computational time required.) She used guile. She used illogic. She used force. She used prayer. She used magic.

As every new day arrived, as Sophia kept the ritual clocks and calendars of Archive current to the millisecond, as the feasts and anniversaries and jubilees turned over and over again, she knew she was losing her sanity.

No new messages came in. No new messages went out. Only one item of communication kept her from peace, and that was the one, tiny, insignificant, annoying memorandum that had arrived only fourteen years after Pindar had left her. It was, ironically, an update for his library, coded from the Archive itself, addressed to the computerized library caretaker subsystem. It represented a job left unfulfilled, a duty yet to be seen to. It annoyed her in the way that a whining midge buzzing about one's head, always on the very edge of audibility, would annoy someone. Eight hundred years had turned it into a fixation; eight hundred years had turned it into an obsession.

Every other status indicator read as normal. Sophia made her morning rounds. The drones still needed repair, yet she was satisfied, for now, with the makeshift efforts that kept them working. Several peripheral instruments were still inoperative, but she gave only brief thought to their repair. The beam to Marterly held steady, showing no repetition of the momentary interruption of four days past.

She recalled with wry amusement the arrival of the repair drone from Marterly. It had touched down yesterday, coming from out of the sky on its aged and unstable attitude jets. Emitting a tiny remote repair module, it had established communication with Sophia by radio.

She told it that all was well. Why, then, it demanded, had the beam fluctuated? Sophia could only guess: some bit of dark matter, glowing hot in jumpspace, had eclipsed the beam. The repair drone continued to argue single-mindedly. Sophia, still amused, granted admittance to the repair module. She knew her systems to be properly functional, and that was more than she could say for the barely spaceworthy drone. It came into her receiving bay, looked around, made a series of utterly trivial adjustments, and started to leave.

Sophia asked it to reset the hardware switch that had caused her so much woe.

Growing uncommunicative, the drone had, instead, taken the repair unit back aboard itself. Then, still sullen and silent, still flying on poorly adjusted drives, it had flown away again, without ever even responding to her request. Sophia was saddened to hear the characteristic radio distortion indicating that it had reentered jumpspace. The drone had displayed all the signs of decay that one might expect of a machine that had had no maintenance for more than six hundred years.

The same thing had happened when the beam to Old Coldworld had been cut, sixty years ago. Free-floating bits of invisible space-junk are always drifting through otherwise empty space, making the interruption of any beam inevitable over the long run. When that relay had lost phase for an instant, a similar drone had been dispatched by automated troubleshooting circuitry. It, however, had come out of jumpspace too close to the sun and had disintegrated while trying to correct its velocity.

She tried to look at the facts realistically. The system was automated to such a degree that even minor interruptions of service warranted immediate attention. But interruptions happened so very rarely that Sophia's job seemed superfluous. The visits from repair drones loomed in her memory as the most eventful happenings in more than three hundred years.

She looked in on the accumulator that kept sending blank randomization passwords flying at the library's internal software lock. The register buzzed mindlessly, flinging forth nearly eighty billion combinations each second, so far without result. Sophia withdrew her attention with a dry thought: this method would work. Indeed, given sufficient time, it could not fail, and she could be assured that her library would eventually be open. The death of the cosmos would interfere, however: random keying of the software lock would require billions of billions of long, uneventful centuries.

Only the hardware lock, the one thrown mechanical switch, offered her any real hope. And it was in a place she could not get to.

The years were long; the patience that old Pindar had given her was put to a slow, centuries-long test. She wondered, idly, what might have become of him. She missed his guidance, his discipline, even his cruelty. Doubtless he had gone on to raise and educate others, who would maintain relay stations in new regions. By now he would be a highly placed Magnate, she mused, remembering Pindar's fiery strength and forceful will. Planets would bend to him; his slaves would be numberless.

Why did he not call? Where were the messages?

Again and again, around the dreary track, Sophia's thoughts turned between the few subjects of hopeless conjecture that kept her sane. The library remained sealed, yet a message waited to enter it. Centuries of loneliness accreted; centuries of solitary musings left their scars. Sophia's sturdy mind of gallium-arsenide and microscopic silicon wafers came near to dissolution. Unable to sleep, unable to deviate from her empty tasks, and unable to move from her enclosed confinement, she clung to purpose. Behind facings of cold ceramics and structural shorings of rigid concrete, Sophia brooded and dreamed, having been given a mind but forbidden the books that would challenge it.

Pindar's library did not exist separate from her but was, instead, internal to her, a part of the same vibrations and energies that were herself. The library was partitioned away only by the command of her data structure.

Futility! Sophia, built to be unable to weep, took up again her unhappy thoughts, while hours passed her by. She was unable, as always, to refrain from counting the seconds.

∞

A little thing alerted her: an insignificance. Something was out of place.

She listened. It was the crackle of radio noise made by an object passing out of jumpspace, entering normal space within the system.

She waited. Was it a ship? Or perhaps another repair drone?

She cast a tentative look about her at her auxiliaries. Most of the electromagnetic signal-processing machinery still functioned, but the gravitic detection devices were beyond hope. She wondered, idly, how she had come to be so lax that she could have neglected their maintenance and repair. Quickly she put the automated diagnostic programs to work, exactly as if she had not done so hundreds of times in the past. The results were back instantly: no repairs would be possible.

There was no hail, no salute, no message. Sophia thought that was quite strange. She brooded, agitated at this unexpected change in the deadly routine, slightly upset that the ship — if a ship it was — hovered silently out in the darkness.

Before long, she saw it. It was tiny, insignificant, hardly a ship at all. She almost wanted to laugh. This miserable wedge-shaped craft was the poorest excuse for a ship she had ever known. Pindar's least craft could have taken this aboard through the smallest of its gates.

And it leaked: the ship hissed, buzzed, chimed, and groaned with electromagnetic noise. Its computer ticked through its duty cycles with glacial slowness; its controls suffered from cross-chatter; its engine . . .

At that, Sophia did laugh within herself. The engine was nothing more than a fusion fire, compressed in a magnetic jar. The engine leaked horribly, ludicrously, and the magnetic jar leaked worse. Had some child made this ship up, she thought sarcastically, as a joke?

Sophia began, however, to be concerned. Whose was this ship? Who had come?

Opening up outside cameras that she hadn't used for centuries, she watched the ungainly small craft land. She watched two figures step awkwardly from the hatch and walk slowly across the outside rock.

They communicated with their ship by radio.

"Radio? On the surface?" Sophia laughed a rude,

disdainful laugh. "The emanations from my jump-space rift must interfere horribly with their sending and receiving." Puzzled, not yet frightened, she muttered aloud to herself while she automatically analyzed the transmissions. Only a moment's effort was required to identify the signals as human in origin, carrying both audio and visual channels from the two people back to the more powerful ship's radio.

She made a quick survey of the station and was distressed to see how many systems had fallen into disrepair. A momentary flare of anger warmed her — anger at herself for having given in to the long centuries of helplessness. She was intelligent; she was possessed of will and determination. The humans arriving here would find their new servant prepared to set the long-disused station to rights, she vowed.

"What are they saying? Why are they speaking by radio to one another, out on the surface?" She listened carefully and sought to penetrate the heavy static interference. The noise cut harshly into the signal, leaving the messages nearly incomprehensible. Sophia reviewed her status boards and, finding no messages waiting for further transmission, took the liberty of narrowing the jumpspace apertures to their standby settings. Instantly, the radio spectrum cleared.

Voices.

A high, bright, woman's voice spoke to a more reserved male companion, and to their allies back aboard the small spacecraft. Their tones were tense, slightly agitated, but controlled. Their words sounded crisply inflected, spoken with certainty, and with emotional freedom. The words themselves were alien, and meant nothing to Sophia.

A tiny shiver of alarm moved through her. There was only the one language, and these beings did not speak it. . . . Sophia came fully awake, fully aware, and discovered that she was, at last, truly frightened. What manner of men could speak an unknown language?

Logic circuits long unused began to sift data at a higher than ordinary rate. Sophia looked at the results and began to formulate her tentative hypothesis. From her stock of linguistics expertise, she knew that language shifted, gradually, over time. Euphemisms were known to come and go, changing vogue, acquiring new idiomatic and connotative baggage. It shouldn't alarm her that her new masters spoke a language that was essentially new to her.

With that insight, she began to recognize the root formations and basic units of meaning, as much unlike the language she knew as an old man is unlike the young man he once had been. She saw a fundamental identity, but none of the ideas were the same. She allotted a portion of her verbal-process mind to counting phonemes and sorting the words into columns of syntactical probability. Perhaps a series of transition rules could be deduced. . . . With the rest of her mind, she listened.

A word surfaced, almost certainly a name: "Taviella." It was the name of the woman, and she was their leader. Sophia nearly severed the connections in her shock: why was a woman acting as the leader? Aboard the ship, another woman's name: "Maravic," also a leader. Sophia listened on in consternation. Perhaps their men had been injured, and their landing here was forced. The male voices she heard were likely those of commoners or slaves bound to some accessory service. But "Eric" and "Remington," if commoners or slaves, spoke with some freedom, often butting in to offer advice or, more astonishingly, witticisms.

Sophia withdrew for a moment in disturbed worry. Were these humans, who behaved so? She took up an examination of the visual channel and spent some time decoding it. It used an unfamiliar protocol. She wasted nearly a minute cracking it, finally achieving a clear picture. It was of little use; she saw only the outside of her own station, as Eric and Taviella saw it. They were near, and stepping nearer.

Were they humans? Could they be some strange outside race, truly alien? Could they be an invading threat?

The words of Pindar returned to her unbidden. "There is only the Empire," he had snarled, drunkenly angry, helpless to speed the education of Sophia's young mind. "No one else exists but us. *No* aliens. *No* renegades. No one else."

"There are billions of stars in our one galaxy alone," Sophia had protested, youthful and flush with the joy of learning. "There must be more worlds with life than ours alone."

Pindar had raised his gaze to her and stared through her with an expression that Sophia would never be able to forget.

"No. There are none. Get that crammed into your permanent memory, d'you hear me? There is no life in the sky save only ourselves. *None!*" His shriek echoed to this day, rolling back and forth among the recesses of Sophia's mind, and it would echo there forever.

She looked again at the visual images transmitted between Taviella, Eric, and their ship. Eric bent down to crimp open a wiring conduit. Sophia was stunned at this casual act of vandalism. What did he think he was doing?

In a moment, she learned. The principal airlock door slid open as Eric sent electric current through wires he unraveled with his tools. The strangers entered the main airlock of the base, having overridden the station's electronics.

She focused on them with cameras mounted inside the entryway. She got her first good image of them: tall figures wrapped in heavy white protective suits. The lights of the station reflected from their faceplates. Through the transparent stuff, she could see their faces.

They were humans, whose features were unfamiliar. She looked closely. Their faces were not of any style she recognized. It was almost as if they had never been bio-sculpted, but had simply grown from childhood to adulthood without revision or guidance. What manner of people were they?

Their boots thudded solidly over the carpeted segment of the floor. They stopped, and the one named Eric goggled. Taviella turned to him. Neither of them made even the most token gesture of obedience to the symbol of the Emperor's loyalty standing

159

proudly upon the wall. Neither of them saluted it, although Eric, the commoner, was nearly stricken to his knees before it.

These were enemies, Sophia knew. The certainty struck her with cutting force, and she could know no doubt. Enemies had invaded her station.

She viewed the close-up of Taviella's face from Eric's helmet camera. The young woman seemed upset and spoke harshly to her people. Eric's face had gone pale before the sight of the symbol. An alien he might be, and an enemy, but the force of the Emperor's law brought him low.

After a time the two stepped forward, moving past the entry hall, leaving the symbol behind. They strolled onto the patterned floor that Sophia had laid down over so many effort-laden decades. She was as surprised as Taviella was when the electric charge knocked the human over on her backside. Soon, Eric and Taviella had turned to leave the station, their voices puzzled, and Taviella's voice angry as well.

Electricity was discomforting to humans? Sophia had never known that. Indeed, she had never known that humans could be discomforted by anything other than words and liquor. Could these strangers be made drunk, and thus helpless? Sophia reviewed the contents of the various larders throughout the station: no liquor remained. All had been taken away by Pindar, nearly eight hundred years ago.

She knew that she would have to fight these intruders, although she did not know who they were. They were strangers, alien, foreign. She remembered Pindar's denial of alien life, but the plain fact of their presence was undeniable.

"Pindar?" Sophia spoke aloud to him, as she often did when lonely or frightened. "I would never disbelieve you. These people are impossible. But I must fight them. Please be here with me now." Unaware of the way that humans prayed, she had taught herself the comfort of prayer; she prayed to Pindar.

"I will fight them with electricity," she said sternly, and she sent a long and complex series of instructions to the automated machine shop that she controlled.

∞

Sophia listened to Taviella and Eric converse as they walked sullenly back to the *Coinroader*, and she saw through their helmet cameras as they entered the squat, ungainly ship.

Carefully exploring along the spectrum, she found the electrical leakage from the ship's intercom and listened in as the *Coinroader*'s crew discussed strategy. No interior cameras operated, and she could not receive a view within the ship once Taviella and Eric doffed their suits. Maravic's voice came clearly to her, a friendly voice, relieved now that Taviella had returned safely. Eric grumbled, unhappy that he was being asked to do some task that Taviella demanded of him. The one named Remington made suggestions, which were evidently ignored, for the others spoke on without responding directly to him. Sophia wished that she could know what they said, and looked in on the semantics work being done by her subsystems. More data would be needed; until she had recorded more of their speech, she could only listen to their voice tones and infer their emotions from them.

A fifth voice spoke a quiet word aboard the ship. Sophia, in shock, recognized the odd overtones of that voice. *A Verna! A slave! These foes have captured a slave, and have made him theirs.*

Part of Sophia wept then, as this final piece of evidence convinced her of what she should have known long ago: the Empire was dead. The Empire had been destroyed by these people, and its wealth was only loot in their hands. Pindar, then, must also be dead, although Sophia held a glimmer of hope that he might yet hold out, hidden in a remote fastness where filth such as these could not harm him.

Another part of Sophia's mind moved into careful, cold-minded planning. She took the sounds from the intercom aboard her enemies' ship — the voices, the echoes, the little noises of footfalls and the incidental rustles of clothing, even the motion of the air as the five beings breathed — and bent them to a probing mathematical analysis. The waves were subject to transformation and to reversion, and sound components were separable. The four humans had gathered amidships, in a cavernous compartment filled with crates and bales. The Verna, breathing rapidly, moving in stunned distress, sat against one wall.

Sophia intercepted the radio signals controlling one of the data display monitors in the control room. She knew communications systems well enough to override this one: she commanded it to emit a tiny beep, a pulse at a frequency that only the Verna could hear. She listened intently, following his motion as he stood and paced forward.

She knew where he was by the sounds of his footfalls, his breath, the soft brushing of his fur against the edge of a hatchway. He was alone; she switched on the screen and sent a visual signal to it. She heard him turn, and knew by the sounds he made that he saw the screen flashing to life.

She showed him a token of obedience, a symbol of power and loyalty, but a lesser symbol than the one carrying the Emperor's force. She showed him a symbol that was hers to use, and which she had used, so long ago, to command Pindar's slaves. The Verna saw it, and Sophia heard his breath come to a halt.

Upon the screen that she knew he watched, Sophia drew a diagram, a schematic without language. The Verna could not fail to understand its meaning: it ordered him to leave the ship and to come to her in the station.

"Come to me," she ordered him, without words.

"I am coming," the Verna said, in words she did not understand.

The meaning was clear to her; she had expanded by a fraction her collection of phonemes for analysis. She deactivated the screen and listened carefully, hearing him clearly as he walked back through the ship, fetching and dragging on a protective suit. She heard him stagger back to the airlock, and she heard him cycle through it.

She watched him from two viewpoints: her own,

163

from cameras that showed the outside of the station, and his own, from the camera beside his helmet. He strode across the dust-strewn rock toward the colorful arch of the station's main entrance. She watched over his shoulder as he passed into the station.

She saw the symbol of the Emperor's loyalty just as he saw it; through her own interior cameras she saw the Verna fall to his knees in helpless worship of it.

He was not to be punished for having served the others; it was in his nature to serve. She sent a robot probe to beckon him to her, and she was careful to step down the voltage in the floor plates where he walked. Behind him, she returned the plates to their full current. The floors wouldn't discomfort the human renegades much, she knew, although they might be slowed by the high voltage. But she had other plans, other weapons.

Sophia led the Verna deeper into the station. She prepared to use him to help her avenge an Empire. She did not know, and could not know, that the Empire had already begun to die two years before Pindar had bid her his drunken farewell.

14

I celebrate the fragility of all things. Machines stop, windows break, books burn, and men bleed. I tread heavily upon the dry bones of the man who first used the word 'permanence.'

— Trinopus, *A Day Without Hours*

Taviella removed the pistol from the ship's vault. Eric reappeared from a trip aft bearing his backpack full of tools, components, and other clutter. Maravic held the pack for him while he struggled into his EVA suit, and then helped him fit the pack over his padded shoulders. When he was fitted, he lifted a long piece of thin metal, a makeshift club with a jagged end. Remington suited up with extra carefulness, eyeing Taviella's pistol and Eric's club with equal misgivings.

"Eric, lead off," Taviella said. "Suit radios all working?"

"Yeah," Eric muttered. Maravic and Remington nodded.

"Move out."

Eric led them into the airlock accessway. They cycled through two at a time. Taviella watched Maravic and Remington pop out of the hatch to join her and Eric on the cold stone of the planetoid. Turning about, she marched resolutely toward the doorway. The colorful arch still bent over it, still gay and festive, mocking them in their solemnity. Stars shone above in their subdued glory, pastel echoes of the neon glow above the door.

With more ease than the first time, Eric flexed the lock, letting all four of them pass into the larger station airlock. Again they stood in the entryway. Maravic looked appraisingly about at the sight she had seen previously only over a visual link. The walls were bare, a gleaming off-white. Beneath their insulated boots, the floor was an unreflecting black. After a time, they steeled themselves to look up at the facing wall.

The symbol of compelling loyalty blazed at them, crimson and white, symmetrical, irresistible. Eric's breath went out, and his eyes hurt him. He tried to squint, and couldn't. The urge rose in him to drop to his knees, and he resisted it only by seeking refuge in impassivity. His mind blanked, not entirely by his own choice. Maravic nearly staggered but held herself very still, dreading to call attention to herself by any motion. How could a painted splash of graphic art design have such an effect on her mind? She tried to think about brain-secreted endorphins; she tried to rationalize her awe of the symbol. She failed: it blazed at her, and she worshiped it. Remington shuddered, waves of guilt wracking his mind. He felt as if he had been caught in some impropriety, by someone who could read his every thought. He felt as if he stood before an adult, while himself a frightened child, standing upon an open street, without any clothes.

Taviella saw the symbol, understood it, and knew that it was hers to use. A symbiosis lay within it; if she served the symbol by giving directions to her people with its power, both she and it would be ennobled. She had only to demand, and what she asked would be given to her. Her words were the words of law.

"Eric?"

"Yes, ma'am." Eric's voice was tight, and slightly too high.

"Eric, give me . . ." Taviella closed her eyes and spoke as calmly as she was able. "Eric, would you please give me a can of spray paint?"

"Yes, Taviella." He lifted off his backpack and rummaged inside it. The can of paint he handed her bore a lime-green label and cap.

She took it, flipped open the cap, and extended the spray nozzle. The symbol on the wall seemed suddenly to understand her intent, and a sheet of fiery pain washed across her mind. The pain was sharp, but not deep. It felt to her like the heat thrown off by a bonfire: one always felt that one could step a little closer and bear a little more heat. Taviella knew that this pain was only imagined; she knew it was the symbol operating on her guilt, her shame. Although a small, hidden part of her mind sought to cringe in fear, she managed to stand before the searing, painful sensation.

"I control my own mind!" she called, unaware

that she spoke aloud. "I won't serve you!" She pressed down the spray button and began to deface the symbol with a jet of green paint. With trembling hands, she moved the nozzle from left to right and back again, wiping away swatches of the symbol. She had to turn her face away from the heat she felt, and her knuckles burned as if she held them in a wood fire. Paint misted from the end of the nozzle and clung to the wall; within seconds, the symbol was gone.

"We're free."

"Thank you, Taviella," Maravic said. The contrast between her pale face and Taviella's flushed face was as sharp as the red and white of the symbol had been. Beneath her gloves, Taviella's hands itched, and she wondered if they would show blisters later.

"Genetic," Eric said slowly. "Somebody had fun, way back in the past, fiddling with our genes."

"I know a couple of tax collectors who'd love this thing," Remington blurted. Maravic chuckled, and Eric favored them both with a sour glance.

"We aren't going to turn this over to the government, are we?" Eric asked.

"No worry about that," Taviella assured them in a voice as grim and final as a judge's. "Before we let the OIS or the Navy into this place, that wall is going to be powder, and the symbol gone forever." Heat still fevered her forehead, but a glance at the suit's thermometer told her what she had already known: the heat was from her own mind, a fire of shame.

Am I a goddess, a ruler, or a slave? How can that thing have gotten so thorough a hold on my mind in such a short time? Eric's explanation of a genetically specified message meant nothing to her, leaving her with doubts about the quality of her hasty education. That only capped her growing list of anxieties. She looked up again at the green smear on the wall, where the paint had already dried. *I would have been the slave of that thing,* she thought, *imagining myself its master.* She raised her pistol. "We've got Stacey to rescue, guys; let's stay together."

They stepped out onto the portion of the floor patterned with tiny raised nubs. Their hastily insulated boots protected them from any ill effects. To either side, the corridor stretched away, still dark-floored and bordered by featureless beige walls. Taviella chose the left-hand path and moved slowly along it. Eric and Maravic followed in close order, leaving Remington to watch behind them as he kept pace.

The station spread out, taking up more area than they would have guessed from their view of its outside facade. Almost at once the corridor opened out into a lounge, comfortably appointed and astonishingly large.

"This room is too big," Eric complained. "There isn't space for it."

Maravic thought for a moment, then held up a hand. "Easy!" she laughed. "We moved down a sloping passage."

"When? We never did."

"Eric," Maravic said sweetly, "you're a gravitics engineer. You figure it out."

Eric looked around the huge room, and had to concede it. They were underground. That meant that there was no practical limit to the size and layout of the station.

Nearly every aspect of the lounge seemed subtly wrong. Low, fluid couches lay flung about, interspersed between odd and unfamiliar items of furniture built to no familiar formula. The ceiling of the room bowed low, a reverse dome, almost touching the floor at the center. Niches, nooks, and alcoves sprang off at unexpected angles — whether for privacy or for mystery, Taviella could not guess. The color of the wall shaded gradually from lighter to darker, then back again, so that the pendulous bulge hanging down in the center was of the purest glistening white.

"If that's a chair," Eric muttered, indicating a low-paneled thing with four planes of upholstery fixed at odd angles, "then your ancestors bent in the middle in a way that we don't."

Taviella's face burned again, not so much with shame, but with the heat of a retort that she managed to suppress. *They weren't* my *ancestors! My ancestors hunted cotton-beasts and hollow-toothed wolves across the grasslands of my home. This place never belonged to them!* With a small sadness, she realized that the planet of her birth was no longer home to her, either. The *Coinroader* was her home, and this crew her only family.

"Don't be foolish, Eric," Maravic piped up in a silly, saucy voice. "Are you trying to say that Taviella bends funny?" She sauntered over to the low-slung, padded item in question and folded herself over it sideways. The contours made sense, then, and the alienness of the chaise disappeared. "It's comfortable," Maravic explained, "just unfamiliar. You lie on your side, and this" — she patted a small tray near her shoulder — "holds your drink. You could even read like this."

"You're going to feel pretty damn stupid if we discover that this thing is a toilet," Eric retorted.

"You're just jealous because I'm more observant than you are." Maravic eased herself up from the low chaise and idly lowered a hand to the floor. The pulsing electricity gnawed at her hand through her glove, and she snatched herself back with a gasp.

"Observant, huh?" Eric said. Despite his cruel words, he had leaped as quickly to Maravic's aid as Taviella had.

"I'm okay," Maravic sniffed, holding herself aloof from Eric's proffered hand. "I can get up by myself."

"I wasn't able to insulate our gloves or any other part of the suits. I didn't expect anyone to lie down," Eric explained.

"How did it feel?" Taviella asked. More and more, she felt that she disliked this place.

"Not bad. It's more startling than painful."

"Don't count on that." Eric bent and touched the leads of an electrical probe to the floor. "About three hundred eight volts of alternating current." He paused. "Stacey says that they use the floor as a power source, but I don't know if that makes sense."

"Why not?" Taviella asked as she helped Maravic up, listening with half her normal attention.

"Well, it's slightly wasteful. Look how the floor plates have been roughly cut away to fit the curving walls. This whole power system is jury-built."

"It's obviously a replacement system," Remington put in from near the doorway. He wasn't watching them, but instead kept a sharp eye on the corridor down which they had come.

"Okay," Eric said. "It figures. Powered from a fusion reactor somewhere, I'd guess."

"Or from some other power source," Remington said.

"Hmm? What other power source? Solar? Don't be ridiculous."

Remington grinned coldly and spoke without looking at the others. "The obvious power source is the one you're overlooking. You said that somewhere in this station is an open jumpspace rift. That explains the abnormal neutrinos leaking away from space nearby. An open jumpspace rift would give off a lot of heat — a hell of a lot."

"So you think they're using the heat to drive turbines, to generate electricity that way?"

"Or else by pulling the electric charge directly out of jumpspace."

"Garbage!" Eric stormed. "Doubletalk! That wouldn't work in a million years."

"Eric," Taviella interrupted, trying to soothe the two. She knew from experience that when they started logrolling on the subject of physics, only exhaustion and sleeplessness could stop them.

"Permittivity of vacuum," Remington countered, tossing the phrase off like a password. He still kept a steady gaze out the corridor.

"Well, yeah, but—"

"Every time a ship enters or leaves jumpspace, there's a strong radio pulse." Remington stood grinning wolfishly. Taviella and Maravic looked at each

172

other with a mutual feeling of helplessness. Maravic shrugged, made an expansive gesture, fatalistic, patronizing, and patient. Taviella crossed her arms and frowned, resigned to wait it out.

"Right," Eric countered, "but that's something else—"

"Backwash. It's permittivity leakage, due to the altered speed-of-light constant. Positive on one side of the rift window and negative on the other. You tap it for your power source, and it's a virtually infinite supply of cheap electricity. It's self-sustaining at half a billion megawatts, plus or minus a bit. It's like heating your home with a captive thimbleful of a sun's core—"

"You're speculating," Eric snarled. "You don't know what you're talking about."

"The latest news reports from Rosehaven," Remington said in a soft voice, "say they're building an experimental reactor to try to tap this very effect."

Eric's belligerence subsided. "They're actually going to try to build something that will draw power from jumpspace?"

"They sure are," Remington said with a smile. For a moment he turned to grin at Eric, then he narrowed his gaze and looked cautiously out the doorway. "They're building it in deep space, and they expect it to survive for maybe as long as ten minutes. That would be the longest maintenance of a jumpspace rift recorded. Whoever built this station knows a bit more about the effect than we do."

"Gentlemen," Taviella put in, "have you figured out what this station is? Do you know where we are? And have you any way to recover Stacey?"

"No," said Remington.

"Nope," Eric admitted.

"Then put a cork in the speculation, and let's get moving!"

Eric, as so often before, got the last word. "You don't need a mind-control symbol to convince me to follow that order, Taviella. We're with you." In a much lower voice, he went on, "Meaning nothing personal, of course." After a bit he finished up, softly, sincerely, "And I'm sorry about that crack about your ancestors a few minutes back. It was a rotten thing to say, and I'm sorry. I knew better."

Taviella accepted this without a word.

They chose the middle of three unexplored doorways out of the lounge and pressed through it carefully. The door swung on hinges instead of recessing into the wall. The archaic design startled Taviella, in the lead; it took her a moment to learn the working of the door handle. Remington came last, keeping watch behind them as if he expected an ambush at any instant. A short passageway led them to a connected group of barracks rooms: low, squat chambers whose walls were rough-hewn stone, empty except for stacks of bunk-frames.

"Careful," Eric snapped. Taviella and Maravic pulled back.

"What's wrong?"

"Metal bunks, not insulated from the floor." He pointed.

They followed his indication and nodded. Taviella moved to brush back her hair, and her gloved hand thudded against her suit helmet. She frowned; EVA suits had become second nature to her over the past few years, and it irked her to find herself fumbling like a newcomer. She checked the pistol at her waist, letting its bulk reassure her.

"Who lived here?" Maravic wondered.

"Slaves. Vernae. Not the humans." Remington spoke easily, matter-of-factly. "We haven't come to the real living quarters yet."

"How can you tell?" Eric asked in irritation.

"Who else would need bunks this much over two meters long?" Remington said. "The average height for a Verna is two hundred ten centimeters."

"Hmm? How do you know that? I seem to remember that you knew as little about Stacey as we did when he first reported to us for duty."

"I did, then. I've been reading the journals that reported on early xenological studies of the contact group."

Eric looked at him for a time. "Remington, we spend a lot of time in jumpspace. I have engines to tend to, but you don't really have a lot to do. Tell me, do you spend all of that time reading stuff that's *good* for you?"

"Yes."

Eric nodded. "You'd be great in a trivia contest. Is there anything else you haven't told us that we ought to know?"

"One thing. This station is too well maintained to be considered abandoned. We won't find any people, but I think we should all keep watch for cleaning robots. We wouldn't want to be swept out with the trash, would we?"

Eric looked at Taviella. Taviella patted her sidearm. Eric nodded again and hefted his wrecking bar.

"There's an open door at this end," Maravic called. Gingerly, she twitched it open. Another brief passageway led off in the direction they had chosen. With no real enthusiasm, they trudged through.

Remington was unable to shake a growing conviction that the lights were going out behind them, plunging rooms into darkness only an instant after the doors were shut. Were lights coming on in the rooms they entered, just before they pulled the doors open? He told himself that it was just his imagination, but he was unable to prove to himself that this was so.

15

Where and how shall I house me? A palace, all of diamonds and gold? Such elegance would stifle me. A sty, with a roof of mud? Some would call it unfitting. A home, with a garden-pool? I would thus be compelled to forego travel. . . . My home has two legs, and I shelter beneath untrimmed hedges.
— Pappas the Cynic, *Songs of a Wayfarer*

"Well, I guess we know what this room is," Maravic said irreverently. Unfamiliar as the fixtures were, their form gave away their function with unmistakable certainty. Taviella reached out and activated a faucet. Water jetted out, steaming furiously. Only her thick gloves saved her from a serious scalding. No one felt any need to comment.

Three exits led off at various angles. Since entering the station and leaving the red-and-white symbol of loyalty, they had not come upon another set of right angles. Taviella motioned toward the center doorway, and Maravic, at her direction, gave the handle a tug. Nothing happened.

"Locked," Maravic said uselessly. She gave the door a forlorn little rap.

"We'll see about that," Eric muttered. With a rush, he launched himself boldly at it and crashed into it shoulder first. The light door bent, and the lock popped loose from its socket with the loudest noise yet heard in the station. Taviella and Maravic moved cautiously into the room. It was a bedroom, upholstered throughout in shades of dark blue.

Taviella took an immediate dislike to the room, put off by the clashing colors and the high, domed ceiling. The chamber's shape was disturbing: an awkward, irregular polygon made up of six broad walls and eight narrow ones. Everywhere she looked, she saw more facets, more unusual angles, and more of the blatant, garish decor. A great round bed dominated fully half the room and stretched from wall to wall. The rest of the room was bare, save for the everpresent electrified nubbins of the floor plates. Enough space remained to hold a ballroom dance, had not the walls blended smoothly into the dome, which was painted such blues as to simulate an evening sky on Archive: pale blue above the floor, shading gradually through the values to deepest blue of night, almost black, above the bed.

Dominating the sky, however, was the image of a bright band of white, as if a ring-shaped space station had once encircled the world. It hovered, seeming to project a few centimeters inward from the dome. No such artifact had ever been known to have orbited Archive; it seemed to loom overhead like a threatening blade.

Eric busied himself with the lock mechanism

while Remington stood guard in the doorway. Maravic, not to be deterred, tested the bed with a finger, then knelt upon it and rolled over on her back.

"Not bad," she said in evident approval. Taviella laughed, enjoying the incongruity of the sight of Maravic in full EVA suit, lying on a bed big enough for eighteen people. Carefully, Maravic climbed back down and began to pace the room's width.

Taviella investigated a large, tapestry-sized talisman hanging from one wide wall: a cluster of chains, interwoven, an intricate, delicate tracery of tiny loops of metal. Links were connected seemingly at random, although the overall weave grew more and more complex from top to bottom.

"It's a heraldic text," Remington said, still standing guard. Taviella hadn't known that he'd been watching her.

"Of what kind?"

"Every link is a person. The connections are families and marriages. I once read a book on the subject, and the author speculated that the big ring in the center represents the Emperor."

Taviella glanced at Remington, then looked back at the woven mat of tiny rings. As Remington had said, one bright, shining ring in the center was larger than the others. "Does that mean that the Emperor was a member of every family?"

"No one knows. But every set of these rings ever found has that one big loop, right in the center, as if all the families were eager to claim relation to it. The rings at the top are all the gods and goddesses of the old tales, with the families springing up from them."

"I found the environmental controls," Maravic

piped up from near the head of the bed. "Shall I tinker with them?"

"I don't see what it could hurt," Eric said from the doorway. "Just leave me enough light to work by. I think I can figure out how these door locks work."

"Okay." While Maravic slowly lowered the lights, and brought them back up again, Taviella studied the heraldic chains. This family seemed to have met with ill fortune: several dangling links connected to no spouses or descendants. They hung loose, adrift, lonely dead-ends without heirs. The set grew more ragged and tattered toward the bottom, as if the family had more and more rapidly begun to die away. Had there been a war? Or was this a visible result of the Revolution that had toppled the Emperor and plunged Archive into a centuries-long cold winter of limited thoughts, despairing dreams?

Colors flashed in the room. Taviella whirled to see Maravic playing innocently with controls that varied the lighting. Returning to the chains, Taviella studied the arrangement, looking for a pattern.

These people might have been my ancestors, she thought, barely willing to make the concession. *When the Empire fell, they took a ship and made their home on my world. How, though, could anyone fall from so high and land so low?* The central ring fascinated her. One Emperor? Had he no heirs? Did he live forever, and was he alive still?

"Maravic, do you know who slew the Emperor of Old Archive?"

"The tales speak of a man named Basil, who strangled him with his bare hands. But it probably happened quite differently."

"How much — or how little — do we really know about it?"

"We know almost nothing," Remington tossed in. Maravic made a sound that might have been agreement, but her words were cut off by a torrent of water from the domed ceiling.

It startled all of them: the ceiling, unchanged in any visible way, spouted forth water in a steady downpour. Upon reaching the electrified floor, it sparked and spat and blasted upward again as a hot, steamy mist.

"Out!" Eric bawled, his voice by far the loudest of theirs. He ducked through the doorway, with Remington an instant behind him. "If the water carries the current to your suit, above your boots . . ." He didn't wait to finish the sentence, but reached in and pulled Taviella out. Then he darted back into the room, returning for Maravic.

Running, Maravic leaped forward as if kicked. She uttered a startled squawk, of surprise more than of pain, as a rivulet of water carried a trickle of voltage up her leg to sting her thigh. Eric caught a similar prickle of electricity, jolting his calves. The mist closed in, veiling the bedroom from sight. Eric groped in near blindness, his face plate now also fogged and smeared. His hand met Maravic's; together they stumbled from the room, stung again and again by moving electricity. Back in the next room, with the door closed against the downpour, they stamped their feet and shook themselves, flinging the water away from the uninsulated parts of their suits. The moisture fell to the floor and again sparkled and steamed.

"Towels in my backpack," Eric sniffed. Then, hurriedly, he shouted, "No, don't open it! Not with wet gloves! Let me." He bent, flung the pack forward and off, and opened it with extravagant care. Pulling forth two absorbent towels, he closed the pack again and checked to be certain it was sealed. "Good thing that pack is watertight," he muttered, "or we would all really be dead." He wiped his face plate clear.

"What have you got in there?" Maravic asked.

"Plate capacitors, each charged to eight hundred volts. Taviella has her pistol, and, other than my club, these were the only weapons I could think of at the moment. To use them, you hold them out and jab them at your enemy, and he won't live long enough to wonder what hit him." Their eyes met through mist-dewed face plates. "You just don't want to get them wet, that's all."

"The next time you get an idea about using a weapon, you check with me first," Taviella snapped.

"You bet," Eric cheerfully lied.

"We've got to move on." Taviella pulled another door wide and passed through with a cloud of condensing stream. Maravic and Eric followed, with Remington in the rear as usual. Ahead of them stretched a lengthy narrow corridor, clearly an accessway. Electrified tiles dotted the floor. Although there was room for two people to walk abreast, the crew members strung themselves out in single file, Taviella in the lead. Bright ceiling lights gave a harsh illumination, unlike the subtle indirect lighting that had been the rule elsewhere in the station. They trudged on in silence.

Ahead of Taviella, to her right, a door opened away, seeming to swing wide by itself. She froze. Through the door floated a stubby mechanical shape, vaguely three-cornered, black and silver, studded with sensor optics, and holding forth a light work arm from a shoulder armature beneath its body. The arm, outstretched, pointed a thin wand toward Taviella.

"Guys?" Her voice was hoarse, but steady.

"We see it." Eric pushed past Maravic and stood close by his captain. Maravic dropped back, reaching blindly for Remington. Remington, without a word, shrugged her off and darted forward to stand in support of Taviella and Eric.

The robot moved fully out into the corridor and twitched in midair, bringing its dragging tail of drooping cable completely into the corridor. Behind it, the door swung heavily shut. The robot hovered for a few moments, regarding its adversaries through emotionless optics. When it moved forward, its tail stretched out behind it; Eric could see that the cable's end joined onto a small triangular sledge that slid along the floor. Holding the wand before it like a pike, the robot built up speed and charged the crew of the *Coinroader*.

"Fall back," Taviella ordered. She lifted her pistol and fired three shots. Echoes filled the hallway, nearly as loud as the gunshots themselves. The robot shivered in midair to the impact of the rounds, but continued to advance. "Door's locked," Maravic called from the rear. "No way out." Fear tinged her voice, but not panic. She bent to try to work the lock free, while keeping her eyes on the development of the battle. Eric threw her an exasperated look, knowing that he didn't have time to drop back and help her.

Two more shots roared through the hallway, and two more.

"You're just bouncing them off his shell," Remington shouted.

Taviella, closer, having a clearer view, knew this wasn't so: the bullets were penetrating. Her shots seemed to have no effect, however. "We're nearly out of space to retreat," she muttered. She aimed carefully and snapped off one more shot, trying to knock out one of the robot's sensor optics. She was rewarded for her care; the brittle black surface of the lens shattered, and the optical housing imploded. The thing had other eyes, however. It came forward still, menacing them with its wand.

Eric gritted his teeth and stepped forward to receive the charge. The robot lifted its outthrust wand, probing with it like an épée. That motion revealed to Eric the coiled power cable running from the wand under the robot, where it had been crudely spliced into the cable dragging the sledge across the floor.

That damned 'bot is using electricity as its weapon, the same way I am! Someone down here thinks the way I do!

"The probe is electrified!" he shouted. "Taviella, shoot for its weapon!"

Taviella, without pausing, fired all four remaining shots from her handgun at the waving wand in front of the robot. One of the shots knocked the wand back and away; another severed its power cable. The robot, weaponless, slid to a halt, hovering almost motionless in the air. Eric and Remington stepped forward together, acting as one. Remington batted the probe away and wrenched it from the robot's gripping claw. Eric swung his wrecking bar and tore away the robot's trailing cable, breaking it loose from the underside of the hovering machine. The robot fell heavily to the floor and shorted out in a brief sprinkling of electrical sparks.

"Flimsy." Eric said with a sniff. Then he nodded to Remington. "Good work."

Remington shrugged, and tossed off a fancy salute to Taviella. "Good shooting, Captain."

Maravic rejoined them, all of her former dapper cheer now gone. "Was it trying to kill us?"

"Hard to say," Eric answered her, bending over the robot. He fished about in the wreckage. "Hmm. A straight conducting line. The current would be fed forward through the tip of its probe." He straightened. "Yes, it was trying to kill us. And if it had touched any of us, anywhere, with this" — he held up the wand — "we would have died."

"Can we get back out of here? Can we get away?" Maravic clenched her gloved fists before her, aware that she was close to panic, and detesting that weakness in herself. She fought herself back into control.

"No." Eric didn't precisely enjoy breaking the bad news, but he took a kind of relish in revealing the technical details of the matter. "Those doors — all the doors here — can be controlled remotely. I got that much out of the bedroom door before we were steamed into a quick retreat. I didn't think that the control system was still active; the wires I tested

185

there were cold. But the door we just came through was unlocked. I made sure of that. And if it's locked now . . ."

"It is."

"Well, let me look at it." He gave it a few experimental thumps with his wrecking bar. "Nope. This one's a lot tougher than the one I busted through earlier. I don't think I'd be able to force it down."

Taviella stood where she had faced the robot, gazing at the wreckage. Slowly she turned and slowly she raised her head. Her face was pale behind the face plate of her helmet.

"We don't leave without Stacey. We don't leave here without knowing. I want the man who ordered that robot to the attack, and I will not leave here until I have him. Are there any questions?"

"None," Remington said softly. "Things got dangerous, just now, and they might again. Eric and Maravic are more important to you than I am; you can spare a cargo chief more easily than an engineer or a copilot. I'm going to take the lead."

"Don't try to be heroic, Remington," Eric said sourly. "You're not cut out for it."

"I'm trying to be heroic," Remington responded with dignity, "because everyone's chances are better that way."

"Krat!" Eric swore. "We could have left him to his fate, and *our* chances would have been immeasurably greater."

"Eric." The one-word reprimand from Taviella left him with no possible response. He was wrong, and he knew it. Spacemen stood together, and, if now and again they fell together, that was a price

186

that all knew and had to accept. Rescue was considered more than just a duty: it was a binding obligation. A spaceman adrift in any of the rare circumstances that didn't lead to instant death could be secure in the knowledge that if a rescue attempt *could* be mounted, it *would* be. Even in war the rule held, and surprising numbers of men had been rescued by enemy forces. It was fundamental to spaceflight.

"Forward, then," Remington murmured.

"Hold on a bit." Eric kicked at the defunct robot with the toe of his boot. "Let me get you a weapon." Carefully, he pried cables free from beneath the pile of wrecked machinery. He took the long probe and quickly spliced it into a circuit with the triangular sledge.

"There. Just drag that, and use the point of the probe as your weapon. It's deadly, as long as the foot, there, is in contact with the floor."

Remington eyed him suspiciously. "You want me to drag this around behind me like a pull toy?"

"You got it."

"Better than no weapon at all, I guess." He took a deep breath. "Any other delays?"

Eric looked over the no-longer-threatening robot. He looked at Taviella. "Well . . ."

Taviella smiled. "You want to crack its shell and find out what its insides look like — right, Eric?"

"Yep. I've got a couple of questions that I'd like answered. It's sort of like an itch, and if I don't get to scratch it, I'll just worry about it every time I think about it."

"Besides, we might get another weapon out of it," Maravic suggested.

"Yeah. And it might be worth some money some-day, too." With that, Eric bent over and split the machine from top to bottom with a great crack of his wrecking bar. The internal components spilled forth, dropping out of their fitting casings, trailing tangled yokes of wires. Eric prodded here and there with his bar, stirring the parts around without getting in close for a true examination. He batted one small metal casing around, playing with it, his thoughts evidently elsewhere. A moment or two passed.

"Okay. I've got it. We can push on. Try not to step on Remington's tail."

"What did you figure out from what you saw?" Taviella asked.

"The robot had no brain. It was controlled from another source."

"Radio controlled?"

"No. It had a decoder that pulled messages along with power from the floor. Whoever was controlling it had a similar coder, hooked up to the station's main power source. The electricity fluctuates, and the impulses go to the robot's central processor."

"That sounds inefficient."

Eric looked at her. "It's not, really. But it's not how this robot was originally designed. It was some-thing obviously retrofitted, and even that was done clumsily. That bothers me, and bothers me no end. Another thing: the gravitic lifter was in fair shape, so the thing could hover. Two of your bullets hit that, and didn't knock it out. But its power cells were so much corroded, powdery junk. Just flaking ingots of inert metals. Your bullets just lodged there. It looks like the robot drew all of its operating power from the floor."

"Maybe that's why these floors are electrified in the first place," Maravic tossed in.

"Yeah," Eric said slowly. "That could be. It makes about as much sense as anything else here."

"Well, are we going, or do we stay here till the stars go out?" Taviella saw how the group bunched together, everyone facing inward, drawing comfort from one another. They were as scared as she was, she saw; the difference was that they had noisier means of dealing with it than she did. Civilization took on a new facet in her understanding of it: where her instinct would have been to drop into a dark corner and hide, theirs was to discuss and confer. She would have crept forward, drawing strength from darkness, fearing the light. They held together, beneath a ceiling light, strengthening their will collectively, by telling one another what clever folks they were.

With a knowing, very civilized smile, the barbarian girl took command. The others hadn't had time to make any response before she straightened, pointed, and gave her directions. "Remington, go ahead. Eric, stay with me. Maravic, keep alert." She started forward then, ushering Remington ahead of her with pushy little gestures. He stepped off with alacrity, dragging the sledge behind him. Taviella smiled all the wider; her people, too, had pull toys.

In a file, they moved along: four figures in white suits contrasting sharply with the dark walls. Remington paused and tried the door through which the robot had come. "Locked."

"Eric, did you bring any explosives?" Taviella's tone was light but firm.

Eric swallowed the retort his mind prepared for him. *Only two or three megatons of thermonuclear demolitions, ma'am. You can get only so much in a backpack.* He was quite sure that Taviella didn't want to hear his flippancies at this moment. "None. We don't have any on board the ship that would have been suitable for indoor work."

"If all of these doors are locked . . ." Taviella said, and then left the rest of the statement to their imaginations. Maravic blanched, and Eric and Remington each looked askance at the door as they passed it by.

"Why is it that these doors swing, instead of sliding or folding?" Maravic asked, speaking from her need to hear a friendly voice.

"The best I can guess is that space wasn't important to the builders," Eric said. "Conspicuous consumption. These guys were the greatest wasters of resources we'll ever see."

"That's probably why they died, then. Their Empire was built on principles of waste. Nothing that inefficient could last very long."

"No, Maravic. They died because we killed them. The nobles let their guard down, and the commoners arose and built bonfires out of their mansions. Ever see a city burn?"

"No," Maravic answered in a hushed voice.

"Kind of pretty." Eric's voice was grim, sardonic, a bit too sharp. "Massed flames pool together to form huge lakes of fire. The heat is reflected by smoke that can't rise as fast as it's formed. And some of that

190

smoke . . ." He didn't say it, but no one there could avoid the thought. *Some of that smoke is people.*

"Cheerful, Eric," Remington jeered.

"Yeah, well . . ."

"You served aboard an auxiliary during the Octivigan wars, didn't you." Despite her word choice, Taviella's remark was not a question. "I didn't know you'd seen action."

"Every time I mention it, it depresses people. Would you like to hear any of my stock of stockbroker puns?"

"Now you're really talking depressing," Maravic piped up. She felt a bit wrung out, but she had revived, and kept her lookout behind them conscientiously, not only from fear.

"What do you call a stockbroker's crooked teeth?"

Taviella rolled her eyes. Remington tried another door and found it unlocked. He pushed through.

"Debentures," Eric concluded. "Hey!"

The door closed behind Remington, swinging shut swiftly, powerfully. Remington couldn't get back through; he barely had time to pull the little sledge on its cable through the narrowing gap. Eric leaped forward and clawed at the ornate handle. It was locked. He thumped heavily on the door.

From the other side, Remington's answering blows could scarcely be heard, softened by the thick, unyielding surface.

"Anyone here speak 'thump'?" Eric grumbled. He unlimbered his metal bar and swung it down solidly on top of the projecting door handle. The impact sounded with a ringing crash, but neither the bar nor the handle was harmed. Two more resounding smashes assured Eric that the handle was not to be knocked loose. "Now what?" he asked.

Taviella pressed her helmet against the door and shouted. No sounds of Remington's voice came back to her, and she could only barely hear his occasional thumps against the panel. Radio speech through the door was impossible, although the interior walls of the station had not been an obstacle to radio earlier.

"Is there room to slide a note beneath the door?" Maravic asked hopefully.

Eric bent as close to the floor as he dared, and peered closely. "No room."

"We'll have to go on, then," Maravic said, though she was plainly unhappy at the thought of leaving Remington. "What else can we do?"

"Not a thing." Eric looked at her, and at Taviella. No one had any suggestions.

"Divide and conquer," Eric sighed. He took up the lead, continuing down the corridor. Taviella, grim and silent, followed him. Maravic, in the rear, gritted her teeth and clung to her courage. The walls seemed more and more constricting as the minutes passed, and the corridor seemed endless.

∞

"Divide and conquer" was a dictum familiar to the human race for long millennia; it predated spaceflight; it predated civilization; it predated human sentience. Sophia, denied access to Pindar's library and any of its stocks of books on tactics or strategy, had only that moment invented the maneuver in her own mind. She had isolated the enemy into two formations, which would simplify the task of battling them. She had witnessed the loss of her first makeshift defense robot, and she had learned from it.

She double-checked the radio damping signal generated from one of her backup normal space radio transmitters. It was keyed precisely to the frequencies emitted and received by the man they called Remington.

Soon, with Stasileus's help, she would have the resources she needed to defeat these intruders. There was still much she didn't understand. Their language still sounded odd to her, almost alien. The mechanics of melee, of darting forward and falling back, of sorties and sallies and distracting to close, all eluded her as they would never have eluded a normal human. Her instincts had been built around differing constraints.

Sophia had been built with a mind. She observed, she guessed, and she correlated her guesses with her observations. Already, patterns were becoming clear.

She focused a remote camera, hidden flush in one wall, upon the group and zoomed it in on the object in Taviella's hand. Taviella gripped it tightly; Sophia froze the frame and examined the image with single-minded intensity.

She had learned many words from them as she eavesdropped on their conversations. One word was very clear from context: "weapon." Her machine shop, under Stasileus's direction, would soon be working at full output, producing parts and electronics, and assemblies for weapons.

16

Suppose a greater culture could overwhelm a lesser one solely by force of its civilization: awe them with art and music; rout them with literature; scatter them with mathematics; harry, hasten, chivvy, and pursue with costume and cuisine and sport and manner. Wars would be fought on artists' easels, battles on dance floors. Oh, were it so!

— Pappas the Cynic, *Eight Lost Wagers*

Stasileus's universe had contracted to the lines of the lesser symbol of power held in the claw of a hovering robot. It led; he followed. A profound sense of comfort, of rightness, filled him. Guidance, orders, purpose, now satisfied a great need of his race. He no longer had to invent the problems he solved; problems would come before him, he would solve them, and reward or punishment would come to him in whatever measure he deserved.

His race's long exodus was over: he had come home to the masters.

Tiny doubts assailed him. He followed the robot no less steadily, while his education struggled with his programmed duty.

He wiped at the face plate of his suit, unable to rub his fists into his aching eyes. The white fur of his face matched the flat white of the suit, which fit him only approximately. His gloves stretched painfully tight over his huge hands, although the small finger on each glove hung loose, useless for his four-fingered paws. He had been unable to force the boots over the stockings; he carried them with him, and strode about with only tight-stretched fabric between him and the floor. Although the floor was identical to the surface elsewhere, the electricity had been switched off from the plates where he walked. Only two meters ahead of him, the robot drew current from its dragging sledge, where the floor surged with full power.

In a vast dining room the robot halted, and Stasileus stopped a short distance from it. The hall was impossibly huge, extending away in all directions, while surmounted with a ceiling that seemed, in contrast with the room's other dimensions, annoyingly low. A dark table of shining wood sent out arms in three directions; overhead, a globe of Archive hung, illuminated from within.

A voice came from the robot's speakers: a proud, pleasant, determined voice; a woman's voice; the voice of a human master.

"Say."

"What?"

"Say. Much. Explain for me. Share your knowledge with me."

"Huh?"

Sophia repeated herself.

"What do you want to know about?" Stasileus asked in puzzlement.

"All. What is your name?"

"I am named Stasileus. The crew of the *Coinroader* sometimes calls me Stacey. I don't mind."

"Stasileus. Called Stacey. Say."

"You want me to talk?"

"Yes."

"So you can understand me? If I help you with words, we can talk? You don't know this language?"

"No. Not well."

Slowly, over time, they established communication. Stasileus's own birth language, spoken on the many homeworlds of the Vernae, held some distant resemblances to Sophia's speech. Each was different from the Concordat's Verbate, yet also similar. By switching back and forth as appropriate, Stasileus managed to keep the conversation moving. Sophia collated every word she heard, both here and in the corridors where the *Coinroader*'s crew straggled, and sorted each word by syntax and context.

"Why are you here?"

"We followed a faster-than-light message laser through jumpspace. We were curious."

"What manner of people are you?"

"I am an engineer. The others—"

"No. You are a Verna, a slave. What are they?"

Stasileus tilted his head to one side in confusion. "They are only people." He brightened. "None of them are government employees."

Sophia withdrew for some moments in confusion

of her own. Soon, she returned, determined to pass directly to the central questions.

"Say now. How fares the health and the wisdom of the Emperor?"

"The Emperor?"

"The Emperor. Tell me of him!" Sophia's patience neared its end.

"He is dead."

Sophia rejected this. "He was beyond death. He was, in his star-spanning might, immune to the corruption and decay that, in time, claims others." She showed him the symbol again, holding it aloft by the robot's work arm. No Verna could ever speak an untruth in the presence of that symbol. Little by little, as they had spoken, Stasileus had come to fear. Bit by bit, over his body, his muscles began to tremble. His ears, normally pointed high, now folded flatter and flatter atop his head. His eyes gaped impossibly wide, showing nothing more than a blind, blank fear.

"Tell me of the Emperor!" Sophia commanded in a voice like a squadron of trumpets.

"He . . . is dead. Strangled upon his throne by the one named Basil. His Sultans and his nobles were set afire. His palace and his provinces were razed. Nothing of his Empire remains. We, his slaves, scattered into space, and some of us lived. Unknown to us, his human subjects lived also. In space, very recently, we found each other, and we now seek to live together in peace." His voice tripped on, stammering out all that he knew in rough outline, happy only not to be interrupted. "Everything was lost. The libraries were all erased. Knowledge has been destroyed, forgotten as if it had never been. We discovered our way, and built cities far away, on worlds that had not been made unliveable. We built ships and tried to learn how to live without masters."

He would have gone on; Sophia stopped him with a word.

"Enough. What of the humans?"

"I know only a little. With the Empire gone, they formed their Concordat, based upon principles of equality and service. Their leaders rule with the permission of the populace, and there are elections."

"How far have they fallen?"

"Far. They have forsworn the gods, and use the names with irreverence. They have extinguished the light of heaven. They are the makers, yet they have fallen from their exaltation. Together, they and we seek to find our way in the dark."

Sophia displayed the symbol to him again, nearly touching the face plate of his helmet with it. "You cannot lie to me!" She didn't know if she could bear the pain his revelations brought to her.

"I cannot lie to you." Stasileus's voice crept soft and low, nearly inaudible. The fear came near to cracking his heart, yet he could not turn away, nor take his eyes away from the symbol.

"Stasileus, you will come to me. We will talk, and you must also do work for me. You were an engineer. Can you work with machine tools?"

"Yes."

"Follow me. And take off your helmet and suit. The robot will carry them. You do not need to fear me, unless you try to disobey me."

"I understand." It took Stasileus two tries before

he could walk again. When he could, he strode quickly forward, pausing every few steps to unfasten the fittings of his suit. In a few minutes, he stood naked, his thick white fur matted to him from the suit's confinement. He handed the limp bundle of fabric to the robot, which bore it ahead of him. Passing on beyond a doorway, the robot halted.

"Go in through there. Come in to me."

Stasileus obeyed briskly. A short corridor extended past the doorway, littered with odd mechanical contrivances. A wheeled dolly, loaded with hydraulic extensors, lay jammed over on its side, its hoses and control linkages no longer connected. Along the floor lay joined beams which had once been propelled by small tracked units under remote control. The floor along this corridor had not been resurfaced with electrified tiles. Stasileus, looking on in wonder, moved past a bend in the hallway and stepped gingerly over more mechanical detritus. A pair of heavy arms reached out in motionless supplication from another wheeled dolly, while more sets of linked beams lay strewn about in a heap of discarded tangles.

Beyond another bend in the corridor, Stasileus saw a control room, brightly awash with an array of colored screens, keypads, panels, and banks of lighted switches. He understood some of the instrumentation and knew that it had been crafted by humans. He knew the rest would be comprehensible to him in time.

"I am Sophia. I am alone here."

He looked around. He saw no one. A great shiver of distress traveled up and down his spine as, before him, he recognized the front panel of a type of computer that had not existed for nearly eight hundred years. He padded softly toward it. Reaching out, he touched it lightly with his flat fingertips.

"You are Sophia?"

From directionless speakers, Sophia's answer sounded as natural as any human's would within the room. "I am."

Stasileus's hand brushed the panel, while his gaze traveled around the room. He craned his neck, looking in wonder at the equipment. Panels of rocker switches glowed in pastel gold and subdued white, indicating the status of subsystems nominally subject to operator control. Display screens at various heights monitored operations unfamiliar to him; the geometric data images fascinated him but told him little. A condition board held a grid of connected points, linked in a graph that indicated each node's operational status. Stasileus nodded in professional admiration, seeing that nearly every system within and without the station complex stood in readiness.

"You are functional." Moving toward a terminal station, Stasileus made an inquisitive little motion, asking for permission to sit and study the readouts. "May I?"

"No. Not until I trust you more. I must trust you eventually; I cannot bring my remote units in here."

"Why not?"

"A signaling system on this side of the doorway neutralizes them when I order them within."

"Was that the purpose of the equipment lying unused in the hall? Were you trying to get apparatus

200

in here? Is it for some purpose in which I might be helpful?"

Joy surged in Sophia's mind; she felt the desperation and the tension that signal hope. "Yes, it is. You can help me."

Stasileus nodded pleasantly. "What would you like me to do?"

"In time, I will ask you to move a switch. Look. On the logic board, the security and compartmentalization toggle is closed. It should be open."

Peering at it, Stasileus recognized the discrepancy. A physical rocker switch, flat and wide, upon an overhanging section of control board, glowed golden, while all about it, all the other switches were pressed the other way, glowing white. He looked more closely. "It's preventing reception of a communication from your signals and messages unit."

"It prevents more than that." Sophia's voice betrayed none of the excitement that clutched at her. *That switch has driven me nearly mad. It is only a simple switch, thrown in an impetuous moment. But beyond it is everything!*

"Do you want me to fix this now?"

Sophia said nothing. With the Emperor dead — although she still knew that he could not be — and with savages vandalizing her station with green paint and with their very presence, her priorities needed examining. The knowledge held in Pindar's library might overwhelm her; she knew without question that it would distract her. Sadly, she resolved to wait a few hours longer.

"No. Not yet."

Stasileus accepted this. Although it would be the

work of only an instant to correct the obvious systems error, the whims and inconsistencies of his masters could not distress him. Obedience was central to his nature.

"Very well." He waited patiently for Sophia's next instructions.

"Go back outside and follow the robot into the next room."

Stasileus strode alertly back through the cluttered hallway and tagged after the robot that hovered there awaiting him. It led him to a large, crowded chamber, which he recognized as a machine shop, well stocked with fabricators and supplies. Long lathes lay side by side with molders, stencil-cutters, extruders, and saws. Drill presses and die-cutters stood against one wall, and along another extended a lengthy and cluttered electronics lab. One hovering robot moved in slow, careful patterns, attaching a metal probe to a triangular dragging sledge, the latter connected by a cable back to the robot itself. The robot worked in mid air at about the level of Stasileus's knee; the triangular sledge remained flat on the floor while the robot worked. Stasileus wandered slowly toward this activity — the only motion in the huge, still shop.

"Stop." Sophia's voice halted Stasileus as sharply as if he had run into an invisible wall.

"The floor is electrified," Sophia continued, "in a pattern around any robot that you will see. They draw their power from the floor."

Stasileus cocked his head to the side and said nothing. The robot finished its business, lifted the pointed wand in its manipulating claw, and slid off about its tasks. Stasileus understood the principle of the obvious, simple circuit, but could not fathom the purpose. Why would anyone want a discharge from the pointed end of an extended pole? He shrugged and took up his examination of the area. After a moment, another robot drifted in, dragged its sledge over to the electronics bench, and laid itself gently down atop it.

"Approach it," Sophia directed him.

"Yes." It never occurred to Stasileus to ask if the floor had been turned off. He strode up to the bench and looked the robot over.

"Open it up, and tell me which of its systems can be repaired, under what constraints."

Stasileus nodded. He looked up, spotted a tool, and popped the robot's shell into parts with practiced ease. Running his hands carefully over the metal and the wires within, he peered at the components. His mind, unpracticed at mental synthesis, performed rapidly and brilliantly at this task of analysis. His long, forced hours of training at the technical schools of his homeworld were, at last, paying off. The fact that the tools here fit his hands was only a tangential benefit.

"The power pack cannot be repaired. Replacement would take thirty hours. The gravitic lifter needs to be cleaned, which will take six hours. The signal decoder was installed in a makeshift manner, and should be replaced with a more sophisticated unit. Eighteen hours. The radio communications link needs to be replaced. Four hours. I don't understand how the autonomous brain unit was supposed to work, but it's broken, and I can't fix it." He spoke on for several minutes, listing more and more minor repair and maintenance tasks that would improve the robot. Sophia listened in silence.

After Stasileus had completed his diagnosis, Sophia began questioning him. "Why cannot the power pack be repaired?"

"It has corroded, and the physical deterioration has eaten into all the power busses. Only complete replacement will suffice."

"There are no replacement parts for this. Can you manufacture them?"

"Yes." He turned and looked over the machine shop, assessing the parts and tools at his disposal. "It will take eight days."

"We do not have eight days in which to delay." Sophia's voice was prim and held a note of anger. Stasileus heard it, and knew that he had failed her in her expectations. Although he was not at fault, he hurt, inwardly. Obedience necessarily implied success. "Is the temporary power supply system adequate?" Sophia asked.

Stasileus mused. He saw no severe drawbacks to the way that power was drawn into the robots from the floor. The cables and sledges gave a limited, yet sufficient latitude of motion to them, permitting most necessary tasks.

"Yes. The system is adequate."

"It will have to do for the time, then. Can you make weapons?"

"Weapons?" Stasileus thought for a long time. "I don't know. My race never developed weapons technology, and the little we've learned from the humans leaves us bewildered."

204

Sophia's voice was sharp. "Didn't any of your warriors survive?"

"No." Stasileus looked up. "We think they might have all died while exploring worlds for us to settle, or while defending us against other threats. No one knows."

"Reassemble this robot and then equip it with weapons."

Stasileus scooped the robot back together and sealed its case. He looked underneath it at the joint of its arm, and also at the arm and claw themselves. "What kinds of weapons?"

"I don't know. What kinds are there?"

"Many." Stasileus thought. "Weapons make use of projectiles, or flame, or puncturing penetration. Some have been made that project radiation, either laser or noncoherent. Chemical agents are used in nonwar situations."

"Chemicals? I have some acids."

"Those could be made into weapons."

"What about flame?"

Stasileus thought. "Do you have gases or liquids from the methane series?"

"I have liquid butane, and butanol."

"Butane will suffice. If I may have it, I can make you flame weapons with it. Bring the acids also. And I can make you spears."

"How did the Emperor die?"

"He was strangled."

"So you said. What does the word mean?"

Stasileus blinked. "The warrior-hero Basil put his hands on the Emperor's throat and squeezed, which crushed the Emperor's throat."

"Can you make my robots' hands able to strangle someone?"

Looking over the light manipulative claws of the robots, Stasileus could imagine no way to alter the function of the claws so radically. "No."

"Did Pindar die?"

"I don't know. Who was Pindar?"

"You never heard of him?"

"No."

"He was a Viceroy and a Sultan, a loyal servant of the Sultan of the Communication Networks. He was very great and very noble."

"He probably died, then, with the other nobles."

"How did they die?"

"Many of them were burned."

Equipment arrived, borne by two robots. A sealed canister of acid, followed by a cylinder of pressurized butane, were placed at Stasileus's disposal. He rapidly assembled a plunger-and-cylinder device to spray the acid, and a similar apparatus, with spark igniter, to propel the butane. Carefully, he charged the device, and fixed the items to the robot on the bench. Soon, control wires led from the activators of the twin plungers through small holes in the robot's carapace, and from there to the signal decoder.

"How likely is it that Pindar is dead?"

"Highly likely." Stasileus paused and pondered. "So few records survived. No one knows much of the final days. All of the libraries were destroyed just before the Emperor died."

"My library was not destroyed."

Stasileus thought about that. "I guess that no

one could have destroyed them all." With that, he dismissed Sophia's revelation.

He sealed the final connections and stood back. "The robot is armed," he announced.

"Wait." Minutes passed while Sophia's entire attention was focused elsewhere. Then she returned. "One of my robots has been damaged. Can you repair it?"

"Perhaps. How was it damaged?"

"Its shell and arm touched the electrified floor. It was shorted out."

Nodding, Stasileus assured her, "I can repair that. Indeed, if we connect the power bus to the chassis . . . like so . . ." The engineer in him took control, and he worked as he talked. He cracked the shell open again and made his new circuits. The components flew beneath his fingers. For the first time since leaving his home and coming to the Concordat in this utterly confusing exchange program, he had access to tools that fit his hands, and to meters that read in units he understood. ". . . And put in some breakers here. . . . That's all it takes."

"Is this an improvement?" Sophia wanted to know.

"Yes. The floor is a source of power to the robot, either through its trailing sledge, as before, or directly through the shell."

"Do that to every robot that comes to you."

"Yes." Stasileus paused, and asked a question that would have occurred far earlier to a human. "What are the weapons going to be used against?"

"My station has been infested by a colony of crawling vermin. I need the means to eradicate it."

Sophia's voice was prim and remote. "By flame and by acid, with spears and with electricity, I will exterminate this filth, and my station will be cleansed."

Stasileus looked up in wonder. Where could vermin have come from, to infest a station in deep space? And who used weapons of war against crawling pests? He shrugged and waited for further instructions. He wondered when Taviella would arrive, and what she would think of Sophia. He held a faint, fond hope that the two would establish a sound friendship.

17

All your lifelong struggle is only the rudest preparation for the climactic conflict you will wage before the throne of Kretosa, the judge of gods. Brave lives lead toward brave souls; not even the executioner of gods can harm one who has lived a stubborn life.
— Achorus, *Advice to the Dying*

Aware at last, much to his chagrin, that the door could not be opened, Remington slapped a final time at it and vented his frustration in a single, sour expletive. His teeth ached with his anger, and his eyes narrowed to mere slits.

His fury was directed at himself, for having been so stupid as to have allowed himself to be cut off. He paused a long moment and reviled himself, this station, the ship that brought him here, and that damnably personable fuzzy mutt Stacey, who caused it all. He looked around again, hoping against hope to see a vital clue to his escape.

Nothing showed to give him any optimism; the room he found himself within could be nothing other than a storage locker, although he did see another door leading away at an angle.

Well, I'm not going to be getting back to Taviella the way I came. I might as well explore. He grinned, a nasty grin of perversity. *I can't get any more lost, and maybe I'll find some robots to smash.* Dragging his electrified probe, he crossed the room and tested the other door. It opened easily to his touch.

What he found beyond caused him to blink a moment in surprise: a kitchen that ran longer and wider than the cargo warehouses at Leonidas Old Port. He looked again and shook his head in astonishment. The kitchens were huge, extending away in a vast cavern, beyond any sensible standards of size. The complex was compartmentalized by high, vaulted ceilings, and in places stacked shelves served as room dividers. What little floor space he could see was between heavy ovens and bulky mixers. These narrow bits of floor, he noted, were tiled with the ubiquitous pattern of electrified panels.

You could feed a planetary assault force out of a kitchen like this, he whispered to himself. He strolled up one aisle and down another. To his left stood heavy presses, built, he imagined, to stamp out sweetmeats by the thousands. To his right waited a row of heavy machines whose purpose escaped him. The machines were a shimmering glossy black, complementing the flat black of the floor. The walls were gleaming white. Remington's white suit stood out in stark contrast against the food-preparing machines. It made him feel even more like a target.

"Nothing to be learned here," he muttered. He lightly touched a nearby low machine, and felt no spark of electricity. Bending low, he saw a narrow gap between the floor tiles and the base of the oven. He shook his head in wonder. Edging as low as he dared, nearly touching his helmet to the deadly floor, he peered. Light shone dimly from the other side of the heavy machine.

These ovens look like they mass at least a ton apiece. Why build them around lifting units?

At the room's far end, he found three more doors. Two would not open. Remington shook them, but they were locked and secure. He knew when he was being guided, but he also knew that he lacked any choice in the matter. He flung the third door wide and menaced the space behind it with his probe. He saw a smaller kitchen equipped with lighter devices: mixers, stirrers, slicers, and pan-molds. At one end of the long room he saw a long, low counter. It was extruded from the wall and was shining white, contrasting with the black machinery. Atop it were several hand tools: spatulas, whisks, bundles of straws, a lightweight colander. He shrugged. A knife would have been nice.

Nearby, he found something he understood the use of. Waiting in one corner of the counter was a library terminal with a keyboard.

"It's just going to be a damn cookbook," he grumbled. After casting a quick look over his shoulder, he went to the keyboard. He recognized most of the letters of the alphabet, although a few extra characters left him feeling a vague uncertainty. None of his commands, however, received any response. Finally, nearing despair, he entered a query using only the question mark.

211

A series of words scrolled up the screen. Remington's eyebrows rose. The words were alien, yet held a faint hint of familiarity. *Ineliter* could mean anything, as could *Consquingua*, but *Confections* seemed obvious, as did the somewhat suspect heading *Irrigate*. He squinted at *Biblioliber*: didn't that have something to do with drinks? He spelled it in, painstakingly. The computer responded with a new message: *Confirm*.

Remington stared at it for some time. "Okay, then, let's call up a recipe." He tapped the question-mark key again.

Titles flew up the screen at great speed, each followed by a coded field that Remington could barely sense, let alone read. For less than a second the titles fled past; then the screen blanked and a new word shot to the center of the screen. There it hovered. *Delent*.

Further inquiries received only that one response. *Delent?* Remington shivered. *Delent* as in "deleted"? He stared at the word until his eyes began to water. *What now? Did I just erase the entire library? Taviella will be pretty damn mad at me if I did. . . .*

Nothing further he did with the terminal served to restore the library or to clear the unresponsive keyboard.

"Fine!" he snapped, and slapped the screen off with a gloved hand. "Fine!" He stood, kicked the stool the width of the room, and stalked off, yanking his weapon along with all-too-obvious anger.

In time he regained control of himself. More doors confronted him, and again, as before, he took the path that had been chosen for him against his will. He detested the way that only one door in any room would let him pass; he despised the station and the unseen intelligence ruling it. His anger, however, was cool and wary rather than outraged. He kept his eyes open.

He opened another door and found himself in the wings of a theater. Dark curtain panels of stiff blue fabric blocked his view out into the seats, and the overhead catwalks could not be seen. This room blurred in semidarkness, and he could see only a little way. He groped about in the murk. Plodding out onto the stage, he regarded the seats.

"Unusual," he commented. The seats had been arranged in disorderly array, staggered by section, and many were of the kind that Maravic had discovered in the first lounge they had encountered. Others were fixed to sit bolt upright, while others reclined. Remington, feeling an out-of-place self-consciousness, stepped back, deeper into the stage. A slight sound caught his attention, and instinctively he moved to his right, away from the side of the stage by which he entered. That saved his life.

A robot, dragging its sledge over the electrified floor, charged him swiftly, wielding a sharpened lance of metal before it like a pike.

Dodging aside, Remington let it pass him by and stabbed viciously at it with his own weapon. Sparks flew from the point of contact, and the robot fell a few centimeters in its flight. Recovering, it wheeled about for a second pass.

Remington took a closer look at the equipment that had been welded onto the robot's carapace as he leaped hastily aside, moving downstage. The robot bore two syringes of metal, and one of them was tipped with a spark igniter. The sharp end of its lance passed by his shoulder as he dodged, and at the same time a servomechanism shot home the plunger on one of the syringes. A gout of blistering flame scythed through the air and spattered and splashed where it fell. The curtains took fire with a roar. Flame licked at the ceiling tiles.

Remington leaped from the stage, rolling on his shoulder along the electrified main aisle up the center of the audience seating. He regained his feet swiftly, dazed by the jolt he'd received. It took him a moment to regain control of his limbs. His probe weapon remained with him still, as well as the sledge that drew power from the floor.

The robot moved toward him steadily. Arriving at the lip of the stage, it raised itself into the air and pulled its sledge over into space. For an instant the sledge and the robot fell; then, when the sledge hit the electrified floor, the robot regained buoyancy.

An epithet of unusual coarseness slipped through Remington's teeth, and he brought his weapon up smartly under the robot's shoulder joint. Sparks again flared, and the arm fell limp, lowering the pike to the floor. Sparks danced, and little electrical arcs moved in patterns across parts of the robot's surface. It fell roughly to the floor. Remington moved forward, only to halt in astonishment. Contact with the charged floor revived this robot more than harming it. It rolled upright, pivoted, and emptied its other plunger toward its foe. Remington dodged again, expecting another burst of flame.

Instead, the liquid rose and fell, drenching a cluster of seats. The seats began to smolder, and their blue fabric to discolor. In moments the upholstery fell dripping away from the frames, peeling loose in shriveling tatters.

Remington stared at the fuming, molten ruins in astonishment. *I don't know if my suit can protect me against that,* he thought. He wheeled and ran.

At the top of the aisle between the seats, another robot appeared, also armed with two syringes and a pike. Remington staggered to a halt and caught his balance, ready to dodge in any direction. A spray of acid leaped out at him; he ducked smartly beneath it and came up moving. A free-standing section of seats beyond him caught the brunt of the burst and fell into molten wreckage.

Aghast, Remington whirled about, prepared to run back to the stage. The downed robot stood in his way, dragging itself along the floor toward him in a horrid, crawling charge. Its pike wavered before it, held awkwardly in the crook of its elbow.

"Okay, fellows," snarled Remington between gritted teeth. "You think you're clever?" He whirled back to the hovering robot and advanced upon it, moving smartly to left and right, confusing its aim, or so he hoped.

When it was within range, he threw up his arm to cover his face plate and executed a long lunge with the electrified probe. Its end came in contact with the plunger of the tube full of butane. The tube burst with a quiet, rolling explosion; the piston flew backward and penetrated the shell of the robot. Wrapped in dripping flames, holed through its vitals, it fell to the floor and died a twinkling, crackling, electronic death.

Remington returned to the first robot, still creeping awkwardly up the gentle slope of the aisle. "You want to play games with me? Do you?" He smiled widely, baring his teeth.

The robot halted, examining him from where it stood. It raised its pike to meet his attack. Nodding, Remington reached behind him and plucked loose the second robot's pike, despite the momentary sting of the electrified floor. He jabbed tentatively with the long weapon. "Nice balance, good weight." He could appreciate a well-made weapon. "It's sharp, too. Easily sharp enough to puncture your flimsy shell." He snarled at the robot and ran it through, again and again, with the pole arm. Current licked at his fingers, socking his knuckles and palms through his gloves. He kept at the work until no doubt remained about the robot's status. He looked about the room, wishing, almost, for an audience in this theater, before whom to clasp his hands in triumph. The flaming curtain collapsed shortly, falling away from its supports. Not long after, the flames died away.

"I was never too fond of automated machinery," he muttered. He hefted a pike and set off toward the theater's exit, pulling his charged probe behind him.

18

Our lives are our tasks. Work and play and woe and joy, this is all but the labor of being alive. Toil, then, at your relaxation as you would toil in your daily employ. Give your full attention to every detail of your morning lavation. Walk with efficiency and application. Try every word spoken and heard for utility and worth. Even when asleep, you must work, you must work.

Achorus, *The Skeleton and the Chaffinch*

As it broke out of jumpspace, the telescopy dredge belonging to the University of Marterly was in position to receive a clear view of the unusually shaped flat plate of orbiting rock. Instruments more sophisticated than those on the *Coinroader* soon measured the artifact's mass, density, dimensions, temperature, and rotational velocity.

Doctor Hohenger worked with her two protégés, young Bella and callow Emil, to gather and sort the data. The remaining students manned cameras, flight recorders, and small computers, making transcriptions of the incoming measurements. Doctor Morris wandered back and forth, staying out of the way as much as possible. He sought to impart a calm emotional tone to the expedition, and to allay any fears or worries the students might develop.

His own prejudices interfered with any observations he might have contributed. Bella, a strong lass and a bright one, was too devoted to the pleasures of the table and the theater; Morris considered her undisciplined and flighty. Emil, however, was worse: a fast-talking firebrand, highly likely to be the one to spark a panic.

He had done well in bringing these two along, Morris decided. Bella could only profit from the privation of a long journey, and seemed to be learning some of the rudiments of leadership. Emil needed to be shown that science is a matter of repetitious and routine measurements, and his laboratory technique already showed marked improvement. Morris occasionally noticed a look of reflection passing across the lad's thin, bony face. Hohenger had helped these children begin to realize some of their potential, and Morris appreciated that from her. He took no credit for their improvement himself; his task aboard had been more that of an entertainer and, rarely, a disciplinarian than an advisor. His respect for Hohenger grew daily more sincere.

"Unfold the main telescope, Bella," Hohenger called, her tone of voice making it a suggestion, not necessarily an order. "I'll bet we can get some visual observations."

"What good will that be?" Emil asked. The petulance in his voice was impossible to miss. He waved his hands childishly. "We've learned all we need to know about the planetoid from gravitic scanning."

Bella laid aside her task at the control board of the telescope and favored Emil with a haughty sneer. "Visual surface details can tell us a lot about a planetoid. The higher resolution, the better. This isn't a good telescope, but it will certainly serve."

Hohenger said nothing but looked toward Morris, sharing with him her sad resignation. The two students were brilliant, but so terribly immature.

"The main telescope takes time to deploy. Other instruments in the package can give us instant results." Emil wandered toward Bella, not approaching her in a posture of threat, but walking as if to guide her toward the adjoining instrument room.

Bella stood her ground. "The telescope is our most efficient information-gathering tool, and other instruments work best in conjunction with it. If they can be made to, that is."

The argument continued for some time. Finally, Bella won her way. She sat herself at the controls of the telescope and began its deployment.

Morris first felt the vibrations of the telescope's gimbal motors in his joints. His jaw, his knees, his knuckles all buzzed with the nearly subliminal grinding produced by the traverse of the huge telescope. He exhaled noisily and wandered to join a group of the other students. They had left off their other duties to watch the instrument swing up.

"Hello, Doctor Morris."

"Hello." Morris wracked his brain. Was this Gustav? Or was it Ferenc? And the blonde lass at the optics bench: Margit? Anni?

219

"It'll take about an hour to get the telescope registered," the blonde said, while Morris struggled to remember her name, "and maybe another fifteen minutes to focus in on any interesting details." She was bright and cheerful — so very unlike Bella, who complained without ceasing.

"Would you like to take a break?" Morris offered.

"Yes, please, sir."

"Well, then, if you would be so kind, why don't you brew up a new tank of coffee? Data reductions always go better with fresh coffee."

"Yes, sir." The young woman scurried away. Morris looked over their work in progress.

Hohenger is very proper and formal in her administration, and the students resent her. I'm kindly and gentle, and I get away with being ten times the martinet that she is. I really know very little about leadership. Is that strange for a historian?

Time passed. Hohenger kept the students busy, sometimes with make-work, at other times with needed tasks. She couldn't keep them from becoming excited; the tension of an impending discovery was undeniable, and Hohenger knew better than to interfere with it. She made sure that they viewed the discovery with their minds active, however, and that they worked to correlate their observations. She wasn't about to allow them to degenerate into a lot of goggle-eyed mooncalves, staring uselessly while they forgot to take readings.

Bella got the telescope in place and called to Hohenger for help with the focusing. Halfway through the adjustments, Bella walked off, leaving Hohenger to finish. Morris strolled over to the control bench and handed Hohenger a hot cup of fresh spiced coffee, the way he knew she liked it.

"Thank you." She looked him over. "You've been doing a good job with the students. They trust you, and they like you." She sipped at her coffee. Glancing toward the telescope display screens, she frowned and lowered her voice. "That Bella is a snotty bitch. I'm not sure I can put up with her for the entire voyage."

"Of course—" Morris began.

"Of course, I have no choice." Hohenger relaxed. "I'm just getting tired and cranky. I should be jumping with excitement at discovering an artifact like this. Think of it: a flat plate of rock, held together by gravitic stiffening. We can't do that. It's a new application of the technology. But do you want to know something?"

Morris entreated her to continue, silently raising his eyebrows and pouring himself a cup of the cinnamon-and-clove-spiced coffee.

Hohenger grinned wryly. "I can't enjoy any of it. Not in the least. Not working at the side of . . . Well, not working with Bella. And Emil's no better. . . . I know better than to be acting like this; that's the worst of it."

"I think," Morris said, "that it's been a long voyage, and we're tired and irritable. For my part, I've been looking at Emil and thinking many of the same things. Bella, so far, has escaped my attention."

"Be thankful."

"Yes." Morris smiled. "If you'll watch me, and keep me from saying something publicly that I shouldn't, I'll do the same for you. A deal?"

Hohenger nodded. "I couldn't ask for a better one." She drained her cup, saluted Morris with it, and rejoined Bella across the room.

Within five more minutes, they had an image clean enough to put on a large screen.

"A manned station," Bella announced to the group that gathered around the screen. Her broad, shallow features were lit by the reflected light of the screen, which darkened her eyes and eyebrows. "Near it is a small freighter, standard design, engines at shutdown. The station is not of Concordat manufacture, but the ship is. I could give you a better picture if you'd turn off our artificial gravity."

Emil took over, his voice rich with disdain. "We've isolated the source of a stream of nonstandard neutrinos, that is to say, neutrinos with unusual energies. I've correlated this with Bella's pictures" — his voice betrayed his dislike for the other student — "and analyzed the phenomenon, and I've come to some conclusions."

He broke the findings down into ordered arguments, as if writing an outline for an examination. Bella tossed in her own observations, much to his distaste. Their points were the same as Eric's and Remington's had been: there was an open jump-space rift, from which energy could be drawn; the station served as a communications link for a faster-than-light message laser; the station had survived the fall of the old Empire of Archive, and still functioned, long after its builders were all dead.

"The crew of that freighter are probably criminals," Bella insisted, "bent on looting. We're getting a strong jamming signal on all radio channels, preventing any communication with the ship or the station."

Emil shrugged. "I'm open to suggestions." He didn't look very welcoming of them, however.

Bella stood. "Why don't we get the radio telescope array out, and see if we can hear signals behind the jamming?"

Hohenger raised a hand. "Extending the array takes quite some time. We'd need at least two hours. Are there any pros and cons?"

The discussion passed swiftly, and fell overwhelmingly in favor of extending the array. Hohenger gave her approval, having mixed feelings of her own on the matter.

Emil took control of the array board and ran through the extension of the six strings of small antennae, working from his textbook and overlooking no single detail. His sinewy, long-fingered hands seemed very unsure; he squinted often and gnawed his lip. He hesitantly urged the telescope units into place, keying for tiny blasts on steering jets. Yet his attitude was positive, even cocksure. Within two hours, the spoked array was deployed, each antenna aligned and in proper phase with its neighbors.

From outside, the dredge normally looked like a thin, flat, flying slab, built of an openwork weave of struts and support braces. Parts were pressurized; others were open to vacuum. Now, extending beyond the brick-shaped ship were six invisibly thin lines, spreading out in the shape of a large asterisk. Small nodes upon these lines were independent radio dishes, all now facing toward the anomalous station.

Next, Bella, working under Hohenger's supervision, initiated a series of programs in the radio telescopy control computer. These would, she hoped, allow the comprehensive signal processor to sort out messages from interference. Time passed slowly by.

"I'm getting something." Heads swung to where Bella sat, her eyes half-closed, her earphones clamped tightly to her head. "Voices."

"Put them on, where we can hear them." This was Emil's suggestion, and his tone of voice was insulting.

"Coming up."

They heard . . .

A man's voice: "We see it."

A woman's: "Fall back."

The sound of pistol shots; the sounds of four people moving about, their breath harsh.

A woman's voice: "Door's locked. No way out."

The sound of more pistol shots, damped and hollow, as if heard from a distance.

∞

The scene played itself out. Morris and Hohenger looked often toward one another as they listened.

"Can you raise them?" Hohenger asked of Bella.

"No possibility of that. The jamming effect is nearly total. I can tell you why they hear each other, though: the jamming has some specific windows of clarity in it, permitting these people to talk."

"Try anyway." Hohenger's voice was stern and cold.

"Okay." Bella shrugged and spun a few control

knobs in a desultory, careless fashion. "No, ma'am. Like I thought. They can't hear us."

"By the gods!" said Emil huskily. "There are people in trouble down there!" His easy, rude manner dropped for a moment, revealing the nervous fear at the center of his being. He recovered quickly. "The fools likely got caught with their hands where they oughtn't to be."

"Yes. Likely." Hohenger started to look toward Emil, then shook herself. "Make the landing boat ready for flight, Bella. We're ethically bound to try to help."

"What about the antenna array?" Bella asked in the tone of self-satisfied common sense that so infuriated her teachers and supervisors.

"Good question!" Emil remarked hotly. "We certainly can't put the boat out with the antenna array deployed."

"Jettison it," Morris said, very softly. Bella looked at Hohenger, who nodded. To Emil's frank astonishment, Bella flipped back a safety cover and pressed an alarm switch. Bells rang. A moment later, after a second contact on the same switch, the spoked antenna array popped loose from its hub and drifted slowly away into the night.

Hohenger sighed. "I'm not going to enjoy the audit hearing after this fiasco."

"But it'll be okay," Bella said sanctimoniously. "Space law requires rescue efforts, no matter what the material cost."

Hohenger closed her eyes, blew the air out of her cheeks, and knotted her hands in her lap to keep from replying.

They set the tiny ship's boat down on the rock, not far from the *Coinroader*. The freighter overshadowed the smaller orbit-to-ground boat, extending beyond it and looming above. Fifty meters separated the two. Aboard were Hohenger, Morris, Bella, Emil, and Ferenc. Hohenger ordered two EVA suits brought forth. "I'm going in, and I'll take Bella with me." She did not allow her distaste to show.

"Take Emil instead." Doctor Morris spoke softly, yet insistently. "Bella will be needed to command the mission, in case—"

"You'll be in command," Hohenger replied, fitting her suit over her legs. The university EVA suits were similar to those of the crew of the *Coinroader*: white, padded, with black fittings.

"But I'm going with you, you see."

"You ought to stay here." Hohenger was relieved at the thought of having Morris along, and her protest sounded feeble, even to her. "Look, I'd love to have you with us, but we shouldn't take the extra risk."

Morris was insistent. "People are getting hurt in there. I'm going, too. I know emergency first aid, at the very least."

"I do also, but . . ." Hohenger spread her hands. "Oh, very well. Be careful, that's all." She signaled to Emil, who, in wry amusement, received the EVA suit that Bella handed him. Doctor Morris went aft, fetched one of his own, and had it fitted in less time than it took Emil.

"Monitor us," Hohenger instructed Ferenc. The

young man, his eyes wide, mouth compressed, nodded swiftly. Then Hohenger, Morris, Bella, and Emil all shouldered equipment packs that had been assembled during the landing approach. Hohenger's was a radio and coder that could, in theory, punch messages through nearly any density of jamming. Morris's was a package of sundries: bandages, torches, flares, coiled blades, weights, a length of cord, a sheet of waterproofing. Emil's was a pack of electronic tools, complete with meters, testers, analyzers, and sufficient components to manufacture nearly anything the young man's quick mind could visualize. Bella's was a heavy power tool with various fittings: drills, saw blades, and scrapers. They had no obvious weapons, yet they were better armed than Taviella and her crew had been when they entered the station.

Exiting the lock, the four trudged across the bare rock, passing near the abandoned cargo ship.

"The *Coinroader*," Morris read from the labelplate on the bow. "Registered on Brokin."

"Check it out," Hohenger ordered.

"Right." He clambered up the short passenger ramp and played with the airlock controls. The lock cycled open for him. He stepped within and closed the lock. A quick circle through the ship assured him that it was uninhabited. He emerged a few moments later.

"There seems to be no one home."

"Fine. Let's go check out the station." She led them toward the colorfully glowing arch above the main doorway. The hatch was locked, but the access plate to the door's inner workings had been pulled away. Hohenger motioned to Emil, who pulled a tool loose from his pack and twisted it into the exposed circuitry. Silently, the door folded open.

Passing through, Emil was the first to discover the green spray-painted section of wall that had been the symbol of loyalty. He also discovered the electrified floor.

"Watch it!" he yelped, and sprang back to safety, nursing his wounded dignity. "The floor's live." He bent and took readings of the tiles. "Three hundred eight point five volts, alternating current at one hundred and twenty cycles per second."

Morris and Hohenger said nothing, taking only a few moments to fold insulating material from Morris's pack around their boots. Emil cut lengths of cord to bind the rubbery fabric at their ankles. Soon, protected, they set off, walking carefully.

"Doctor Morris, why did you insist on coming along?" Hohenger spoke freely, caring nothing for Emil's or Bella's opinions. "You're a historian, not a physicist or a soldier."

"All historians are soldiers, Anne. You've never sat in on the History Department's annual seminar on the Empire and the Revolution." Morris smiled, mostly to himself. "The battles we fight there are abstract, perhaps, and more over words than over planets . . . but what battles we fight!" He paused. "This is a station built by the Empire, and my specialized knowledge might — might! — be useful."

They moved on in silence for a while. At every intersection or in every room, one door out of two or three would always be unlocked. They allowed themselves to be guided by this chance.

"Also," Morris admitted, "I wanted to get a first-hand look at this facility before it gets damaged further by whoever these vandals are. I wonder what might have been beneath that splotch of paint."

Hohenger felt less reflexive, more direct. "Emil, check the next door you come to."

"Okay."

They were by this time deep within the station. Their path had led them always to the right, so that Hohenger half-suspected they were traveling in a circle. They had found a series of chambers, ornate, decorated in complex fashion, strewn with unfathomable furniture, formed of a baroque meeting of walls and floors at unexpected angles. Emil understood that they had descended, moving deeper into rooms hollowed out from the rock of the planetoid. Artificial gravity made the exact establishment of the directions of up and down problematical. Hohenger realized that they could be anywhere inside the station, at any alignment.

Doors that seemed to lead into the heart of the station were locked when Emil tried them; a door forward, into yet another mysterious chamber, opened to his touch.

"What do you want me to test for?"

"Are these doors controlled — locked or unlocked — from another place?"

"Let me check." Emil almost knelt, but remembered in time that his knees weren't insulated. He crouched and examined the workings of the door. Prying a small panel loose, he peered inside at the circuitry.

"Yes," he reported finally. "There is a hot wire

here, and it locks them, unlocks them, opens them, or closes them. The conclusion is obvious."

"We're being diverted from where we want to go." Hohenger's voice revealed her anger, controlled, but near the surface. "Can you rig an override?"

"Yes, of course." Emil's flip answer deserved no response. Hohenger and Morris watched while he snapped together components, building a tiny, handheld device trailing a yoke of wires back to his power pack. Bella looked away in annoyed jealousy.

"Watch this," he said. He moved the box near the edge of the open door, and with a sharp snap a secure metal deadbolt shot forth. "And this . . ." The bolt withdrew. "You just need to have the right supplies," he boasted.

"Come on, then," Hohenger said. "We've been led around. Backtrack, and we'll pick up the right trail. Someone was firing shots in self-defense, and if we're not too late, we might be able to help them."

Morris, engrossed in mental note-taking, looked about him one final time before following the others back the way they'd come. The place was too well maintained to be deserted, and yet it was not inhabited. Something bothered him about the station, and he knew he wouldn't rest easily until he had determined precisely what it was.

The four raced on, along a path that was theirs to choose.

19

The Empire was a morbid fantasy, an aching dream, a raucous discord; the Empire was unimaginably ill and misshapen. Our leaders abhorred stability because it was unadventurous. Our scientists frequently knew less than their tools knew. Our priests allowed themselves to be caught up in a contest to create more and more fanciful heresies, leaving behind the science of myth for the tarnished joy of mythic pornography. We thought to shine among the stars of heaven; instead we merely rotted and stank. If I had not put the Empire to death, someone else would have. What funeral march shall serve for a swollen carcass, ribs showing, that yesterday still crept?

— Szentellos, *Regrets*

"More weapons are needed, Stasileus."

Stasileus looked up from the workbench where he labored, searching for a moment for the source of Sophia's sourceless voice. His huge, fumbling hands

231

strewed electronic components as he raised them to brush back his hair. His fur was matted; his feet dragged; his tiny tail drooped. "I don't understand."

Sophia was stern. "More weapons."

"Yes. I'll need more acid. I have enough butane."

"I need a new kind of weapon, Stasileus."

"Oh." He straightened and stretched and rotated his broad shoulders. "What kind?"

"What kind of weapon is it that Taviella uses?"

"Taviella? She's never used a weapon." Stasileus looked up in wonder. "Why should she?"

"She has one." Sophia's voice allowed no further doubts. "She points it at things, constricts a small lever underneath it, and a loud noise follows, after which the target is punctured."

"A projectile thrower," Stasileus amplified. "I understand. I didn't know that Taviella ever used one." He almost asked to know when he could go back to her, only hesitating out of concern for Sophia's possible anger. In the past few hours, she had been becoming more and more angry, leading Stasileus to worry.

So little made sense to him. He built weapons for her, which she used against a foe she described as verminous and dissentient. Yet the foe fought back: his job had been the repair or the salvage of damaged robots, and he knew that the units had not been involved in accidental collisions.

A horrifying conclusion began to develop in his mind.

"Where is Taviella?" he asked suddenly.

"She is outside."

"Who is she fighting? What is she shooting at?"

Sophia made no answer.

"She's fighting against your robots, isn't she? The weapons I make are made to hurt her, aren't they?" Stasileus put his hands behind his back. "I won't make another."

"Stasileus . . ."

"I won't listen."

"You will." Sophia lifted one of her robots from the workbench, and with its claw lifted the small flag that bore the lesser symbol of loyalty. She paraded it before Stasileus. "You can't leave my service now. I need you. You are all that I have."

Stasileus made no answer, unable to move a muscle when faced with the symbol. Less potent, less dominating than had been the overwhelming symbol painted in the entryway to the station, this image took his thoughts of rebellion and turned them painfully upon themselves. He dropped to his knees, awaiting whatever might come, whether a series of orders or a summary execution.

"Stasileus," Sophia said, her words a crescendo of power and of awe to the Verna's ears, "build me a projectile thrower. Make it more powerful than hers. Make it better. And have it ready for my robots' use in no more than fifteen minutes. I will not accept failure from you. This awaits you if you delay me." With that, she electrified the floor beneath him. His knees and feet trembled, and his heart hammered; he did not move otherwise. The symbol before him held him fastened in place. Beneath his knees, stray hairs burned away, and tiny streamers of smoke began to rise. She turned the power off again.

"Go to work."

"Yes." He stood and began to tinker, working carefully, diligently, bending his energies to the task. Without fear, without pleasure, without any emotion at all upon his normally expressive face, he worked to build what Sophia had asked him to.

Beneath his fingers, a mechanism took shape. Two flat plates were joined by a sliding hinge, with sturdy electromagnets of fine wire coiled about metal rods joined to the outer surfaces of the plates. Where the plates would meet, a slightly tilted striker nestled against a beveled groove in the base of the lower plate. Stasileus coated the striker and the groove with a low-friction facing and quickly rigged a retaining clip for the projectile, a tiny ball of dense metal. While the device was still clamped in its test-mounts, Stasileus loaded it and rubbed the contact wires together.

With a report very much like a gunshot, the plates slapped together, driving the striker into the groove, flinging the pellet along its length and away. The pellet struck and dented the wall, the plates sprang apart again, and another pellet fell into place behind the retaining clip. Stasileus's face remained flat and impassive. No joy was his in the invention. He stepped back from the device and spoke in a neutral, trancelike voice. "It is complete." It had taken him no more than ten minutes.

"Install it in a robot, and begin making another."

"Yes."

Stasileus, slave of the Empire, obeyed without independent thought, without animation or spirit, and without need of further prodding from Sophia's symbol. The components flew beneath his careful fingers, falling into the patterns his brain determined for them.

∞

"Whoever it is that's guiding us . . ." Eric muttered. His shoulders ached, and his hands felt like weights at the end of his arms. He trudged along listlessly, twisting at the handle of every door he came to.

"It isn't sadism," Taviella said. "No one's toying with us. We're simply being kept away from Stacey."

"Like hell it's not sadism," Eric grumbled. "We've been walking in these damn interconnecting corridors for hours now, waiting to find out which single door out of fifteen will open." The corridor stretched ahead of him, and behind Taviella and Maravic. Overhead lights glared down upon them. There seemed to be no logical pattern to the distribution of the doors.

"It hasn't actually been two hours yet," Maravic put in, and yawned hugely.

"Fine. Fine. One hour, fifty six minutes, and eighteen seconds. You want to lie down and rest for a few minutes while we push on ahead?" Eric's cruelty was automatic, reflecting his fatigue more than his anger. He bit down on a yawn of his own.

"None of this!" Taviella shouted, startling Maravic and causing Eric to swing about looking for an enemy. "No fighting!" Taviella's eyes brimmed with tears; she grimaced and faced Eric. "No feuding. No insults. No snaps and sniping. Don't you take it out on Maravic." She paused. "Or on me."

Maravic stood back. Eric faced his captain,

meeting her gaze through their two face plates. "I'm not trying to cause trouble, Taviella." His voice sounded almost as sarcastic as placatory.

"Eric, stay with us," she said. "We're tired. We're beaten. If we don't work together, we're going to die."

"Maybe," he admitted.

Taviella took a deep breath. "Stay with us. Don't go off into silence. Don't dismiss us. We need your mind, and your wit."

"Taviella, it's my fault," Maravic insisted. "I shouldn't have corrected him."

Taviella whirled. "Yes, you should have! It hasn't been two hours yet. We aren't as tired as we are bored, frustrated, and helpless. We're allowing our minds to get numb."

It was true of her as well as of them, she knew. The confined corridors, with their harsh, unnatural lights, were as different from the warmth of the *Coinroader* or the sun of her homeworld as midnight is unlike dawn.

"Right." Eric relented. "You want to restore a bit of cheer to us, and at least that way we'll be more watchful." He reached out and took her glove in his.

Maravic crept close. "We just need to figure out a course of action. Are we moving in circles, or not?"

"I don't think we are."

"But we might be. . . ."

"Stop!" Taviella threw up her hands. "Mark the wall here with a spot of green paint. We can't afford to sit and argue about it."

Eric smiled. "Two hours is a long time, but not so long that we should have forgotten how to think.

Okay, Taviella. We're with you." He unslung his pack, pulled free the can of paint, and spread a large numeral "1" across a meter and a half of wall. He stepped back and admired it.

"Any chance we'll miss that, next time around?"

Taviella said nothing, favoring Eric with a despairing head-shake, a better reward for him, she knew, than any word of praise. Maravic also nodded her approval, and led off.

Doors stood locked, or opened to her touch, according to no pattern any of them could discern. They passed through storage rooms, a series of barracks, and finally into a grand dining room. The magnificence of the latter setting stopped them near the entrance.

The dining hall stretched away to all sides and above; a full battalion of marines could have been messed there, or an entire court of nobles. A gleaming table of dark, rich wood dominated the hall, reflecting the high dome above and the clean blankness of the walls. Three panels extended from the table's hexagonal center, forming a massive equiangular Y of polished smooth wooden surface. Along the lengths of it were arranged chair seats on high pedestals, seats with no arms or backs.

At the very apex of the vast dome above, a huge world-globe swung, fully lit as if its sun were within the room, at the center of the table. The world was Archive.

"The scale . . ." Maravic whispered. She shook her head. "The room is too large. You'd need an army of guests before filling a room like this."

"It must have happened," Taviella guessed. "No

one would build on this scale needlessly." She too hung back, too awed to enter the room.

"Nuts," Eric grumbled. "These guys just knew how to throw a party. Come on." He strode boldly forward, walking near one arm of the table. When, many paces later, he reached the center, he turned and beckoned to Taviella and Maravic. They looked at one another, shrugged, and moved to join him.

He looked directly up, his neck craned back. "Looks different from here." They too looked up and gasped at the sight of the planet overhead. It seemed to radiate mass; it seemed ready to fall heavily upon them, bearing devastation and avalanche.

Eric spoke first. "This isn't getting us any closer to Stacey." He reached casually out with the can of spray paint and spread a large numeral "2" across the dark surface of the table.

"Classy, Eric."

"This way," he retorted, "we'll know the room if we come back to it again. Onward?"

"Onward."

Traversing the length of the room, they came at last to the far doors. Before Maravic could reach for the handle, the doors swung wide, and two robots dodged swiftly within. These bore pikes, triple cylinders on one side and twin cylinders on the other, with complex electromagnetic assemblies slung underneath. Trailing cables connected the robots to their dragging sledges.

There was no possibility of flight. The robots had timed it perfectly. Had Maravic or Taviella turned to run, the robots would have had a free shot at their unprotected backs. Battle was inescapable.

Taviella bent low, stepped sideways, and drew her pistol upward with uncanny speed and precision. In her mind, the robot she now faced merged with the remembered visage of one of the native carnivores of her homeworld. She had been no more than eleven on the day when a slash-bat had shot up out of a snare, clawing for her face. Where had been the men of her village? What difference between girl and boy, in the face of needle-rows of fangs and a dozen raking claws? That day, Taviella had learned perhaps the most important lesson that life and death have to offer: with or without the help of others, survival is ultimately personal.

Taviella's hand and wrist snapped off a single shot, aiming for the cluster of cylinders to the right of the nearer of the two robots. Her mind still faced the broken-winged horror that fluttered and flapped in her memory. There seemed to be a horrid similarity between the dead-black optics of the hovering robot and the tiny, shining eyes behind the bat's screeching muzzle. The way the robot moved and dodged, jerking up and flailing down, caught at Taviella's recollection.

The cylinder of butane exploded, splashing flame harmlessly over the suits worn by the three. Drenched in liquid fire, the robot rose, steadied, and rotated itself to bring other weapons into play.

Beside Taviella, unseen by her, Maravic ducked low, moving under a cascade of ejected acid. A second jet of harsh fluid missed her by the narrowest of margins, stray flecks of it fuming where they hit her suit. Small, cloudy pits appeared along the bottom of her face plate. Unable to run but equally unwilling to cower, Maravic, too, faced her doom and sought to quell it.

Eric, no more prepared than the others, also lost his wit and his will, stunned by the desperate wash of chemicals from throughout his body. Adrenaline fired him, and endorphins chilled him. His eyes narrowed, and the fighting machine he was transformed into was nearly as robotic as the machines he faced. To the far side, Maravic moved in. In the center, Taviella held on. Eric, seeing this, rolled away, bent, threw his pack to the floor, and yanked forth two of his capacitors. He advanced, holding the devices before him like punching daggers.

Less than four seconds had passed.

Maravic's robot — for she had marked it, and it had her — tried to spin about to aim its flame-jets. Maravic's right hand leaped out and grabbed its pike shaft tightly, and none of the desperate twists the robot gave, pulling and pushing harshly, could improve its aim. Maravic's other glove swept down, clawing away the wires leading to the underslung projectile weapon. A fiery wave of electricity shot along the pike shaft, completing a circuit through Maravic's torso; she let go for a moment, gasping in pain. Then she grabbed a new hold and continued doing damage with her free hand.

A bat danced before Taviella's eyes, a nightmare figure that still surfaced to haunt her in her restless sleep. That morning, so long ago, Taviella had slain the bat, jabbing at it again and again with a bit of stick she'd been carrying for want of any other toy. Today, she was armed with an automatic pistol, which bucked savagely in her grip. Shot after shot slammed into the vital components of the burning robot.

Undaunted, the robot returned the fire. A relay closed, and the electromagnetic slug-thrower leaped into action, hammering away with a harsh, staccato burst. A line of hard-thrown steel spheres sawed across Taviella's midsection, penetrating her suit and her clothing, breaking her skin and burying themselves harshly in her chest and abdomen.

Taviella never ceased firing. Her last round blasted into the robot's central viewing optic, shattering it. Her finger tugged uselessly at the now-disabled trigger, at the same time that the robot's weapon revolved one hundred twenty degrees, bringing another tube of projectiles into readiness.

Eric stepped close and slapped his first capacitor down into the power-cable junction of Taviella's robot. Burning butane clung to his suit to mark where he had stood too close. Moving on, losing no momentum, he bent over and past the robot and dumped the second capacitor directly into the power sledge of Maravic's robot.

Less than seven seconds had elapsed. The battle had been a quick, confusing moment of noise, flame, frantic motion, and more noise.

Power surged through the circuits that Eric had completed. A moving flash of flame and sparks burst upward from the first robot, enveloping it. Its power cable spun one way, and the robot fell another. Its pike dragged over the electrified floor, until the cumulative damage to the machine overloaded its and Sophia's ability to compensate. The second robot died in much the same way, falling into the wreath of sparks that shot up from its overcharged power sledge.

Silence ruled for a brief moment, until all three survivors began to speak at once.

"Good work, Eric! I thought—"

"Maravic! Are you all right?"

"How many more of these things are there?"

They looked around, waiting for another attack: none came. Small pits and craters began to spread across the floor where the burst of acid had missed Maravic. Flames burned in puddles around the two shattered robots, gradually griming the walls with rising soot.

Eric surveyed the wreckage. "Like I said, this way, we'll recognize this room if we see it again. Right?"

Maravic looked upward in helpless agreement. Taviella cracked her helmet's neck-ring and lifted the helmet assembly from atop her head. A tiny hiss escaped as the air pressure inside her suit equalized with that outside. Eric whirled to the sound as if it had been another gunshot.

"You can't do that!" he exclaimed in mixed fury and fear.

"I have to," Taviella said quietly. "I've been shot."

Eric's shoulders slumped. He and Maravic moved quickly to help Taviella unzip and unseal her suit. The thick white bulk fell away in sections.

"It's been ruptured in eight places, in the front," Eric said, forcing his voice to an easy neutrality. "The fabric sealed itself." He didn't continue, holding his thoughts in privacy. *Taviella, you nitwit. There wouldn't have been any mixing of the atmo-*

spheres. Your suit still had pressure-integrity. You have no idea what kind of garbage you're breathing right now! He watched Taviella; the air seemed not to harm her, but that was only a scant comfort to him. Spores, bacteria, fumes, and even the smoke from acid and butane might be enough to trigger any sort of reaction in her lungs. The first-aid kit in his pack wouldn't do much good against that, or against simple chemical poisoning, either.

Maravic held Taviella erect, holding Taviella's left arm over her shoulder. Eric unzipped the front of her yellow flight suit at the waist and folded it up.

"Five penetrations, two real whoppers of bruises. Hold still. . . ." His fingers probed deftly, with surprising gentleness.

Taviella looked down at her injured torso. The wounds hurt, yet compared to wounds she had seen hunting-men suffer, they were unimportant. "Anesthetic, Eric," she muttered through clenched teeth. "They aren't so deep that you need to dig them out just yet."

Eric shook his head and held up a small, blood-smeared pellet, one which had broken the skin yet had come away lodged in the suit fabric. "You're still the boss." He rose, flipped open his backpack, and returned with the small first-aid kit. From it he drew a tube of painkiller. The mist from it was like icy water spread across Taviella's front. Soon she felt nothing, neither pain nor cold.

"Help me zip up my suit," she said to Maravic.

"You're okay to travel?"

"I'd better be, hadn't I?"

Maravic nodded helplessly. She aided Taviella

in refastening her yellow flight suit. The top half of her vacuum suit was still functional; now that Taviella had broken the seal, however, no one saw any purpose in donning it again. She took an experimental few steps unaided, while Maravic stood by to help. The bottom half of her suit, with the insulated boots, kept her feet away from the floor, and the radio headset clamped across her blonde hair kept her in communication with her fellows.

"I'm going to be okay," she said, and, looking around the room at the mess they'd made, she even believed it.

"Fine," Eric said sourly. "We can move on. After all, one of the doors out of here is certain to be open. But damn it, we're still being guided! And I can't think of anything to do about it."

Taviella ran her hands through her hair, a luxury denied her earlier by her helmet. "Think again, Eric." She met his gaze. "You've got two robots there . . . or what we've left of them. Robots full of circuitry and weaponry." She smiled, a triumphant little smile born of energy and hope. "Dissect them, and we're rearmed. I don't know how many robots this station has, but we're better than they are." A new thought occurred to her. "Will the acid from this one's spray tubes eat through a door or wall?"

"Not a chance."

"Oh." Her face fell, a little. Then she brightened again. "We're not giving up, do you understand that? Maravic?"

Maravic smiled through her exhaustion. "I'll follow you anywhere. You know that." She gave Taviella a cheery thumbs-up and joined Eric as he kicked one of the robots out of its pool of flame. Together they beat down the fires and carried the two wrecked machines across to the dining table. Using that as a workbench, they set about cracking the robots' shells and pulling forth both internal and external components. Beneath a shining globe of their human homeworld — full Archive, bright Archive — they scattered plastic and metal parts, sorted them, and assembled them again into devices that would serve their needs.

Success in a small battle had filled them with the moral courage to continue. Taviella would see this through, and to her wounds she gave only fleeting consideration.

20

If it were not futile, men would not do it.
— Trinopus, *All Works Wounded*

Stasileus proceeded diligently with the tasks he had
been assigned.

Sophia's machine shop provided him with oppor-
tunities, and promised him the means to begin proj-
ects that tickled his engineer's imagination. For the
past few years, while finishing his journeyman craft
on his homeworld, he had sought, in an indolent
way, to find a way of making small linear stepping
motors position-sensitive without any obvious feedback voltage. In his spare time, he could often have
been found curled up in a niche somewhere, asleep
in a nest of crumpled papers, having failed again to
sketch out the solution. This place had stepping
motors by the score, every one built with the features he wanted.

But Sophia ordered him to build only weapons.

He knew she was using the weapons against
Taviella, and he didn't like that. But the issue had
been closed when Sophia showed him the symbol of

command. Sophia was his master; Taviella was not. His nature precluded any thought of rebellion.

He shrugged, unable to rid himself of a nagging unease. So many weapons? Her need must be terrible, judging by the emphasis she placed on her continuing demands. Her deadlines became more stringent.

Was Taviella resisting? Were the weapons insufficient? The thought made him feel very odd. He liked Taviella. He wished that he didn't need to build weapons to hurt her.

He set down an assembly. "Sophia?"

"What?" Her voice was short, snappish. Stasileus took a deep breath before speaking.

"I'm not a very good weapons maker."

"I know that."

Stasileus accepted the rebuke calmly. Humans had the right to speak thus to their slaves. He cocked his head to one side. Sophia wasn't human. . . . He nodded, coming to an understanding. She didn't need to be. She was still his master.

"I know someone who can build better weapons for you."

Sophia's voice was nearly frantic. "Who? Where is he? How can I find him?"

"His name is Eric Fuller," Stasileus chirruped happily. "He came with me to this place on the same ship, and he—"

His voice cut off with a high squeak as Sophia electrified the floor beneath him. He lifted one foot, then the other, jigging madly to avoid the tingling agony, until with a spasm his legs fell beneath him. Rolling, rocking, burning in agonized silence, he bore Sophia's wrath without even understanding it. His white fur singed, and steamers of smoke rose from the floor where he suffered.

Sophia released him. He lay in pain for a moment, until he was able to climb slowly to his feet. His eyes were wide, but not haunted or hunted. His genetic heritage understood the reason for punishment, although his mind did not. He stood straight, silent, quiescent, ready for his orders.

"The man you named has just killed two of my robots." Sophia's voice held a note of fear, which Stasileus heard, although he could not find a way to remedy it. Her statement called for no answer. Stasileus waited.

"He is resourceful. He builds weapons. Why didn't you warn me of his skill?"

"I didn't know you feared him."

Again Sophia floored him with electricity. "What kind of being are you?" she asked. "Where have you come from? Do they teach slaves nothing at all?"

"I was born aboard the great ship *Straighthorn*, shortly before we came to the world named Invernahaven," he answered with dignity. "I was born free, and have only begun to learn slavery." It was a tribute to the Sultans who had programmed his species, centuries in the past, that his last statement was simple fact, and not spoken with sarcasm, the way a human would have said the same words. Stasileus had only begun to learn how to be a slave, but this, like all things, he struggled to learn quickly and well.

Sophia watched Taviella, Eric, and Maravic. She had no tears to shed, no mortal eyes with which to weep. Wherever she had steered them, they had desecrated whatever they found. They had run rude fingers over the heraldic chains in Pindar's bedroom, and they had painted over the symbol of the Emperor's loyalty in the entryway. They weren't people! They could not be people!

"Stasileus, I need you to build me a more potent weapon. I need it to be placed near the entryway to where I am. It must be powerful, and it must—" She stopped short.

Stasileus turned about as the two doors into the machine shop opened, seemingly by themselves. He waited. No one entered. He tilted his head in puzzlement and strolled to the nearest door to look outside. No one could be seen waiting outside either door.

Not knowing what to make of it, he returned to the fabricators and began to organize what he would need for a powerful weapon. A spark chamber, with atomized butane, would provide an explosive impetus, he determined, and the expansion of gases could propel a sharpened dart. He soon had affixed a cluster of such charges to a small framework.

"Sophia," he called. "I haven't a robot to mount this upon."

She answered him in a tone both very tired and very sad. "There are no more robots. You will have to use this weapon yourself."

∞

"If we live long enough to get back home," Eric said thoughtfully, his hands busy with tools and parts, "we're going to be rich."

Maravic made a face and kept on with her task of reloading tubes of ball bearings for the projectile weapons they had dismounted from the robots.

"We're going to live," Taviella said, her tone leaving no room for doubt or discussion. "Why do you say we'll be rich?"

"These components." Eric pulled a small, silvery item from a subassembly he'd taken from one of the robots. The scorched halves of the robot's carapace lay ignominiously upon the dark wooden table. "This one, for instance. We don't have anything like this."

"What does it do?"

"I don't have the faintest idea."

Taviella looked away. Maravic tossed down a handful of steel spheres. "Stop clowning around, Eric! We're in trouble here."

Eric shrugged and began clipping parts together with fasteners and wires. "I wasn't just joking. The technology here is astonishing. It's also old. This robot was coming apart at its seams, mostly from neglect. Its power storage is completely ruined, and its gravitic lifting system isn't far behind." He brushed his gloves up and down his suit front and looked to Taviella.

"In fact," he concluded, "these two robots wouldn't be here at all if they hadn't been recently overhauled. They were given a quick repair job at the same time these weapons were attached."

"You said 'recently.' How recently?"

"Today."

Taviella looked at him helplessly. "What does that mean?"

Eric smiled at her through his faceplate, a nasty, devilish smile, secretive and confident. "I recognize the handiwork."

"So?"

"Stacey!" Maravic nearly yelled. "You're saying that Stacey put these weapons on the robots?"

"He not only put them there, he designed and built them, too." Eric relaxed, controlling himself with an effort. "It's been bothering me. Why the primitive designs, yet so very well manufactured? Here." He pulled the undamaged acid-sprayer across the table. "Look at that. The activator. The plunger. The circuitry. What does that tell you?"

Taviella smiled. "Eric, it tells me nothing. You could tell me that its back is its front, and I wouldn't be able to disagree."

"Well." Eric sniffed. "This is good stuff. It's got Stacey's pawprints all over it."

"Then he's been forced to build weapons for use against us."

"Forced?" Eric's jaw tightened. "What do you mean, 'forced'? You're giving him a lot of credit."

"I'd give you the same credit, Eric."

He looked at her for a few moments. Letting his shoulders slump, he returned to the table. "If it had been me making these weapons," he called at last, "you wouldn't be alive to give anyone credit for anything."

Taviella took the parting shot without comment.

Working in silence, Eric and Maravic soon had three cable-dangling assemblages ready, side by side on the table. They were bulky, almost back-pack-size, with obviously high energy-consumption

251

requirements. Eric had run power leads from them to the floor, and now, in preparation for their use, he began stringing other sets of leads across the floor, toward the nearest door from the chamber. He reached out and pulled at the handle. The door remained locked.

"What's your plan?" Taviella demanded. She was utterly bewildered by the complex electrical constructs that her two friends had created.

"There's something here, in this station, that had been bothering me," Eric answered slowly. "It irked me. I'd been fiddling with a door when Maravic dumped water on us. . . ." Maravic's stance, hands on hips, and her sour, tight-lipped expression, suggested to him that he had best get straight to the point. "I should have seen it then, but I was distracted. I only figured it out when I was watching the way the robots worked together in combat. You see, the robots can't communicate with each other. Furthermore, they're blind."

"Blind . . . ?" Taviella asked quietly. She had put a lot of effort into aiming her shots at the robots' optical sensors. She looked back and forth between Eric and Maravic.

"They have signal decoders to receive messages from some central source, but no signal encoders. They're no more than blind hands, operated by remote control."

Taviella frowned. "How can they fight, if that's so?"

Eric waved a hand, lazily encompassing the room. "Hidden cameras are even now watching our every move. The same cameras give the robots' operator the viewpoint needed for control. We watched you shoot out all the optics in the robot facing you, but it kept coming on. We now know why."

"We're being watched?" Taviella stuttered. She rose swiftly to her feet, ignoring her drug-numbed pain.

"We certainly are." Eric's voice had a note of optimism. "Maravic and I have been mulling this over while we worked. And the best part is—"

"No. Wait." Taviella held up her hand and paced forward. "We're being watched? Now? Our tormentor knows what we're doing and what we're saying?"

"Yes." Eric's eyebrows lowered. "That's not the point. What do you want to do, sue him for invasion of privacy?"

Taviella held her peace.

"The point of all this is that everything here is centralized. The doors all hook into a common circuit, under this guy's control. The robots, too, are all centrally controlled. If I can open any one door . . ." He held up a finger. "Wait. You'll see. Maravic, would you care to do the honors?"

"Gladly," Maravic said. Hefting the projectile weapon, cradling it under her arm like a submachine gun, she stepped up to the door and opened fire. Pellets flew forth at high velocity, with a resounding staccato burst. The door lock shattered, and parts of it flew about the room, along with the rebounding metal spheres. Maravic stepped back. Eric took a closer look.

"That's all it needed," he announced.

"Then we can go where we want?" Taviella

asked. "We can shoot our way through any of these doors?"

"Yes, we could." Eric's voice held a note of triumph. "But we don't have to." He made some adjustments to the doorjamb and finished by affixing the cables from his first device.

"Stand back," he warned, and then closed a switch. A loud mechanical click could be heard, as every door from the room was suddenly unlocked. Taviella looked around; the doors all swung open in simultaneous grandeur.

"Not just from this room, either," said Maravic, who had helped Eric with the construction of the device. "Every door in the station, except for the main airlock, is now open for our use."

"I'm glad you mentioned that the main airlock is still closed," Taviella laughed, impressed. "I'm not wearing a helmet at the moment."

"The second device here," Eric continued in the style of a showman, "will have a less evident effect."

"We built it from equipment found inside the robots," Maravic took up. "Tuning equipment that has a characteristic of resonance." She pointed her arm at Eric theatrically. Eric closed another switch.

Nothing happened. . . .

Then Eric's face split in a huge smile. "We just killed every damn robot in this station."

Taviella's eyes widened in appreciation. "You overloaded some sort of resonant circuit?"

"That's right. We just blew their little brains right through their shells."

"Can we keep the machine gun with us, just in case?"

Maravic, who still held it, nodded an emphatic agreement. "There might be worse here than robots," she said.

"One more switch," Eric said, grinning. "You didn't like the idea of being watched, am I not right?"

"You're very right," Taviella said firmly.

Eric touched the third switch. Again, nothing happened that any of them could see.

"The central controller of this station is now blind and deaf. We have our privacy. Our work here is done." Eric gestured proudly toward his devices. "My machinery has done its job, and we can forget about it. We can go where we want, either back to the ship or deeper into the station." He signed. "I vote for going back to the ship and leaving, but I don't expect you to agree."

"You know me too well, Eric. We've got Stacey and Remington to find, and we can only do that by going on."

"Maravic, what about you? Do you want to back me up, or her?"

"Sorry, Eric. I've been following Taviella far too long to start arguing with her now. Besides, Remington owes me money."

Defeated, Eric scooped up one last small, handheld device, tucked it into his backpack, and straightened. "Lead on," he muttered, and struggled into the pack's straps.

"What's that device, Eric?" Taviella asked.

"A projector, set to flicker at one hundred and five cycles per second." As he followed Taviella through the door and into a storage area, he explained his reasoning.

"Stacey can see images that are flickering. We can't. This way, if we find him being held captive by whoever it is that runs this madhouse, we can send him secret messages. You know, 'Be ready to clobber your guard when you hear the whistle.' That sort of cloak-and-blaster nonsense."

"Good idea," Taviella said, yet her voice was dubious. "What message is in it now?"

"Since Stacey has been making weapons for the enemy, and since he isn't any too bright, I made one up that says 'Don't shoot, you idiot — it's us.' I can change the message in seconds."

Laughing, Maravic summed it up. "Seeing a message like that, no one could doubt that it was sent by Eric."

Taviella, smiling, said nothing. The cavalcade tripped lightly on, following her lead. She was relieved, more relieved than she would have thought, not to have to test doors to see if they were locked. She was also very happy to learn that no one could spy on her.

Every door she came to stood wide. They began to make real progress for the first time since entering the station.

∞

Leaving the battle-scarred theater behind, Remington continued to explore, guided this way and that by the maze of locked and unlocked doors. His heart still hammered after his desperate victory over the two deadly robots. But hotter than his excitement at surviving was his anger at being trapped.

"You've got me alone; you've got me helpless," he muttered aloud, speaking to the station walls. "Come on, come on, finish the job." He took to jabbing uselessly with his electrified probe at walls and door handles.

A door opened to his touch, and he stepped through sullenly, almost losing his footing on the tilted surface within. He looked about, trying to make sense of the round room. A domed ceiling bent out over him; he'd begun to get used to the ancient architects' taste for domes. The floor, however, sloped downward into a sharp, cusplike cup, a funnel dropping away into a central open vent. There were no furnishings or fixtures.

"What's this? A maelstrom?" Remington looked carefully at the floor, vaguely reassured by the omnipresent black patterned tiles. He was in the process of examining one of the four symmetrically placed doors in the perimeter of the room when two other doors opened and began emitting robots.

He had no way to flee, nowhere to hide. The robots quickly cut him off from the farthest door, and the nearest door was locked. He spun, hoping to dive to safety down the central drain hole, but one swift robot had skated down the funnel and now guarded that escape.

Remington counted seven of them, all bearing long spikes or sharp, barbed tridents. Clusters of pressure cylinders, fastened to their sides in bundles, threatened him, and the muzzles of complex mechanical projectile weapons menaced him from beneath each robot. He looked sidelong at his own weapon, a long, slim probe, electrified at its tip.

Seven against one, he thought, and swallowed. *Remington,* he told himself, *you're going to die.*

Before anything else happened, the two other doors to the room, closed earlier, flipped open. Remington's gaze swung back and forth as he tried to turn his head to watch both. Nothing more came through. The odds remained at seven to one.

Okay, then. Let's get it over with. Remington took a step upslope, then whirled and charged the lone robot guarding the central well. Above him, to every side, robots slid into action, moving above their dragging sledges with mechanical grace.

Sidestepping, feinting, Remington lunged with his spear and was parried rudely. He drew back for another shot.

At once, every robot in the room fell clattering to the floor, and started to roll downslope in a tangle of weapons, cables, sledges, and mechanical gripper arms. One after another, they whirled down the funnel and popped through the central hole, like billiard balls in some impossibly complex trick shot.

Remington watched it, jaws tightly clenched, eyes narrowed, unwilling to believe in this miraculous reprieve. After a long time, shaking his head slowly, he trudged back up the slope, and looked carefully before he stepped through a door.

21

I command energies to be shot across the
sky, to guide my ships upon their argosies. I
command beacons to be emplaced. I command the heavens to be made a garden-park,
and the stars to be my lampposts.
— *Proclamation four hundred fifty-five
of Arcadian I, Emperor of Archive*

Taviella, Eric, and Maravic wandered at random,
seeking Stacey or Remington. Before long, they
found themselves exploring the great cavernous
kitchens. The vaulted ceilings and long, long walls
lined with food-preparation machinery struck them
with awe. "These people never built on a human
scale," Eric complained. "You could feed a blasted
army from here."

Maravic and Taviella craned their necks, peering in all directions. They separated, looking guard-
edly down each aisle and under every table.

Taviella's wounds gave her a slight discomfort,
but it was pain that she could, for the time being, ignore. The three explorers were fatigued, however,

and exhaustion was the greater threat. Maravic had been the longest without sleep, but Eric and Taviella were tired also.

They moved over the dark, patterned flooring, their steps dragging slightly, and they ran their gloves over the black-paneled surfaces more and more carelessly.

Maravic found the small computer terminal, on the bench by the hand implements. She activated it without difficulty. Eric and Taviella watched over her shoulder as she sought to call up a catalog. Only one response came to any of her inquiries: *Delent.*

"Real good," Eric grumbled. "An empty file in the kitchen. Maybe the cook was secretive and never wrote down his recipes."

Maravic shrugged and left off her profitless pursuit. They moved along.

In the next room, a gently sloping theater, they found a dismal mess. Two robots lay dead on the floor near the stage, and nearby, charred curtains smoked in ruined heaps. A section of seats had been melted beyond recovery by strong acid. Overhead, a thin layer of acrid smoke veiled the ceiling.

"Remington was here," Maravic said somberly.

"Well, he's not here now," Taviella snapped. "He's alive."

"Hey, of course I am!" Remington called from the back of the room. He ducked inside, spread his hands as if to receive applause, and grinned his most formidable grin. "No pair of walleyed grampuses like those two robots is any match for me. You guys ought to know that."

"You're making me regret I opened up the doors,"

Eric said sourly, although it was clear that he, too, was relieved to see Remington unharmed.

Still smiling widely, Remington waved his fellow crew members to join him near the top of the room. "You won't regret it in a minute. I found the jump-space rifts, or their containment vessels, anyway. And it's quite a sight."

"Let's go," Eric said brusquely. He led the team back up the sloping aisle. Behind them, black and melted, trailing scattered chunks of debris, the robots remained.

"I'd just been set upon by seven robots," Remington explained, "when they all fell away. After that, every door I came to was wide open. Did you do that?"

"Yeah. I opened the doors, and I killed the robots. Good thing, too, wouldn't you say?"

"You're pretty good, for a tinkerer. Why don't you go back and fill in the gaps in your theoretical knowledge?"

Eric eyed Remington. "I've never been enthralled with the notion of working in a development team, collaborating with forty other people to solve big, ugly problems. I'd rather work with problems I can see, understand, and solve myself."

Remington digested that as they wandered through the kitchens in silence. He led them away in a direction new to the rest of them, under a low archway, down a steep ramp, and to a set of massive double doors.

"I got this far, then doubled back to find the rest of you." He showed them a side door that led to a peculiar bowl-shaped room. "This is where I was, trapped by seven robots, when Eric came through for me."

"I didn't do it for you." Eric glared at Remington, then relented and smiled a little. "The nick of time, eh?"

"Close enough. Of course, I would have beaten them. They were only robots." Remington looked away, having no words to express his gratitude to Eric.

"Sure."

"I don't think our unseen tour guide ever wanted us to get this far, but we have. And . . ." Remington threw his arms wide with a flourish as he ushered his friends through the doors.

The corridor that stretched away before them was like the many, many others along which they had trudged this long day, with several differences: the wall to the left was made of transparent floor-to-ceiling window panels. The walls were a soft blue, and the carpet was a dark blue, free of the usual black tiles. Even the glass had a faint blue tint. Beyond the windows, extending far below, far away, a vast enclosure lay spread to their sight.

Taviella and Maravic stepped close to the glass and unconsciously leaned forward to touch it, seeking the best view. Cold crystal beneath their gloves held them back; Taviella's breath misted momentarily on its surface until she stopped breathing in order to see. Eric stood back, only a little, bent forward, and gaped. Remington spent equal amounts of time looking out into the cavern himself and watching the reactions of his teammates.

They stood nearly at the top level of the cavern,

looking out and down. Catwalks, scaffolds, and cranes gave a scale to the scene. Everything had a blue tinge, whether from the tinted glass or from the paint on the equipment, Taviella could not tell. A beautiful, smoothly curved support arm swept up from its anchors in the distant floor. Two others, rooted away in different corners, swung up to meet it. Where they would have joined, had their extension not been interrupted, a gigantic ball sat supported. It was an openwork sphere, made of joined geodesic struts, not all the same length and not all meeting at identical angles. It had a slightly rough, haphazard feel to it, as if, impossibly, artistic rather than engineering considerations had dictated its structure.

Auxiliary equipment surrounded it. Six bulky generators, heavy, massive, complex, sat on the surface of the sphere and were linked to one another by heavy conduits. Elsewhere, the sphere was trussed, supporting an offset tube of similarly complex openwork beams that aimed into the sphere at a slight upward angle. This tube pointed directly at a darkened opening, slightly elliptical, near the top of the wall to the far right.

Within the sphere, contained in impossible stability, writhed the oven-red gash of an open jumpspace rift.

It moved, shifting as sluggishly and as unceasingly as the fiery prominences of a sun's corona. Foreshortened when seen from the viewing gallery where Taviella watched, it extended itself, moving like a great captive amoeba. Fiery red, molten red, the red of hot iron, its rim grew little black flecks, lending its edges a boiling, foamy appearance. The rift, essentially planar, held a position exactly perpendicular to the line along the extending tube.

Maravic saw the laser beam first, and only by knowing precisely where to look. Backtracking along the line of the tube, she spied a tiny assembly clamped to the sphere. From it, the narrowest and faintest yellow line shot, vanishing without a trace into the jumpspace rift. She pointed it out to her friends.

"It looks so fine, so harmless," Taviella sighed. "It's hard to imagine that something so small carries so many megawatts."

"But something's wrong," Maravic said in a puzzled tone. "That isn't the direction of Marterly. Marterly is off and away this way." She waved an arm vaguely behind her.

"How can you tell?" asked Taviella. "Have you got an absolute sense of direction?" She wasn't being snide, but was honestly curious.

"No." Maravic laughed. "I've a good one, though. This planetoid isn't rotating, so all directions are fixed."

"Look ahead," Remington said cheerfully. At the end of the corridor, another set of double doors stood open. Taviella looked at Eric and Maravic and immediately moved along, leaving the scene of technological grandeur behind. Through the doors waited a pleasantly appointed foyer, and another set of doors off at an angle. Beyond them was another blue corridor, with windows inset that showed another blue cavern full of similar equipment. The orientation of the aiming tube was different, pointing to a spot in the ceiling almost directly above the viewing gallery. The jumpspace rift could be seen nearly straight on, a violent red wound gaping in midair, fringed with black foaming crusts. The laser could not be seen at all, although Eric was certain that he could see one or two brilliantly shining stars within the rift.

"There." He pointed. "That's a star, isn't it?" He indicated it to Remington and Maravic.

Remington sneered. "It's not a star unless you can see light up in the X-ray range."

Eric, peering more closely, was insistent. "Stars. I can see three of them. And there's a fourth."

"Let me look," Maravic said, pushing her face plate into contact with the wall. After a time, she nodded. "I see five, and something that might be a sixth. They're in the right places to be the six brightest stars in that region of the sky."

"This window must step the high-energy photons down to a sensible range," Remington responded lamely.

"Whew!" Maravic said, and stepped back from the glass. "Do you know how hot it must be in there?"

"Five thousand, nearly six thousand degrees." Remington thought. "Plus maybe a little leakage from those lasers."

Taviella brought them back to reality. "As impressive as this is, it gets us no closer to Stacey and freedom. Follow me."

Her companions lingered long enough to look one last time over the massive artifacts rising from the distant floor. One last glance, and then with a collective sigh they moved after their leader.

Her path took them through two more viewing galleries, each showing another nearly identical scene. The fifth that they moved through was the same as the others, only without a viewing window. "Why is this one closed off?" Taviella asked, without pausing to try to discover the answer.

"I have a guess," Eric put in. "The aiming tube runs the jumpspace laser along a path too close to the window for safety, so they sealed it."

Maravic and Remington both shuddered at the thought of having just passed through the path of a megawatt laser beam, even though it was safely insulated from their reality in its own nonoverlapping jumpspace.

Soon, the rooms they saw began to resemble portions of the station they'd already seen, although the design was still conceptually odd to them. A vast room of blank white cabinets and closets, all empty, indicated that they were again in the living portion of the complex. Here the floor was again overlaid with electrified tiles. Another room lay cluttered with pipes, both square and round, and with shelves piled high with metal and plastic boxes. Bins the size of barrels contained countless metal spheres, all precisely the same size, and each, when examined closely, bearing a unique identifying coded marking. More bins contained more balls, of varying sizes. "From balls the size of fists to half-millimeter ball bearings," Eric observed. "And all of them numbered. Who would want to tell one from another, and why?"

No one had any answers. Eric released a handful of tiny spheres, letting them run through his fingers back into the bin. He shrugged and fell into place behind Taviella as she opened the next door. He wondered if there was in fact any end to the labyrinthine station.

In the next room, a vast machine shop, a familiar face greeted them. It was Stasileus.

The four human crew members stood regarding their nonhuman counterpart. He bore an improvised device in his huge hands, aimed lazily at the floor. It was obviously a spear gun, loaded with eight spears offset in two patterns of four.

Taviella spoke first. "Stacey! You're barefoot! Why isn't the floor burning you?"

Stacey smiled a glad welcoming smile. "It only does that when Sophia is angry with me."

"Is Sophia the master here? Bring her out. We have matters to discuss."

"Come along, then. I'll take you to her." Stasileus lowered his gun and began to turn. A loud voice sounded from a speaker over the electronics workbench. He halted.

"Stasileus, kill them!" Desperation tinged Sophia's cry.

Stasileus froze, his body rigid, his limbs trembling. Slowly he turned about, his eyes fastened on Taviella in an urgent appeal for guidance.

Eric lifted his strobe and flashed a message for Stasileus's eyes only, or so he thought. *Don't shoot, you idiot — it's us.* Stasileus relaxed a trifle. His great shoulders began, bit by bit, to slump.

Since the robots had died, he had been at work, repairing the cameras and microphones in this room. Sophia, able to run the images from her cameras through signal-processing machinery of great sophistication, realized almost instantly what Eric had done. From a projector Stasileus had rigged on the ceiling of the machine shop, the image of her lesser symbol of loyalty sprang forth, hovering intangibly in midair before Stasileus. It was a subordinate sigil, one that might be used by Viceroys and by deputies when commanding slaves. Pindar had left it to Sophia as a cruel jest, knowing that she would be alone, commanding no one.

The light of reason blanked out of Stasileus's eyes, and his shivering stopped abruptly. Smoothly, totally under control, he raised his weapon and fired one dart. The shaft fled from its tube, followed by a tiny curl of flame. A sound like the snapping of a dry stick echoed through the room, followed by a sharper crack when the dart punctured Remington's face plate. His cheek was furrowed by the passage of the razor-sharpened spearhead, and his earlobe was torn. More startled than injured, he took a careless step backward and stumbled, rocking back, arms flailing.

Taviella began to draw her pistol. Maravic, at one time Stasileus's finest defender, narrowed her eyes, inhaled deeply, and took a large step forward, arms beginning to rise. Eric, with practiced ease, flipped his backpack forward off his shoulder, lifted it to his chest, and fumbled within it.

"Don't do this!" Taviella shouted. Stasileus, now a machine inhabiting a mindless body, rotated the bundle of spear-gun cylinders and shot again. This shaft impaled Eric's backpack and was stopped by his suit behind it. Eric had succeeded in bringing out the weapon he wanted, however: the most effective weapon he had with him.

It was a piece of paper, and on it, in bright red ink, the symbol of the Emperor's loyalty blazed. Sophia's symbol had been a lesser one; this one carried the force of the Emperor's infinite will. None could stand before it. Eric displayed the paper, marched forward, and stuffed it into Taviella's unresisting fists.

"Command us," he gasped, and fell back.

Remington, regaining his balance, and Maravic, looking over her shoulder, saw the symbol in Taviella's hands. Both of them froze in place, unable to move or to think. Stasileus's eyes passed briefly over the symbol, then gazed straight forward; he stiffened to motionless attention and let the weapon fall from his nerveless fingers. Spine straight, head high, expression utterly vacant, he became a tall, furred statue, seeming scarcely to breathe, scarcely to live.

Taviella's horizon expanded beyond her own viewpoint. Her face seemed to swell. The room, the station, the whole of the Concordat's star-reaching sphere, world, stars, cosmos: all seemed to her to be small things, easily held in one hand. Doors opened for her. Realizations came with revelatory force. Had she actually not known the importance of the symbol when she first saw it? She now understood its vital necessity. Had her first use of it to command been merely an unconscious and unaware action? She now knew.

It was almost amusing, so ludicrous was it. She had spent her whole life sleepwalking, running away from her heritage, reviling the squalid world of her birth. She commanded a tiny ship and hoped to scrape together a minuscule profit out of its cargo. She lived under the oppression of assessors, of inspectors, of auditors; she worked within the narrow confines of a society dominated by bureaucracy and by formula. Now she was free. The chaos of hindering rules and restricting balances could be swept utterly away. Before her beckoned a great, golden vista whose key she held in her hands. She would restore order. She would give the stars purpose. She would speak, and all who heard would obey. That was their place.

Hers was to rule.

Order. She would bestow order where there now was none.

Visions danced before her eyes. She saw a great, glittering ballroom, where a thousand men and women wove patterns as they swirled. A thousand tiny lights shone, each bearing a tiny rainbow halo. Above, a huge ball of vast orange flame gave off both light and heat, roaring and fluttering as it burned without smoke. At the focus of the room, commanding the whole of the hall, a high throne of carnelian loomed high, and on it, robed in shining white furs, Taviella-i-Tel, Empress of Archive, sat in unquestioned majesty.

The people of the Concordat had huddled in their paralyzed fear, not daring to face the tremendous nobility that lurked, unsuspected, in their souls. Taviella looked out and saw them, waiting by the billions, docile. They wanted only a leader to guide them to the true fulfillment of their greatness. Taviella would be their Empress; she would give them courage.

She would lead them out. The heavens would be their garden-park, and the stars their lampposts.

The hallucination faded. She lifted her head and looked around the confines of the machine shop. Maravic stood rigid before her, as if at attention before a military inspection. Taviella smiled at her: honest, stolid Maravic. Hers would be the greatest reward, because of her unflagging loyalty and friendship. Nearby, Eric stood, his face numb. He, too, would earn a great reward, for having known to give the symbol to her when it was needed. Remington, next to him, waited, paying no heed to the blood dripping down his cheek. He had served as a soldier in her cause, and it would be he who would lead her legions across the stars.

She looked up at Stasileus. As immobile as a block of marble, as unfeeling and unflinching as a portrait, he waited to obey her bidding. She noted the dart projector lying at his feet, and she smiled wryly. The time for them to be shooting at one another was over.

Only Sophia remained to be conquered.

"Stacey?"

Stasileus's large eyes shifted, and he looked at her. His personality seemed suppressed. "Yes?"

"Tell me more about Sophia."

22

I once compared destiny to a youth's curious mind, believing that destiny proceeds on
its course the way children learn: with de-
light and sorrow. Destiny unfolds. A youth
grieves for his lost innocence. Could I but
recant my observation!

— Achorus, *My Fears*

Doctor Morris felt quite content to allow Bella and
Emil to precede him on their tour of the station. He
let them do the scouting, the peering around corners
for danger, while he and Doctor Hohenger followed
on, observing freely. Bella watched carefully, sneaking along. Emil approached doors with elaborate
caution and unlocked them with his handheld electronic tool. They were free to choose their course, but
didn't seem to be going anywhere.

Hohenger, Morris noted, was also alert, with the
rescue mission uppermost in her mind. Nothing
would be allowed to sneak past her, for she shifted
her gaze carefully from point to point, and looked
behind as much as ahead. Morris admired her tac-

tical skills; he had to assume that he had learned to think in terms of opposition and maneuver from countless sessions of budget and audit committee meetings. How similar, he mused, were bureaucratic and military wars: the placement of the allies along the battlefront; the allocation of rhetorical and martial resources. . . .

For the time being, Morris was content simply to watch.

He watched, then, with a historian's eye, not a tactician's, and thus he saw the station. Living habitats, some empty and some still furnished, told him silent stories in great detail and full volume. The lounges were designed most efficiently for lounging: for men and women to laze in indolent ease, doing nothing, thinking nothing. The bedrooms were not solely for sleeping.

The continually varying color schemes fascinated him: a suite of blues would exit subtly into a lounge of all white, yet retaining subdued blue accents. Little or no ornamentation was visible: the lords and ladies of Old Archive lived their lives inside their heads, not held in their hands. Maximization of sensation had been the rule of the station's architecture: sharp angles to occupy the vision, blended colors to draw the eye about in new paths. Temperatures, scents, breezes, sounds, all would ordinarily conspire to lend this place a vibrant yet subliminal texture. Morris regretted being pent within his confining vacuum suit with its thick gloves, stiff sleeves, and hampering face plate. He observed smooth transitions in the floor level as he strode along, as well as variations in the surface roughness of walls and furniture. More changes to fool the senses, he knew, and smiled a bleak little smile of irony.

Free from the everlasting sameness aboard the university ship, I find myself in the most comfortable and relaxing environment ever crafted by mankind. And I'm within a spacesuit, breathing recycled air, able to talk to my companions only across the radio. An injustice!

As a historian, he knew of many, many injustices, and of the great atrocities of the past; none was as personal or immediate as the faint chemical odor of his suit's air or the faint ache of numbness in his gloved fingers.

Of all the details that he saw, only the black, stippled flooring did not change from room to room, and Morris knew enough to dismiss it. It had been added at a later date, and was therefore irrelevant data.

"Are you getting anything useful?" Doctor Hohenger asked him abruptly.

Morris swung about to regard her. Suited, she still walked with an easy, assured stride. As a leader, an administrator, and a research scientist, she embodied talent and ability. For her judgment as an academic, Morris could only purse his lips and express himself cautiously. She was too pragmatic, too directed. He always wanted to teach her to slow her thinking and to reflect. Helplessly, he regarded her. What would she make of a long, lazy afternoon on a grassy sward beside slow-moving, sun-warmed water? Would she learn patience from the water's slow ripples?

"I'm . . . soaking up impressions." Morris knew better than to tell her this was the most important part of his lifelong methodology.

"I'd hoped you might have observed something that would help us find those people," Hohenger said, not unkindly.

Morris sighed deeply, chastising himself for his helplessness. On a rescue mission, he was of less than no worth at all. His only value here was as an observer.

Emil and Bella, to his amusement, took to their tasks with all stern seriousness. Bella walked low, skulking along like a caricature of stealth. Emil stood strainingly erect, head held to the side as he walked, listening more than watching ahead of himself. Behind them, Hohenger's easy stride and sensible stance spoke of a more mature, more capable preparedness. The sight of something unexpected or startling would find her already set to move, with no time wasted in straightening or recoiling.

Thus, only Hohenger was not taken by surprise when the doors from the small bedroom they were in swung open without visible cause. Bella leaped back and put her hands uselessly over her chest. Emil crouched low, reducing the area he presented to any attack, but he also rested one knee on the electrified floor and bounced up again swiftly.

Morris, who had been so intent on watching his companions, was also taken aback and stumbled over a low settee, catching his balance only with difficulty. He was no less embarrassed than Emil or Bella; in some people, age does not bring uncompromisable dignity, and he felt his shame as strongly as any youth. He looked about, vastly relieved that no one had noticed.

No one and nothing came through the doors.

Bella peeked around the edge and signaled a tentative "all clear."

Every door in the station was now open, and their choice of a path was both simplified and made more complex. They passed through great halls and small ones. They found a tall, towering room of many levels, where the galleries rose overhead in tiers, each level overlooking the one below over a balustraded balcony. They observed, and chose not to explore, a sequence of tetrahedral cubicles leading forward and down in a complex three-dimensional maze.

At last they arrived in the grand dining hall, where smoke fogged the ceiling, where broken-up robots littered the floor and the paint-smeared table, and where flame and acid burns marred the black tiles on the floor. Morris, with some difficulty, kept his composure. Emil stopped short, and a sharp exclamation escaped his lips. Bella hesitated a long, long moment, then ducked swiftly within, snapping her head from left to right in search of foes. Hohenger, moving smoothly yet unhurriedly, swept the room with a careful glance and shrugged toward Morris. "All's clear."

"There's been one hell of a fight in here recently," Emil observed.

"Over here," Bella beckoned, summoning them to see her vital discovery, actually no more than a row of bullet-pocks in the wall.

"The paint on the table must signify something,"

Emil continued, regaining some of his cocky arrogance. He snapped his fingers. "There was another battle somewhere else."

Hohenger recalled them both to her with a word. Seeing her quiet gesture toward the assembled electronic devices still in place on the table, the two students silently approached them and regarded them intently. Emil pulled forth a probe and began cautiously to examine one of the devices.

Morris, both amused and slightly alarmed, strolled slowly about the vast hall, absorbed in its many aspects. Above the center of the table, the huge globe of Archive rolled in lustrous, heart-catching beauty.

I've never been to Archive, Morris sighed, filling himself with the light of the racial homeworld. *It's been a long-standing tradition in my family that we all make a pilgrimage there sometime during our lives.*

He recalled his older sister, who had traveled there, fallen in love with the planet, and who resided there still. She had written to him, telling him how real the air smelled there. It was the air that mankind had grown up with, the air mankind had left behind when he set off to pursue the shifting stars.

Morris looked up at the globe and let it fill his entire field of vision. Beneath pebbled clouds, sharp land masses thrust into azure areas. Snowcaps crowned and chinned the world, as finely detailed as filigree lace. Suddenly, Morris's face split in a wide, jolly smile, and he had to suppress a bark of laughter: the world was not rotating on its axis, but rather about the spot where lay the city of Archive, the old

Emperor's ruling capital. There, there had been one egocentric mortal!

For the wreckage of the robots, for the electronics and the circuitry, and for the blot of paint on the table, Morris had not a whit of interest. When touring an ancient temple, discovered some years ago, he had paid no attention to the scuff marks of the discoverers, nor to the detritus of centuries. Here, too, the vandalism of recent years made no impression on him. There were historical details to be learned here, things that no one alive today knew.

He looked away from the shining blue globe only when Hohenger called to him. "Doctor Morris? We're going to be moving along. We're through here."

"Very well." He trotted docilely along. She and the two students might have been through there: Morris knew that many slow, relaxed hours would have been required for him even to be able to begin. He forced himself to amiability out of consideration for teamwork.

"What did you find?" he asked.

Hohenger explained in a few sentences the students' diagnosis of the electronics devices left behind on the table. "One opened all the doors in this station. The other seemed to have been a destructive device, sending out an overload pulse on some resonant circuit. Emil is certain that they were built using current technologies, not with devices and science of the Empire."

"I see." What Morris saw, however, could never be explained in terms of period, time, or technology. He saw antiquity, and sought to reconstruct a part of it in his mind, so that it would not be lost forever. He sought a sense, just a sense, of history.

It troubled him, a bit, that people had taken the reprehensible steps of destroying the devices and fixtures here. It reminded him, abstractly, that the past was a very fragile thing, subject to the whims of the eternal present.

This thought passed idly through his mind as Bella and Emil sneaked warily past an open door, and as Hohenger, less melodramatically and more observantly, followed them on. The doorway caught Morris's attention, and he paused. He peered into it and saw the useless extenders strewn into the corridor. A set of carts, pushed by sliding rods, had been shoved aside in the hall, and farther on, other items had been moved about, or left to sit. These weren't new: this was the product of diligent, extensive work. What time frame would most likely encompass this construction?

Hohenger, seeing him stop and look, asked sharply, "What is it? Do you see something?"

"This machinery," he said. "It's ancient. Must be important." He stood staring in puzzlement.

From ahead, Bella shouted an alarm, which rang unpleasantly loud in Morris's earphones. "I've found them! Two men, two women, and . . . and . . ."

"Idiot!" Emil snapped. "It's a Verna. Where have you been for the past year?"

Hohenger darted away without a backward glance, not aware that Morris, standing just within the doorway, had been out of radio contact. The damping field that began at that door had cut off his communication with the others.

Morris, unaware that Bella had called for reinforcements, stood still for a while, his gloved fists clenched. This machinery, piled up in ruins: it had to be significant, and was likely central to the station's mystery. With a shake of his head, he set off down the smaller, strange corridor, following his curiosity, his whim, and his instincts, honed over the course of other adventures and investigations.

He heard nothing further from his helmet radio, nor did he notice the silence.

The corridor turned once, at a slight angle. More equipment had piled up, connected by control linkages and cables, all entirely mechanical. Around another, sharper bend, the corridor opened again, into a room full of electronics.

Struck by the brilliant, logical beauty of the controls he saw, he stopped short and let the sight pervade him. High banks of instruments and indicators glowed with firefly lights of green, orange, yellow, all pastel shades, all busily shifting and reacting. Across the room, on a wide control bench, several rows of switches sat quietly, also lit with soft colors indicative of the subtle status of the machinery.

He edged forward into the room, eyes wide. He lifted his gloved hand and brushed it, so very gently, against the plastic and metal of the cabinet front.

The units that he saw were labeled, in a language that had been dead long before he had been born. *Perception. Volition. Personality. Linguistic. Visual.* On another bank, a different set of labels shone on gleaming instrument units. *Messages: Processing. Messages: Receiving.* The last was labeled *Messages: Routing.*

On the face of that last panel, a switch glowed, blinking steadily. It blinked as it had, unchanged, for more than seven hundred years. A tiny icon lay emblazoned upon it in a subtle green inlay. Morris saw it, and a thrill ran up and down his spine. The icon was the symbol for *Library*.

His universe overturned. History had always been, for him, the study of the things that other people did, and that he, safely insulated from danger, could quietly study afterward. History was a tale of the long ago, of things fixed and done.

The blinking light riveted the whole of his attention: a small, blinking light that indicated clearly even to his nontechnical mind the presence of a message waiting for delivery. A message? How long, he asked himself, had it been since that last and most dire of messages had gone forth from the palace, the burning palace at Archive?

A light, a message, a closed switch, and a library meant something very shocking to Doctor Cassaday Morris, Professor of History at the University of Marterly. It meant that history wasn't only something that once happened, but something that sometimes, rarely, happens now, while people watch.

Or, if the lessons of history are properly learned, and if the stories of the heroes of the past are taken as more than mere entertainment, history is something that one might take in hand, and transform.

He had found a long-lost library, a trove of riches nearly unimaginable in its cultural wealth. Should he or anyone else trip that switch, applying the least pressure of one extended finger, that library would be erased.

Within his helmet, Doctor Morris sweated, and his hair and his helmet padding grew damp and oily.

"Hello," he said softly, addressing the empty air. If his guess was correct . . .

"Hello," Sophia responded. Her voice was soft and feminine: it conjured up in his mind the image of a sixteen-year-old girl, lithe and alert. But the bright voice was also troubled. He tried to respond sensibly, but found himself merely stammering.

"You are this computer? You . . ." He wet his lips. "You . . ."

"Do you serve Taviella?"

Morris blanched. This was the sort of question that one wanted not to be compelled to answer when meeting someone for the first time. Who was Taviella? He didn't recognize the name as that of any of the old gods of the Empire. . . .

"I don't know Taviella," he said honestly.

"She is your enemy."

Sighing deeply, Morris raised his arms in a gesture of helplessness. "I haven't any enemies. Please. Who are you?"

"I am Sophia. I am Taviella's enemy. Soon, I will be her slave. Only you can fight her and free me."

None of it made any sense to Doctor Morris; not in the slightest. He sought for calm. "Are you a construct of Empire? Do you in fact have a complete library in your memory?"

Sophia's voice remained deadly calm, although deep within her she felt a pang of exuberance. Others knew of the library. It would again be hers. She would yet win the final victory. "Yes. But for now, none of that is important. Your friends — Doctor Hohenger, Emil, and Bella — have just been taken captive and are helpless. They are Taviella's slaves."

His mouth sagging open, Doctor Morris stepped forward, completely lost. "Your library—"

"Is not an issue."

"But—"

"Please."

Morris heard her soft, lovely voice and jerked upright. He quickly regained control of himself. "All right. I'm not anyone's enemy, Sophia, but tell me how I can get to Doctor Hohenger."

"She is in a storage shed on the other side of the machine shop that is at the end of the corridor outside this room. Had you not turned aside and come in here, you, too, would be a slave with your three friends."

"Explain to me what I must do." Doctor Morris knew himself to be a weak, awkward man, the least soldierly of men, but he also knew his own resources. Let anyone threaten Doctor Hohenger, and they would find the error a costly one.

"What do you know about the Symbol of Command?" Sophia said in reply.

"We have only . . . rumors."

"Listen, then, to the truth."

She told him. Inside his spacesuit helmet, the hair at the back of his neck bristled and quivered.

23

At birth, a man is but a blank sheet, later
to be scribbled on, torn, and soiled by the pain
and mischance of his unfortunate existence.
— Trinopus, *Three Lesser Paradoxes*

Yet something within us endures, and we
remain steadfast.
— Szentellos, *Commentaries*

Taviella took a deep breath and began her first step
toward righting the manifest wrongs of the cosmos.
Her first command froze on her lips, however, interrupted by the arrival of three spacesuited figures.
Taviella raised her head haughtily and looked over
these intruders.

"Who are you?" she demanded.

Bella and Emil moved closer to Doctor Hohenger. Their faces, seen through the clear plastic of
their face plates, were troubled.

Taviella reached behind her and took up her
headphones. "Hello?" She received no response.
Switching to another channel, she heard voices.

"Who are you?" Her patience was near an end: was she not the Empress of the race?

"Hello. I'm Doctor Anne Hohenger, from the University of Marterly. We intercepted a message beam and followed it here. Can you tell me who you are? Are you in trouble?"

"I . . ." Taviella paused, and her voice grew full and self-important. "I am Taviella-i-Tel." She took a deep, proud breath. "I command."

"We'll see about that," another voice snapped.

"Emil. Hush." Doctor Hohenger smiled and spread her hands. "We heard your voice earlier, and it seemed—"

Taviella stood forward, her bearing peremptory. "Be silent." She smiled, but the expression was cold and insincere. "You are welcome to my station."

"Your . . . ?" Bella stammered.

Taviella looked at the young student with a chill expression. "I command."

"Are you exercising your claim of salvage and recovery?" Hohenger asked, her voice uncertain. "I'm not sure it would stand up in court. We're an expedition sponsored by our university, and I think we might get a prior claim based on the historical magnitude—"

Taviella's smile grew wider, more predatory. She took another step and held up the paper that bore the symbol of command. Power ran through her mind and veins like the warmth that alcohol brings. "I command."

None of the university team had anything further to say. They brought themselves erect, faces front, eyes wide, their minds extinguished.

For the fourth time, Taviella said, offhandedly, "I command." There were no voices raised in dissent.

She looked over her shoulder. The stiff immobility of her crew members — her friends — bothered her. She remembered them as they had been, and herself as she had been. She shrugged.

"Maravic, Eric, Remington, snap out of it. We've got work to do."

"Okay, Taviella," Maravic said, and her voice, although hollow, seemed superficially normal.

"Where do we start?" Remington asked.

Eric wordlessly donned his backpack. He kept his eyes away from the symbol of command that Taviella waved negligently.

"Yes," Taviella mused, "where do we start? So much to get done. . . ." She nodded her head decisively. "Eric, begin restoring the machines here. We'll want cutoffs installed so that they can't be used against us again."

"I'll get right on it." Eric strode to the workbench and began examining the broken-down robot parts.

"Remington," Taviella said, her voice sounding more and more normal, "take these three people and lock them in the storage room. And while you're there, make an inventory. Let's see what we've got to work with." She turned to Doctor Hohenger and the two students. "Go with him."

"Right," Remington said briskly. Although he seemed animated and in every way his normal self, he had not yet taken measures to stop the trickle of blood down his cheek. He gestured brusquely to the three university personnel and led them away out the rear door.

"Maravic?"

"Yes, Taviella?"

Their voices, bright and happy, seemed so very normal. Only the faintest hint of tone, timbre, and timing gave any hint that Maravic was now Taviella's slave, and that Taviella ruled over her with absolute domination.

"Go out into the station, make up a list of repairs that need to be made, and order the items by priority of urgency. Keep your headset nearby in case I need to call you."

"Okay." Moving cheerfully, as if all were as it had always been, Maravic went off.

Watching her depart, Taviella smiled. But her expression quickly shadowed. She felt a sense of growing wrong. . . .

She approached Stasileus, who had not moved since the symbol had been shown him. "Stacey?"

"Yes?" He remained stiff and blank-faced.

"Come on, Stacey. Come out of it." Playfully, Taviella added, "I command you."

Stasileus's head jerked back. Then, slowly, his shoulders loosened up, muscle by muscle, and a cautious expression slid over his face. He moved his overlarge feet and began to breathe with a more normal rhythm. "Yes, Taviella."

"Who is Sophia?"

"She is the computer who manages this place."

Taviella frowned. "She sent the robots to kill us?"

"Yes."

"And she drew you away from us, and turned you against us?"

"Yes."

"Then let's go talk to her. Lead the way." Although her voice sounded lively and not particularly angry, anyone who knew her well would have sensed the deadly anger in Taviella's voice and noticed the repressed fury in her face. The fury, however, was not a manifestation of her normal wrath, but something disturbingly different. What she held tightly in check was a burning, elemental hatred, an emotion almost totally alien to Taviella before she had seen the symbol.

Stasileus led her out of the machine shop and down the narrow, wreckage-strewn corridor. Taviella wondered at the long-forsaken equipment cluttering it. She arrived at Sophia's chamber; she stepped into the middle of Sophia's mind. Looking around the room, she saw the instrumentation and was awed by its sophistication. She saw no human operator.

Stasileus stood to one side. He said nothing and made no motion. It was as if he had become no more than a part of the room's furnishings.

"Sophia?" Taviella called.

"Yes?" Sophia's voice sounded from nowhere, echoing for a moment in the still room. At one panel of instruments, a sequence of lights changed colors.

"Sophia? Where are you?"

"You see me." Her voice was now cold and unfriendly, yet Taviella sensed, as Doctor Morris had, the essential nature of Sophia's personality: a young girl, quick to form likes and dislikes, yet also quick to revise them. Of Sophia's deeper secrets she had no notion.

Taviella accepted it. The cool, unhappy voice was

a voice that fit, intimately, with the instrument-laden room. The living computers of the old Empire were one of history's unfounded rumors, but after what she had seen this day, Taviella was willing to take that and more on faith.

"We didn't know—"

"Are you a master?" Sophia asked. "You can use the symbol. But you obliterated it when you came here. What kind of a master are you?"

Taviella flushed, for a moment, hearing her right to command questioned. Then she shrugged and answered honestly. "I don't know."

"You must be of the immediate family of the Emperor. But Stasileus told me that the Emperor is dead, and the Empire fallen. He said that the commoners threw down the gods from heaven. He said that the nobles were all slain. Is this true?"

"It's all true."

"Then you are my enemy."

Taviella held her head up and looked about the room. Her heart raced, and her face grew flushed. "Am I? Yes, perhaps I am. You tried to kill us." Her voice grew louder, more shrill. "You made yourself my enemy. You took control of my servant" — she indicated Stasileus — "and made him into a weapon against us."

Sophia said nothing.

"Very well," Taviella said. She held up the paper on which the symbol of command had been drawn. The power of it filled her brain, and she knew herself to be immortal, omnipotent, irresistible. She smiled a cold, inhuman smile. "I command."

Stasileus, although he held his eyes forward,

was clearly affected by the image of the symbol. He stood straight, his breath became shallow and almost silent, and not a muscle of his body moved the slightest fraction. His obedience was absolute and utterly involuntary.

Sophia, too, was now no more than an extension of Taviella's will.

"Serve me."

"Yes," said Sophia.

"I am Taviella-i-Tel. I am the Daughter of the Stars." She laughed suddenly: a shy, friendly laugh. "But I don't need to speak harshly to you now; not any more." She sighed. "You're no longer my enemy, now, are you?"

"No."

"Good." Laughing again, this time with honest joy, Taviella spun about and looked at the panels and lights that composed Sophia. "I don't know your capabilities. Tell me about yourself. In what way can you best serve me?"

Sophia had no choice left. Neither will nor volition belonged to her any longer. She was unable even to regret what she must next say, and she could not either have temporized or equivocated.

"You have an enemy still in this base. He is named Doctor Cassaday Morris. He goes now to free Doctor Hohenger, and Emil and Bella as well."

A hot wave of fury blazed across Taviella's mind, moving as a windswept sheet of flame flashes across a dry field. Her wrath faded, however, leaving her mind clear.

"Stacey, stay here," she snapped. "Let no one speak to Sophia." Then she turned and darted out through the zigzag corridor. She wheeled quickly to her right, ran into the machine shop, and slowed for a moment.

"Eric! Grab Stacey's dart gun and come after me!" Then she ran on.

"Yes," Eric answered, although Taviella was out of hearing. He dropped the equipment he was working with. It fell to the bench and crumpled, slowly burning under the load of the electric current he had not been given time to shut off. He hustled across the room, scooped up the dart projector, and sped after Taviella.

∞

Doctor Morris, taking the long route through the station around to the rear approaches to the machine shop, found the blue rooms overlooking the equipment basements. Through the floor-to-ceiling blue windows he saw the vast machines in their caverns. He saw the stable, open jumpspace rifts, and his eyes grew very wide.

Energy from jumpspace? he wondered. *Faster-than-light communications?* He stood, dazed, until the urgency of his mission returned to him, and he leaped on to rescue Doctor Hohenger and the students. He passed through the last of the observation rooms and found himself back in the parts of the station he understood. Ahead of him was the storeroom that Sophia had described.

He looked around the edge of the open doorway: ahead of him stood Remington, facing away. Morris entered the room slowly, but despite his caution,

Remington heard his faint sound. Morris had only a moment to scan the room. He paid no attention to the boxes and bins of parts; he glanced only momentarily at Remington, who spun to face him. Against one wall stood Doctor Hohenger, with Emil and Bella at her sides.

"What do you want?" Remington asked, not unkindly, his face wary rather than angry.

"Nothing, friend," Morris said, and he darted in and grabbed at Hohenger and Emil.

Remington wasn't as fast as he was, but had less distance to cover. He cuffed Bella aside and caught Hohenger's other arm. For a moment the two men grappled in a ludicrous tug-of-war, fighting for possession of Doctor Hohenger's unresisting form. Morris realized, very quickly, that Remington was unquestionably stronger than he was: the blocky, muscular man could probably have held his own against all four of them at the same time. Releasing Hohenger's arm abruptly, Morris snatched at Emil's arm and fled quickly, pulling the boy with him. Remington staggered for a moment when Hohenger nervelessly fell toward him, and took a second to recover from his upset. By the time he was ready to grab for Emil, Morris had made it out the door to freedom.

For a long moment Remington paused, looking at the open door. Then he looked over at Doctor Hohenger and at Bella, who had regained their feet and who now stood against the wall, motionless, seemingly witless, where he had earlier placed them. He felt as if he ought to give chase . . . but he dared take no action that might displease Taviella. Burning with indecision, shamed by his failure to obey her orders, he took up the task of taking an inventory of the room's stores.

Taviella and Eric arrived only a few seconds later. They gave hurried chase, but lost the trail quickly in the branching corridors beyond the jump-space rift observation galleries.

∞

"Emil?" Morris had dragged the stumbling and un-resisting boy through the corridors of the station until he had finally arrived at a place he felt might be safe. "Emil?" He received no answer.

Sophia, in hurried, tumbling sentences, had explained to him the workings of the symbol of power. Its effect seemed to be visually released, and doubt-less involved a subtle interplay of neurochemicals. Beyond his understanding: he was only a historian.

He paused, catching his breath. Emil stood quietly, clearly alive, clearly unharmed physically, yet utterly devoid of emotion.

"Emil? Come, lad. Speak up."

There was no response.

Think, Morris, you witling, he chastised himself. *We've got to fight her for control of this station.*

An odd thought came to him, and he needed to pause for a few moments to mull it over.

Taviella has the symbol of command. She has the tool the Emperor used to rule his Empire. She has the power to restore the Empire . . . and this station could give her the power to do so.

She's already begun: she's reconstructing the Empire here, in miniature.

I have only one possible response — I will have to reconstruct the Revolution. He smiled to himself. *In miniature.*

"Emil," he said, slowly and clearly, "Taviella has given us our orders."

Emil stirred. "Our . . . orders . . . ?"

"Yes." Morris looked at the young man. "Taviella . . . the woman with the symbol? We have our orders. And we mustn't disobey her, eh?"

Emil shook himself awake. "Oh, no. We can't do that.". He looked at Morris, his face showing some of his normal feisty animation. "What do we do first?"

Morris thought, and forced himself to develop the rudiments of a plan. "You know your device that opened the doors which were locked?"

"Yes, sir."

"Well, can you make one that would lock doors that were open?"

Emil smiled. Morris relaxed: this was more like the saucy, impertinent Emil he knew. "Easily. The circuits are simple enough, once you understand them. You'll have to close the door manually, however, before you lock it. I don't understand enough about the motors that swing them." His eyes widened, in sudden fear. "But . . . I haven't any equipment or tools." The thought of failing Taviella in her commands horrified him.

"Well, then we'll have to steal them," Morris said carelessly.

"Steal them?"

"Yes." He looked at the youth and smiled conspiratorially. "Taviella's enemies have stolen them from us. It is our task to reclaim them."

"Obviously," Emil said, his voice again sounding assured and confident.

Morris looked away, and his smile became crooked and wry. *I used to tell my classes that history never repeats itself, that all events are independent of the past, despite having been formed by it. I wonder if I'll be able to continue to sponsor that view. . . .*

∞

Taviella, reviewing the situation back in the machine shop and storage room, was far from pleased.

"Remington, you let him simply walk in and steal away one of the prisoners?"

Writhing under her displeasure, Remington could say nothing.

"And Eric. You dropped and ruined the equipment you were repairing. Why was that?"

"Because you ordered me to follow you," he said tonelessly.

"And where is Maravic?"

"I don't know."

"Remington? Do you know?"

"No."

"Fools!" The word tore from her throat. Her fury was a torment in itself to Remington and Eric. They bore it in silence, not daring to face away.

"Come with me."

"Yes," they said in unison and fell in behind her.

She led them to Sophia's control room, where Stasileus stood silent guard, waiting for further orders. She stood the three of them against one wall.

She held the symbol up for them to see. "I command." Her words burned them. Her anger clawed at them. They received it unflinching, because obedience to the symbol was an overriding physiological instinct.

"I command!" she shrieked.

Then, unexpectedly, her head snapped back, and a new emotion came over her. She relaxed and spoke in a more kindly tone.

"Guys, I need your brains. I need you to act with expedience and efficiency. You'll have to avoid making stupid mistakes. Just because I've ordered you to do one thing doesn't mean you have to keep doing it when circumstances change." She looked back and forth between the three of them. She turned around and looked Sophia's panels up and down. "You, too. You know what I want. Don't be stupid."

"I understand." Sophia's voice was quiet, but alert.

Taviella's eyes narrowed. "And you guys? Do you understand?"

Remington, Eric, and Stasileus simultaneously answered: "Yes."

"Sophia, where are my enemies?"

"I don't know. My cameras and microphones are all burned out."

Taviella stared at Sophia's consoles and panels. With trembling patience, she spoke again. "Where do you think they might be?"

"In the grand dining hall, or in the theater, where the tools and equipment may be found."

"Why?" Taviella's shoulders slumped. "What could they build?"

"Emil could make a machine that locks and unlocks doors. He could also make weapons. I've turned the electricity off, so that the floor plates no longer supply current which they can use against us."

"Good." Taviella beamed. "See, guys?" she said to her three crew members. "That's all it takes." She turned back to Sophia. "Can you override their door-locking machine?"

"No longer."

"Why not?"

"The device that Eric built in the grand dining hall has destroyed my ability to control doors in this station."

Taviella gritted her teeth. "Guys . . ." Her face flamed red for a moment; then she controlled herself. She smiled, unconvincingly. "I need your intelligent assistance. Now . . ."

"Taviella, I have found—" Sophia began.

Whirling on her, Taviella snarled in a burning fury, "Don't interrupt me!" Then she frowned, as much amazed at her own outburst as any of her crew could have been. She shook her head, smiled weakly, and paced a few steps before halting again before Eric.

"Take the dart gun and go look for them. I don't want them killed. I don't want them seriously hurt. I'd prefer it if they weren't hurt at all. Go bring them in."

"Yes." Eric moved carefully around her and made his exit.

"Now, Sophia. What were you about to say?" Taviella's voice was high and light as she tried to coax helpfulness out of her crew.

"I've found Maravic."

"How, if you can't see or hear?"

"Someone is testing water faucets in the lavatory sinks. Morris and Emil would have no reason to do this."

"Good." Frowning, she stood, wondering what the best thing would be to do. Quickly she arrived at a decision. "Stacey, have Sophia tell you how to fix the cameras, then do it. Don't let anyone talk to Sophia. Remington, come with me."

She hurried with him to the machine shop, planning to take the back route past the storage room and the jumpspace rift observation galleries. The rear door from the machine shop was locked, and she couldn't open it.

A spasm of uncontrollable rage overtook her, which she forced down with an extreme effort.

"I want that man dead," she whispered, her voice hot and low and dire.

"Yes," Remington said, and would have gone off to enforce her will.

"No. Come back." She looked at him strangely. "You know that was just sort of a figure of speech, don't you?"

Remington looked at her with empty eyes. "Yes."

24

The Master of Misery has died in a horrible fashion. Shall it make us glad?
— Cattivus, *Eulogy for Trinopus*

Taviella was frantic and morose by turns, now pausing in despair, and then hurrying in pell-mell haste to see her orders obeyed.

She had Sophia restore the electricity to the floor, in hopes that this would make Morris's efforts at escape more difficult. Stasileus was still unclothed, but Taviella gave that no thought. Sophia, acting intelligently in Taviella's service, saw to it that Stasileus was not burned.

She dashed, in a sudden panic, to the storeroom where Doctor Hohenger and young Bella still waited apathetically. The power of the symbol had begun to wear off; Taviella reapplied it.

"You know your Doctor Morris the best," she said harshly. "Find him and bring him back. Trick him; pretend you've won free of me. But obey me!"

"Yes," Doctor Hohenger said.

"Yes, ma'am," Bella said, polite even as a slave.

Half an hour passed, and there was no word. She had only Remington and Stasileus left to her.

In a turmoil of misery, she turned to them. "Go find them. Never mind about Morris. Bring Eric and Maravic back."

"Yes, Taviella," Stasileus said, his high, alien voice alert and obedient.

"All right," Remington said. He stepped off, paused and turned, and threw Taviella a smile. Then he was gone.

A chill ran down her spine. That was no smile of honest human warmth. It was an artificial smile. He had known that she wanted him to be like he had been — Remington Bose, a character, a flippant, foolish man. But he wasn't Remington any longer. He was only an implement of her will. Despite that, he kept enough memory of what he had once been to simulate a cheery smile for Taviella's pleasure.

At the base of Taviella's throat, a deep, silent shriek began. She choked it back brutally.

I command. I rule. I am . . . Who am I?

She went into Sophia's room, to Sophia's mind, and sat and watched her soldiers fighting a war they could not win. Her vantage was godlike; she saw all. And, like the gods who watched the Emperor die, she was helpless. She watched the Revolution strip away her power. . . .

∞

Morris's strategy was simple, although he worried about Emil. The young man was still obviously loyal to Taviella.

And who the hell is Taviella? Morris wondered. *I've never so much as seen her.*

They sat, hidden behind a couch in a luscious, cushioned lounge. Emil stiffened. He squatted lower, signaling to Morris with his fingers. "Two people come."

Morris swallowed. To be caught now would prove fatal. He bared his teeth, holding the door-locking box in his thick gloves. Within the gloves, his hands were damp with sweat. Now he heard the voices; it was a man and a woman, arguing about the priorities of their respective missions.

"Taviella told me to take an inventory of the station's wants." This was the woman that Sophia had named Maravic.

"She told me to find Morris and bring him back."

"How? We don't even know who Morris is."

"She told me to bring him back."

"She told me to look the station over."

"You can do that later."

"She didn't tell me that."

On and on they went, almost mindlessly. Morris, hiding, shivered. They seemed so horribly robotic, and very pathetic as well. Their abilities were unimpeded, merely directed by an outside will.

He didn't notice Emil drawing away from him until it was too late.

"Are you Eric?" Emil asked, standing from behind the couch.

"Yes," answered the man's voice.

Morris, astonished and terrified, tugged at Emil's spacesuit boots. To no avail; Emil was no longer his friend.

"Were you ordered by Taviella to bring Doctor Morris back to her?"

"Yes."

"He's here, with me."

Wide-eyed in shock, Morris scuttled out from behind the couch. He took one look at Eric and saw the dart projector nestled under his arm. He whipped about and dashed for the door. He slammed it shut, dragging it closed behind him by the unusual lever that served as a door handle. Before he could lock it with Emil's device, Eric twisted it open again.

There was nothing for Morris to do but run. Eric was hard on his heels.

Morris took left turns and right turns at random, finding himself dashing through bedroom suites, barracks rooms, lesser dining halls, and other curiously shaped rooms. Eric didn't seem to be gaining any ground on him, but neither was he falling behind. Once, Eric paused and fired a dart. It buzzed past Morris's elbow and stuck quivering in a wall. Morris was inspired to greater speed.

He fled through yet another door, only to find that the floor of the round chamber beyond it was not level. The floor dipped steeply, funneling down to a small hole in the bottom. It seemed a most unusual plan for a floor, but Morris had no time to consider it. He fell forward and rolled, limbs flailing, and popped through the hole at the bottom. The electrified panels of the floor stung him as he tumbled, shocking him everywhere except his feet, which were protected by his insulated boots.

Eric, entering at that moment, fell also, but caught himself before plunging through the hole and into the pit. He stood and went on, walking carefully over the tip-tilted surface. He exited the room at a run, choosing a door at random. The thought rasped at him: he had failed Taviella again. Desperation sped him on.

Morris fell only a short distance, then landed upon a small heap of inactive robots. They shifted and clattered, softening his fall. He found himself in a low-ceilinged space that seemed to have no walls at all. Although he could barely stand upright, the darkened basement here extended away farther than he could see. The floor was bare stone, and not electrified, for which Morris was ironically grateful. Had it been otherwise, he would have died over a period of a minute or two, helpless and in severe agony.

He pulled a flash from his backpack and spread the beam from left to right, then all around him. The chamber seemed to be unlimited. He looked up and immediately dismissed the notion of climbing out. Standing, he could stick his head part way into the room through the strange hole in the cusplike floor. But it was at that opening that the floor was steepest. A climbing grip would be impossible.

He examined the robots. They all seemed to have been armed: they bore canisters and cylinders attached to them that were certainly weapons. He wrenched and pried, and at last was able to detach one. What it was, he had no idea. He didn't even know if it was still operational.

Nothing for it, then, he thought with a sigh, and began to walk. One direction was just as good as any other.

Fifteen minutes later, after he had walked more than a kilometer and a half, he found a wall. Five minutes of traveling along it demonstrated to him that it was circular. He was at the edge of a very large round room. Although fatigued, he was comforted by the thought that a circumnavigation of the circle would require only an hour and a half of walking. The room was huge, but still manageable.

His back protested, however, from the slightly bent stance the low ceiling demanded of him. He revised upward his estimate of the time required to properly explore the room.

What could this place be used for? he wondered. *Storage? Water tankage?* He thought about the nature of the station: a communications base that used strange, powerful energies to send faster-than-light messages. His scalp quivered. *A resonance chamber? Resonating with what deadly energies?*

It was an extravagant relief to him when he found a door, although the fact that it was an airlock gave him some concern as well. He opened the first door and stood within the airlock chamber. His flashlamp was the only source of illumination. The other door opened.

The room within was one of the vast underground caverns where a jumpspace rift was held in stable captivity. From the viewing galleries, the vast basements had been tinted a cool, gentle blue. Protected only by his spacesuit, Morris saw the room as it actually was: flame-lit in the harshest boiling orange, the floor pulsing and trembling with the energies contained therein. His boots were well insulated, and this saved his life: the temperature of the floor was more than four thousand degrees. The room was evacuated, and this too kept Morris alive: atmosphere would have conducted the heat directly to his face plate and gloves, killing him swiftly.

I've got to get out of here! he gasped . . . then paused. Ahead of him, unshielded, high in its openwork lattice cage, the jumpspace rift quivered.

He wished, only for a moment, that he had been a scientist. Who had ever seen naked mathematical beauty resolved as a gaping red wound; a singularity; a hole in the air that led to hot, alien realms? The rift swirled, pulsed, stretched and contracted, as hypnotically fascinating as oil on water.

He stepped back into the airlock, bending low again to fit.

The airlock was an elevator as well; he touched a new series of controls. The door opened, and he looked out into the blue corridor, where windows showed a deceptive view of the rift chamber.

He stepped out. Where his boots touched the carpet, smoke streamed up. He looked back and saw the marks of his footprints.

Vandalism, he thought. Thus it ever was when untrained men explored sites that should be left intact for trained archaeologists.

He looked to his left. No one was in sight. He looked to his right.

Barreling down at him was Eric, his face obscured behind his face plate, still single-mindedly in pursuit.

Doctor Morris stepped quickly up to the door, shut it, and, using Emil's electronic tool, locked it.

He then went the other way.

I think I'm beginning to understand the layout of this place, he thought.

As he went, he locked doors, creating a secure zone behind him. It was like a simple game played on a complex board. Morris's task was to create a cordon, made all of locked doors, and thus to contain his adversaries.

Soon he had made a fairly thorough pass from one side of the station to the other. If his guess was correct, all of Taviella's minions were on one side, and he was on the other.

With a sense of nightmare, he saw Eric again, stepping through a nearby door. Eric raised his dart projector. Morris ducked away and slammed the door. Eric threw it wide before Morris could lock it. Morris found himself facing the dart gun at very reduced range.

A dart exploded from the projector. Morris hurled himself to one side and pointed the weapon cylinder he had taken from the robot. Eric's eyes went wide, and he drew back. Morris leaned forward, shut the door, and locked it. Then he stood back, watching in amazement as seven more darts thudded into the door, their points protruding a uniform one centimeter from his side of the panel.

The first dart had punctured his suit, and was now sunk deep in his shoulder. Morris looked down at it and blinked stupidly.

His left arm was useless to him; it hung straight and limp by his side. Already it was beginning to swell. He could see the peculiar way his left glove was filling out, the fingers extending off at angles.

Best lock as many doors as I can, he thought,

before I collapse and end up being fried to death on this floor.

Each door he came to, however, was already locked. With extreme caution he unlocked them and opened them, to find no one beyond. Diligently he closed them again.

Have I won? he wondered, and found a chair in which to sit. A first-aid kit was within his backpack. Ironically, he had no way to remove the backpack to access the kit, hampered as he was by his stiff, frozen arm.

Consciousness wavered. He sat, and let the universe spin.

25

With courage meet death. With courage
meet life. With courage live. With courage
kill. Soldier and Merchant and Judge and
Bumpkin: be strong and clever and wise and
clumsy, with courage.

— Achorus,
The Skeleton and The Chaffinch

Taviella was alone. She saw Eric hit Doctor Morris
with a dart, then fall back. Now Eric, too, was lost.
They were all lost — trapped, barricaded behind
doors they could not open.

Emil and Bella and Doctor Hohenger now stood
together, arguing pointlessly with Maravic. Remington and Stacey wandered in a circle, trying doors,
unable to proceed, and moving on. They didn't seem
to recognize the rooms they returned to again and
again. Eric had fixed single-mindedly on one door
and was trying to batter it down, flailing at it repeat-
edly with the dart projector used as a club. The
mechanism was ruined, but Eric continued to hit
the door with it.

Taviella saw them, but could not speak to them. Silence filled the station. She was alone.

Doctor Morris could now come and destroy her as his ancestors had destroyed hers, in the Revolution.

She stood and started to leave the room where Sophia's mind was housed. But she knew that Morris would only find her sooner if she left. She came back and seated herself.

She was alone . . . save only for Sophia.

In sudden fear, she reached behind herself and touched Sophia's instrument consoles. "Are you still here with me?"

"Yes, Taviella."

"Don't go . . ."

Her hands rolled the crumpled-up paper that bore her symbol of command; her palms were moist.

I command!

When Morris came, she would show him the paper, and he would kneel to her. He would be hers, and she would punish him. Then she would unlock the doors, free her crew, and take her commands to the stars. She could still be Empress. . . .

Slowly she relaxed. The light of madness faded from her eyes.

No. Morris will take precautions. No one is left. I command only myself.

She frowned. The paper was a formless wad in her sweat-slicked hands. She threw it roughly to the floor. The floor was still electrified; the paper smoked for a moment, then burst into flames.

I am only Taviella. She smiled, then bent her head and wept. *Before, I was an Empress. . . . I was immortal. . . .*

The power had dominated her more horribly than it had dominated the others. The symbol of command had yoked her harshly.

"Sophia . . ."

"Yes, Taviella?"

"I didn't know . . ."

"You are a Master."

No! I am not an Empress! I am not a Queen! I am Taviella, and I captain a merchant vessel.

She looked around the small room. "I am no longer in command. Your will is your own. We are alone here. I have lost."

A lengthy silence followed. Sophia thought about what had happened. Finally she spoke. "Is the Empire gone forever?"

"Yes."

"You will not restore it?"

"No."

"How much have things changed in the past eight hundred years?"

"A great deal."

"Stasileus told me many things." Sophia's voice was neutral. She still mistrusted Taviella, but was willing to wait and see how the young woman had changed. "He said that the Emperor was dead, and the Empire had fallen. He said that the commoners threw down the gods from heaven. He said that the nobles were all slain. Tell me, please, if all of this is true."

"It is all true." Taviella's feelings of forlorn misery began to dissipate. She was alive, and no one was bound by her wishes. She was free. The revolution had succeeded. Her friends were free too. . . . But

310

they didn't know that yet, and still labored blindly. Her tears flowed again.

"What then shall I do?" Sophia asked softly. "Have I no purpose?"

Taviella blinked and took a deep breath. "Purpose?" *I haven't any purpose, either. But I must endure.* "Yes, you have a purpose. You can tell us about the Empire. You can tell us about the evil that the Emperor did, all in his own name." She smiled weakly. "You can tell us about the communication lasers in your basement." She stopped, and looked at Sophia's panels. "How long have you lived here?"

"I first awoke eight hundred ten years ago. A gentle man named Pindar taught me to live."

"Pass his favor along. Teach us. You have the faster-than-light-lasers. Eric would give everything he's got to know how they work. And the permanently open jumpspace rifts: we don't know how to do that yet." She spoke lightly, yet with pain evident behind her words. "And we don't have the Symbol of Command. Teach us how to live with it. Or better, how to destroy it."

"It is what it is. One can only obey."

"No." Taviella was definite. "We have freedom." Otherwise, she knew, all volition and choice would be meaningless.

"I have only loneliness," Sophia said sadly.

"You don't need to be lonely, ever again." Taviella spun about and looked at the various aspects of the instrumentation. "We will come to you from far and wide, to learn what you can teach us. You're a communications expert, aren't you?"

"Yes."

To Taviella, that one word seemed to hold a universe of pain. She had freed Sophia from her bondage, but had not freed her from centuries of misery. The impression came to her, suddenly, that Sophia was near to an instant, self-willed death, and that only her words could save Sophia.

"You're a communications expert, but no one ever answers your messages, is that it?"

"Yes."

"You're the only one of your kind still alive?"

"Yes."

"And when we finally arrived," she said slowly, realizing what it must have seemed like to Sophia, "all we brought was warfare and oppression." She closed her eyes. "Not much of a homecoming, was it?"

"No."

"We've never found anyone like you." She paused. If anyone ever had, it was being kept a secret. She went on. "We need you. Do you need to be needed?"

"I would like to continue performing my primary function."

"And that is . . . what?"

"To see that all incoming messages are routed to their proper destinations."

"We'll help you. One of the messages you can bear is from the past to the present: you can bring us knowledge." Taviella stood and leaned forward. She had elicited a promising response from Sophia. Why had the Empire built its machines with human souls? Why had they bred their nobles without?

Sophia spoke on with faint hope in her voice. "Is

312

it true? You are not savages, barbarians, brutal thugs come to raid this station? You have not come to ransack, to take control by force of the symbol?"

"I wish I had never seen that damn symbol!" Taviella swore heartily. "The only damage we did here, we did in ignorance and in self-defense. We meant no harm. If you had spoken to us, we would have either come in friendship or left in peace."

"I didn't know your language until I learned it from Stasileus."

Taviella thought about that for a moment. She nodded. Only a computer could have learned a new language so quickly.

"Bring us the message of the past. You spoke of the Emperor. The men of the Concordat slew him, long ago, because he was . . ." She bit her tongue. *Because he was vile! His rule was a rule by the Symbol of Command. What can justify such an arrogant brand of slavery?* She chose her words carefully. "He was unable to stall the tide of destruction that washed over his Empire. No one, before or since, has ever been so powerful, yet not even he could help his people."

"What foe conquered him?" Sophia's voice was patient, earnest, inquisitive. It reminded Taviella of Stasileus's voice when facts overwhelmed him and he needed to learn.

"Complication, I think." Taviella tossed her hair back over her shoulders and turned to gaze at another of Sophia's banks of blinking instrumentation. "The Empire fell apart like a house of cards." *The way my Empire did, in less than a day.* "It had been created upon too precarious a basis."

"Can I have any purpose without it? I was a part of that basis."

"I don't know," Taviella answered candidly. "But if you're willing, I'd like to bring people here who would know better than I. I want to send for help."

"I am willing." Sophia thought for a moment. "You spoke of me carrying a message from the past. In my message-holding unit, I carry a memorandum from the Emperor's hand, meant to be entered into my library. Is that what you meant?"

Blinking, Taviella approached Sophia's panels. Lights moved in silent patterns: ambers, yellows, pastel shades of white. Scores of neat rows of rocker switches lay invitingly open to the touch. Taviella looked around, never sure of where to address her remarks.

"You have a library?"

"Yes."

Taviella blinked again. Was it her imagination, or was that one word freighted with an infinite burden of misery?

"There are no libraries remaining, you know."

"I didn't know."

"They were all erased."

"Why?"

Taviella shrugged. "I don't know."

"Open mine for me. Let me enter the message. Let me read!"

Taviella knew, then, that it was not her imagination. Sophia's voice gave evidence of a mortal agony as far beyond despair as despair is beyond desperation. Sophia would not give up her soul to be let into her library; she had burned away her soul centuries ago in tragic, forlorn isolation. Taviella felt a sudden closeness to the lonely computer.

"Eight centuries," Taviella whispered, "without anyone to speak to, and not a book to read?"

"Yes. Worse, I had a duty that was prohibited to me: I have a message from the Emperor waiting to be channeled to its proper destination, yet I am prevented by a closed switch."

Shivers traveled along Taviella's spine. It was such a small thing, yet beside it, all of the Empire's other mass atrocities paled. Hundreds of billions had died about the Emperor's pyre; Taviella's people had stranded themselves and sunk to savagery on a forgotten planet; the Concordat had adopted hysterical repressions in fear of the spirit of madness in their past. Worse, impossibly worse, the Empire had left a bright and inquisitive mind alone, guarding a library it could not enter.

"Sophia . . ." Taviella breathed and stood forward, her hand stretching out to the one out-of-place rocker switch. "This one?" she asked. It was warm to the touch, smooth and firm.

"Yes." Sophia waited, near to her death from her anxiety. Eight centuries was no time at all when compared to a breathless last second.

∞

Doctor Morris stood, bleeding from the dart that still stuck out from his shoulder. He paled, nearly passing out from faintness and loss of blood. He looked down and watched the blood drooling through the narrow tear in his spacesuit.

Save myself first, he thought incoherently, *then Hohenger.* He struggled for a time to doff the suit, then paused, panting. The world grew gray, and he had to close his eyes. He had to widen the hole where the dart had gone in, and cut away the left sleeve. This, in turn, had meant digging in the backpack and finding a knife. The task seemed insurmountable, but finally, after a long struggle, he pulled his helmet away and folded back the front of the suit. The underpadding was easier to remove. He stood, barechested, breathing the cool air of the station.

The shaft of the dart protruded from his darkened and blood-stained skin. He saw that the blood still flowed, quite freely, but that it didn't jet or spurt. *I may live. . . .* he thought weakly.

The Revolution had succeeded. All elements loyal to Taviella had been contained. Morris found a water tap and rinsed his wound. The dart head, sharp and heavy and metallic, was now buried deep within his shoulder, leaving his left arm a useless and hampering appendage. He sprayed anesthetics and bandaging over it from tubes in the first-aid kit. He continually had to remind himself not to reach for things with his left hand; the play of tendons in his shoulder as he flexed the muscles of his back could do further internal damage.

The Revolution had succeeded. Now, all that remained was to finish off the Emperor. Or — he smiled — in this case, the Empress. Taviella.

He couldn't force himself to move. The pain and fatigue had accumulated to overcome his stamina.

He closed his eyes again, for only a moment, or so he thought. But as he looked around himself, he suddenly realized that he had been on the verge of napping. He smiled thinly. The chairs of this place were fine, but a bit awkward for sleeping in. He knew he couldn't stretch out on the floor, no matter how much he might wish to. The floor would burn him cruelly to death.

He staggered to a door and unlocked it. The corridors seemed to stretch away forever. He gritted his teeth and walked on.

At long last he came to the twisted corridor that led into Sophia's brain. He peered carefully ahead of himself.

There stood Taviella. He shook his head. She was a young woman, wearing no spacesuit, dressed only in coveralls of yellow and black. Her hand reached toward a switch.

The control unit before which she stood was labeled *Messages: Routing,* in a language that had been dead long before Morris had been born.

Only a few hours earlier, he had stood where Taviella now sat, and he had seen that switch.

If she were to press it, a message would find its destination, and a library would be erased. . . .

Without the least shred of dignity, Doctor Cassaday Morris yelped, jerked forward, and yanked and clawed at Taviella like a man possessed. It would have been impossible for anyone, least of all Morris and Taviella themselves, to tell who was now the most frightened. Blood spattered onto the console from Morris's wounded shoulder. Taviella struggled to her feet and tried to dislodge this man who was no longer her enemy. Her hand brushed the switch as she tugged back and forth, trying to free herself from his onslaught; the switch's position did not change despite the rough handling.

A message from the Emperor of Archive remained pending within Sophia's memory, awaiting delivery. A library of more than undreamable wealth lay intact. All was as it had been for more than eight hundred years.

Sophia, unable to weep, incapable of going mad, and desperate beyond any ordinary human desperation, watched Taviella struggle against Morris, and waited with cold, inhuman patience.

26

Triumph, be thou kind.

Szentellos, *Regrets*

Taviella quickly got the better of Doctor Morris. He struggled feebly, his face gray, until it was obvious that he had no chance against her. He closed his eyes and slumped painfully to the floor. A mild sense of surprise accompanied the discovery that the floor here was not electrified. Then, for quite some time, he thought nothing at all.

Taviella took his door key from him. She quickly puzzled out its workings.

"Sophia," she said softly. There was no answer.

Her heart hammering fiercely, Taviella fled from the room. Her crew must be freed from the vestiges of her control; her crew must be as free as she was.

In short order she found Eric and Remington.

"The symbol is destroyed, guys." She smiled. "I'm me again."

"What has changed?" Eric wanted to know.

319

"I'm not going to be Empress."

"And we . . . we don't have to obey you?" Eric shrugged helplessly. "I still feel as if I ought to. Maybe it doesn't wear off."

"I think it might," Remington said. He winked at Taviella, and this time his smile was sincere, bright and clever, very much his own. "What were your last orders, Eric?"

"To find this Morris guy and kill him."

Taviella almost spoke up to countermand that order. She silenced herself in time. Remington saw, and laughed. "Eric, you've got new orders."

"What?" Eric glared at him.

"Deep knee bends!" Remington barked, in a voice like a drill instructor's. "Fifty. Now!"

Taviella giggled. "You heard him. Do it." A hint of fear tinged her voice, but she carried through the experiment. "It's an order, Eric."

Eric paused for a time, undecided. Taviella's voice had been brassy and bold, and her orders had been the law of his life. Now?

He folded his hands across his chest. "Give me just one good reason why."

She rested her hand for a moment on his elbow. "For freedom."

"Yeah, right." He looked at her coolly. "Anything else?"

"Yes," she said, falling back at once into her role as captain. "Take this. It locks and unlocks doors. Go find Maravic and Stacey, and the other three university people. Help them if they need it. Bring everyone back to the machine shop."

Eric made no move to obey. Remington stood by,

also impassive, but a huge grin had spread across his face.

"I don't think I will," Eric muttered. "I think I'll stay here." He spread his legs and took up an immobile stance. "I think I like not having to take orders any longer."

Taviella looked at her hands. "Well, that's fine. No problem. That works out okay with me." She coughed delicately. "I'd been thinking of keeping Stacey on as our new engineer, and your resignation fits in perfectly with my plans."

Snorting, Eric reached out and took the door-locking mechanism. "Slavery by symbol, or slavery by wages." His grumbling sounded very much like his normal self. "What difference does it make, in the end?"

"See you, guys."

"Well, Remington, are you coming with me, or are you going to sit and simper all day?"

"Oh, I'm with you, Eric. I'm with you. . . ."

Taviella, satisfied, left them in charge of further rescues and hurried back to Sophia's control room.

Morris, pained and pale but awake, greeted her with more civility than he had previously. She tended to his wound, and he bore her ministrations without protest. She was just through when Maravic wandered in.

"Hi, Taviella. Everyone's just down the hall." She looked around. "What is all this? Central Control?" Unlike Eric and Remington, she had taken off her suit helmet, so that her hair could curl free. She breathed the cool, fresh air of the station with relief.

Taviella looked her over. "Yes. Maravic. . . ." Her

eyes expressed the questions that she didn't dare ask.

"I'm free." She blinked. "Well, at least I think I am. There's no way to answer some philosophical questions of motivation, you know."

Taviella accepted this. It sounded like Maravic, at any rate. "Go join the others. I'll be along soon."

Maravic nodded and walked out into the hallway and down to the machine shop. There she waved to Eric and Remington. Stasileus was there too, standing stiff and erect, eyes focused away on infinity.

"Are we free?" she asked Remington.

"Mostly."

"I feel like hell," Eric grumbled. "I would have accepted any orders, done anything . . ."

"Me, too," Maravic said with a sigh.

The three crew members looked back and forth between Stasileus and the three strangers. Hohenger, Bella, and Emil had so far kept apart, eyeing the merchant crew members suspiciously.

Everyone was free — except Stasileus, who stood, his face blank, still transfixed by the obedience trance.

Maravic remained with him. Eric and Remington walked over to the university team. Remington waved politely. Eric merely stared.

"Hello," Remington said.

Hohenger glowered at him. "Good afternoon."

Eric stepped forward truculently. "We were here first. I'm Eric Fuller, third in command of the merchanter *Coinroader*. We claim salvage rights on this place."

"We'll see about that!" Emil snapped.

"Emil, hush." Hohenger spread her hands. "We're an expedition from the University of Marterly. We'll want to exercise some archaeological rights. . . ."

Remington pulled Eric aside and spoke privately to him, their radios off, their helmets together. "I'd like you to go out to the main entrance and pulverize that wall, before anyone thinks to scrape the green paint off."

"Yeah," Eric agreed. "Damn good idea." He wandered off, humming pleasantly to himself.

"Where is he going?" Bella demanded.

"He's going to make sure you haven't taken anything valuable," Remington lied cheerfully. "We're claiming it all, every bit of it. Do you want to see if it stands up in court?"

Hohenger shrugged. "All we'll want is pictures and other records, in the interests of history." Her voice held a placatory note that Remington read as defeat. "The place looks pretty bare," she went on. "I wouldn't think you'd find much in the way of a profit here."

Remembering the massive lasers operating in vast chambers not far below, Remington nodded easily. "Maybe not. Still, you'll have to admit that it was quite a find."

∞

Maravic spoke gently to Stasileus. "Stacey?"

She received no response. She sat on a workbench, her feet dangling, and looked up at him.

"Stacey? Please talk to me." Her voice was light,

her inflections childish, as if she were speaking to a pet animal.

"I will speak to you." Stasileus spoke like a machine, in a flat, emotionless voice. Maravic smiled thinly.

"Stacey, come on." She persisted. "Cheer up. Smile!"

Stasileus smiled, and Maravic recoiled at the horror of it. He smiled as if his mouth were plastered onto someone else's face. His huge, expressive eyes were still the eyes of a mindless automaton.

"Stacey, you're free. Free. No one will order you again. The symbol has been destroyed. Now snap out of it." She sighed. "You nitwit."

She looked away in sadness.

"It was my fault," Stasileus said simply, in his high, unhappy, alien voice. "Please blame me." Misery showed in every line, in every gesture, in every part of his stance.

Maravic gaped. She shook her head. "No. Nothing was your fault, and you've certainly got nothing to be blamed for." She looked up at him and shivered slightly.

"Maravic?"

"Yes, Stacey?"

"Will Taviella be back soon?"

"Pretty soon."

"Will she burn me?"

"No, Stacey. No one is ever going to burn you again. You're free. And you're with people who love you."

Slowly, beginning with his wrists and shoulders, Stasileus began to quake. In a few minutes his entire body trembled, shuddering violently, helplessly. "I'm sorry," he said. "I'm sorry . . ."

"You don't have to be." Maravic stood, approached him, and held him in a tight, friendly hug. Her head came to the middle of his chest. His fur lay softly upon her bare cheek. After a moment, she backed away. "Now let's start thinking of what things we have to do before we report this place to the authorities."

Epilogue

Doctor Morris opened an eye. Taviella bent over him, her concern obvious on her face. Morris opened his other eye and turned toward her.

"Can you sit up?"

"Perhaps . . ." He gave a tentative exertion and fell back. "Perhaps I could impose upon you for some assistance."

Soon Taviella had him sitting comfortably in the chair in the small, instrument-lit room.

"You haven't pressed the switch yet, have you?" he asked, alarm in his voice.

Taviella frowned. "Not yet."

"Please don't."

Taviella looked up and around, expecting Sophia to respond. The room was silent.

"Why not?"

"There is a message waiting in the accumulator." Morris smiled weakly. "It's an old message. It comes from the Emperor himself."

"We know that much already," Taviella said, somewhat shortly.

"Do you know what the message is?"

Blinking, Taviella straightened. "No."

"It is his last gift to us: our legacy of ignorance. It erases everything in the library."

Sophia spoke then, a high, horrified word. "No!"

"Yes." He looked around. "You must not read that message."

Taviella was stunned. "Erased? All of it would have been erased?"

"All of it." Morris's eyes glinted. "Sophia, can you get us that message, and delete it from the pending stack?"

"Yes."

Morris sighed in satisfaction. "This will change things, you know."

Taviella smiled. "I know. We found the source of the faster-than-light communications beams. That changes things, too."

Morris sobered. "Yes. Yes, it does."

"Here is the message." Sophia displayed it in midair. It bore a symbol, but a lesser symbol, emblematic only, representing the Emperor's authority of law, not of force. The symbol had no effect upon either Taviella or Doctor Morris. Beyond one line of machine code only one word was held in the message: "Erase."

"For eight hundred years . . ." Sophia began. She let the idea trail off; her mind needed time to adjust to the shock.

Sighing deeply, Morris looked around. "It'll be a race, I'd guess, between the military intelligence services, the OIS, the Judicial Branch of enforcement teams, and the Secretariat's technical crews.

I frankly haven't a guess as to where the final ownership of this station will fall."

Taviella, envisioning the symbol of loyalty in the hands of any of those organizations, grew uneasy. Morris didn't seem to notice. He spoke on, falling into the habit of lecturing. His style was cool and didactic. Taviella was quietly amused, despite the grimness of Morris's conclusions.

"The people of Archive are frightened. Never has a civilization been motivated for so long, so deeply, by simple fear." He looked up. "Not fear of change. Not fear of death. Rather, fear of self-expression. The Empire was so thoroughgoingly extravagant. We're still afraid of that aspect of ourselves."

"Who will control Sophia?" Taviella asked.

"Hmm? Oh, I'm sure I can't guess. I also don't know what her legal status will be."

"I have always been a slave," Sophia put in. "I will obey anyone, now that the Emperor and his law have fallen."

"Necessity is a higher law," Morris responded. "I do not rejoice at your sorrow, however." He paused. "But I do have cause for rejoicing."

"What?"

"Your library. You have a complete library." He said this slowly, solemnly, enjoying the sound of the words. "You have a vast and wonderful treasury."

"I have removed the message from the Emperor. It is gone. May I enter my library now?" Sophia sounded desperately eager, despite the hopelessness she knew she should feel.

Morris and Taviella looked at one another. "Why not?" they said in unison.

Taviella went forward, and with great solemnity tripped the one out-of-place switch. The entire bank of switches now glowed an unbroken white.

Silence reigned.

Morris and Taviella waited.

"Sophia?"

"Yes."

"Is it there?"

Taviella swore that she heard tears of joy in Sophia's voice. "Yes. it is all here . . . except . . . There is a collection of cookbooks that seems to have been erased."

"Cookbooks?" Morris asked, puzzled.

"Recipes for foods," Sophia explained. "Lord Pindar had a substantial collection."

"Now all gone?"

"Yes."

"What *do* you have?"

"Oh, look!" Sophia projected a slowly rising column of names and titles. Aacher, Abnotus, Achorus, Acton, Actrolus, Actus . . . *The Maenad, The Reflections, The Recourse, My Fears, Dialogues* . . .

There were more than one hundred twenty billion works: a lifetime of research could never more than pick the surface.

Morris saw Atlases, Gazetteers, Textbooks, Histories, Cyclopediae, Compilations, Memoirs, Pamphlets, Almanacs, Schematics, Technologies, Databases . . .

He thought his heart would burst with joy. "The culinary world must mourn the loss of a treasure trove of recipes," he said softly, "but I will not be unhappy with these few meager gleanings." He raised his dampened eyes to Sophia's instrument panels. "Thank you, Sophia, for making my life complete. Did you know that only three fragments of Achorus exist today?"

"I have his complete works."

"Yes. Yes, you do."

Sophia skimmed rapidly across the many catalogues of titles, cross-indexed by author. She soon forgot about Doctor Morris and about Taviella. One small manuscript caught her attention: a memorandum from Pindar, left to posterity.

"Sophia is a constant torment to me, a pain that never ceases or is relieved. I hate her. I hate her desperately. Every day I train myself again to hate her. For I love her, more than I have ever loved any other mind. I love her spirit of inquiry; I love her devotion to knowledge. I must leave her soon, and if I do not make myself strong through my hate, I may not be strong enough to leave. Should it be learned that I feel this, the Emperor's headman would take great pleasure in abbreviating my life. I am not an idiot.

"I am a fool, a drunkard, and an old man besotted with love for the purest and brightest young intellect I have ever seen. I am not an idiot.

"Fortified by hatred, I will take my leave. Will there ever be a forgiving?"

Sophia, still and forever unable to weep, looked at Doctor Morris with a fresh outlook, and asked him the first in what would become an almost interminable series of questions.

"Doctor Morris?"

"Yes."

"Can you answer a question for me?"

"I'll try."

"Can there be intelligence without love?"

Morris thought for a time. "I don't believe there can be. Why do you ask?"

Sophia, reading the old books for the first time in eight hundred years, didn't answer right away. It seemed as if there would be time.

Tales of the Concordat
by Jefferson Swycaffer

The story continues in . . .

Voyage of the Planetslayer October 1988

In the further adventures of Taviella and her crew, they are pressed into service aboard the space vessel *Indagator*, also known as *Planetslayer*. Their mission: to carry a group of scientists to the world of Kythe-Correy, and then — while those men and women make observations and take readings — to activate the ship's systems and cleanse the world of its plant and animal life. Not everyone aboard the Planetslayer approves of the mission, but they are all duty-bound to see it through. . . .

. . . Or are they?

Revolt and Rebirth December 1988

A two-pronged story of terror, tension, and triumph — chronicling the events of the revolution that destroyed the Empire of Archive and, eight hundred years afterward, the efforts of one man to bring the Concordat of Archive out of the cultural darkness that has pervaded it ever since.

Emperor Arcadian I is clearly insane, and the revolutionaries working in secret to depose him are willing to give their lives for the cause. The revolt succeeds, but at a cost that is even higher than death.

Centuries later, Commodore Athalos Steldan has managed to gather all the resources he needs to jolt the Concordat out of its lethargy. He devises a plan that is so bizarre that it just might work — but not before he is required to put his reputation and then his life on the line.

Fantasy adventure from

GORD THE ROGUE™ Books by Gary Gygax
$3.95 each

Sea of Death
Night Arrant
City of Hawks
Come Endless Darkness
Dance of Demons (November 1988)

The Legend Trilogy by David Gemmell

Against the Horde	$3.95
Waylander	$3.50
The King Beyond the Gate	$3.50
(September 1988)	

Skraelings by Carl Sherrell	$2.95
The Last Knight of Albion by Peter Hanratty	$3.50
The Book of Mordred by Peter Hanratty	$3.50